PRAISE FOR ZACHARY JERNIGAN'S NOVELS OF JEROUN

"To call Zachary Jernigan a fearless writer is an understatement. His universe is one of gods who make worlds only to torture the inhabitants, demigods who turn on their father, nations exterminated, wars in which the dead take sides. But what floors me is the ease with which he travels this strangest of landscapes. We pass from the mythic to the mundane and back again in the space of a paragraph. We come to know his characters with unsettling intimacy, even as their identities come under magical siege. We sense the solid ground beneath our feet and the presence of forces that could (and do) blow it back into atoms. Jernigan is part of a wave of authors breathing new life into the epic fantasy tradition we love."
—Robert V. S. Redick, author of *The Red Wolf Conspiracy*

"A science-fantasy epic that's as of a much perverse hybrid as it is an homage to an earlier era when those genres weren't so strictly segregated, *No Return* is set on a world that bears wizards and astronauts equally. It also pulls no punches in its rich, visceral depictions of sexuality, martial arts, punk energy, and the philosophical quandaries of power and identity that speculative fiction uniquely exploits—and that few up-and-coming speculative writers outside Jernigan tackle with such guts."
—Jason Heller, *The A.V. Club* (*The Onion*)

"Vivid, varied, and violent. At once beautiful and terrible to behold."
—Nickolas Sharps, *SF Signal*

"*No Return* needs to be noticed. There is so much more to it than the accoutrements would imply. Populated with a fair amount of face punching, as coded by the visceral cover, it contains a tenderness and at times overt eroticism that's often ignored in science fiction and fantasy. Zachary Jernigan has something unique to say, a voice we're not hearing from anywhere else. I dearly hope more readers, and award aficionados, take an opportunity to listen to him."
— *Tor.com*

"A visionary, violent, sexually charged, mystical novel—*No Return* challenges classification. Clearly, Zachary Jernigan has no respect for genre confines. His tale of gods hanging in the sky and a "constructed man" with glowing blue coals for his eyes and a motley band of fighters navigating a harsh landscape peopled by savage creatures and religious zealots . . . Well, it's pure genius. Here's hoping it's just the first of many such works from this guy."
—David Anthony Durham, Campbell Award-winning author of the Acacia Trilogy

"Be careful picking this one up, because once you join with the adventurers in this strange and stunning debut novel, there will be no going back to familiar precincts of heroic fantasy. Zachary Jernigan starts at the very edge of the map and plunges deep into uncharted territory. Mages in space, do-it-yourself gods, merciless killers in love and a mechanical warrior with a heart of bronze await your reading pleasure. For thinking readers who like swashbuckling with an edge, *No Return* delivers."
—James Patrick Kelly, winner of the Hugo, Nebula, and Locus Awards

"*No Return* asks the kinds of questions speculative fiction should ask, and provides the kinds of answers that literary fiction thinks it owns. . . . It is, in fact, the most daring debut novel of 2013 . . ."
—Justin Landon, *Staffer's Book Review*

"*No Return* is a rich, diverse, inventive fantasy, in a style that reminds me in some ways of Tanith Lee's Tales from the Flat Earth books. Zachary Jernigan has created a stunningly original world and I can't wait to see where he takes it next."
—Martha Wells, author of The Books of the Raksura

"Zachary Jernigan's genre-defying epic raises the bar for literary speculative fiction. It has the sweep of Frank Herbert's *Dune* and the intoxicatingly strange grandeur of Gene Wolfe's *Book of the New Sun*, with a decadent, beautifully rendered vision all its own. One of the most impressive debuts of recent years."
—Elizabeth Hand, Nebula and World Fantasy Award-winning author of *Available Dark* and *Radiant Days*

"[A] fascinating exploration of how atheism might function in a world where everyone knows that God (or at least, a god) exists."
—Amy Goldschlager, *Locus*

"[A] hypnotic sort of read the evokes a lot of the same awe and wonder I felt reading Gene Wolfe's stuff; the Elizabeth Hand blurb tells you all you need to know. If you love the shock and awe of science-fantasy and don't care much for paint-by-numbers plots, pick this up."
—Kameron Hurley, author of *God's War*

"Jernigan's first novel, the opening gambit in a saga of religious war, magical science, and martial combat, is a mixture of epic and sword-and-sorcery fantasy. The author's style, with its sensuality and, often, erotic ambiance, calls to mind the novels of Tanith Lee's Flat Earth series as well as the eclectic imaginings of Michael Moorcock's Eternal Champion novels. A promising voice."
—*Library Journal*

"[A] fascinating world, nicely-executed plot . . . and a wonderfully squishy and twisted aesthetic. *No Return* is an excellent fit for readers of Mark Charan Newton's Legend of the Red Sun series or those who enjoy the fantasies of M. John Harrison, Gene Wolfe, or Jack Vance."
—*Pornokitsch*

"Jernigan's debut is full of wonder: a smart adventure, with measures of philosophy and violence and lust. For all its strangeness and far-flung setting, *No Return* is a very human novel. Like Samuel Delany and Gene Wolfe, Jernigan can write a rousing, literary genre story that pushes boundaries and transgresses categorization."
—Brent Hayward, author of *Filaria* and *The Fecund's Melancholy Daughter*

"The greatest pleasure a reader can have is for their expectations to be confounded, to find their eye drawn word by word down a different path to the one anticipated. Genre fiction is too often comfort food, and the palate can grow complacent. *No Return* is not a complacent book and it took me somewhere unexpected and new."
—Martin Lewis, *Strange Horizons*

"Jernigan has really unleashed something unique on the world with *No Return*. It doesn't fit nicely into any boxes or cookie cutters. It's quick moving, subtle yet bold, and absolutely R-Rated and raw. . . . It's bold and vivid and it will probably make you uncomfortable, but that's not a bad thing. Jernigan takes you on a one-of-a-kind journey and he leaves you breathless, gasping, and full of new thoughts."
—Sarah Chorn, *Bookworm Blues*

"*No Return* displays the kind of prose, worldbuilding, and depth of characterization that place Zachary Jernigan securely within the top tier of Fantasy authors. The prose pulls you in like a piece of art, forcing you to slow down and observe. The world-building makes you imagine maps, bar room brawls over differences in customs, kids praying to the god who lives on the moon, women making sex spells, warriors becoming one with their self-controlled, mutating body suits . . . all in a way that separates the world in *No Return* from generic fantasy—this world is alive!"
—Timothy C. Ward, *Adventures in SciFi Publishing*

"Zachary Jernigan writes with a flair for the weird and makes it endearing enough for readers to feel familiar with it. *No Return* is a magnificent debut that straddles fantasy and SF genres seamlessly and makes itself into a jewel faceting both fields."
—Mihir Wanchoo, *Fantasy Book Critic*

Also by Zachary Jernigan

No Return: A Novel of Jeroun

SHOWER
OF STONES

A NOVEL OF JEROUN

ZACHARY JERNIGAN

NIGHT SHADE BOOKS
NEW YORK

Night Shade books may be purchased in bulk at special discounts for sales promotion, corporate gifts, fund-raising, or educational purposes. Special editions can also be created to specifications. For details, contact the Special Sales Department, Night Shade Books, 307 West 36th Street, 11th Floor, New York, NY 10018 or info@ skyhorsepublishing.com.

Night Shade Books® is a registered trademark of Skyhorse Publishing, Inc.®, a Delaware corporation.

Visit our website at www.nightshadebooks.com.

10 9 8 7 6 5 4 3 2 1

Library of Congress Cataloging-in-Publication Data

Jernigan, Zachary, 1980-
    Shower of Stones : A Novel of Jeroun / Zachary Jernigan.
       pages cm
    ISBN 978-1-59780-817-0 (hardback)
1. Imaginary wars and battles—Fiction. I. Title.
    PS3610.E738S58 2015
    813'.6—dc23
                                    2015006849

Print ISBN: 978-1-59780-817-0

Edited by Jeremy Lassen

Jacket illustration by Alvin Epps
Cover design by Claudia Noble

Printed in the United States of America

For my mother, Betty Jernigan.

THE MONTHS OF THE YEAR

Month of Ascetics
Month of Alchemists
Month of Mages
Month of Sectarians
Month of Fishers
Month of Surgeons
Month of Sawyers
Month of Smiths
Month of Drowsers
Month of Financiers
Month of Bakers
Month of Finnakers
Month of Soldiers
Month of Clergymen
Month of Pilots
Month of Royalty

PREVIOUSLY, IN
NO RETURN

Unlikely allies Vedas Tezul, the constructed man Berun, and Churli "Churls" Casta Jons journey to fight in the tournament at Danoor. Doubt, violence, and guilt follow the companions, and the seeds of this doubt prompt Vedas to consider speaking out against the God Adrash if he wins the tournament.

While Vedas and his companions are on the road to Danoor, the mages Ebn bon Mari and Pol Tanz et Som are engaged in a war of wills and resources. Pol sees an opportunity to gain the upper hand, and allies with the prophetic dragon-tamer Shavrim Coranid. This alliance eventually results in Ebn's death and Pol's transformation into an ascendant god.

Heady with this newly gained power, Pol attacks Adrash, not only wounding the god and stealing secrets from his mind, but knocking the Needle—a collection of iron spheres large enough to affect the tides on the planet below: a weapon of incalculable power—out of alignment. The attack drains him, however, and he must flee before the god can summon the energy to kill him.

In Danoor, the travelers split up. Churls is forced to flee. Vedas enters the tournament and prevails despite grave injuries, while Berun follows him in secret. Vedas's victory speech starts a riot, which erupts into even greater violence when the broken Needle rises into view. Berun takes

Vedas to a secluded valley outside the city and then retrieves Churls from her hiding place, bringing with her a rumor that a man with a dragon is in control of part of the city.

Far above the planet's surface, Adrash recovers from his battle with Pol and stabilizes the spheres of the Needle that most threaten the planet. He relives his millennia-long life, recalling the prophets he has encountered and the distinct ways each coveted his power. Realizing finally that it is not one prophet, but several—Pol, Vedas, Churls, and Berun—he readies himself for the battle he assumes is coming . . .

SHOWER
OF STONES

PROLOGUE

THE 4TH OF EVERPLAIN WATCH
SENNEN, BOWL OF HEAVEN, NATION OF ZOROL

They labored on a vast concave plain, under the bluegreen sun. Side by side, the four of them: she, her mate, and the two men they both knew but had never met before the previous day. They pulled sweetroot from the earth in silence, depositing their vegetables in the long furrows that ran poleward to poleward for nearly forty leagues. It was repetitive, backbreaking work, but they were content.

How did she know her companions were content?

She sensed it, just as she sensed the coming and going of her own thoughts.

She and her mate never looked up from their work. Now and then, she would delay for a second after picking her sweetroot, or he would finish his task a moment too quickly, and use the opportunity to touch one another's arm or leg. She would smile, and know that he too smiled.

Newly arrived and unused to the plain, the newly arrived men would occasionally rise, stretch the kinks from their backs, and turn in slow circles, peering with shaded eyes at the world around them—for no practical reason, surely. The sun arced overhead so slowly as to be still in the sky. The breeze came consistently out of the bottom pole, bending the sea of golden grass with nary a ripple.

The only objects surrounding the plain were the tall, thin wind-gatherers clustered to the right-up-poleward, a series of low purple hills to the left-bottom-poleward, and next to the hills the bleached skeleton of the abandoned tensii warren.

The wind-gatherers were simply wind-gatherers. Mindless, immobile beasts stretched to the task of collecting energy, they could be found anywhere. The hills, too, were not special. They folded upon themselves without so much as a rocky outcrop, only subtly changing color as the sunlight crawled in glacial inches over them.

The warren, she supposed, was a unique thing, looming over the near horizon like a massive wooden cage, like the trap for some immense crustacean. The world possessed only five such structures, monuments to an unknown race. People had once devoted their lives to its study.

But it too never changed. It never had in anyone's memory.

In her younger days, she had done as all local adolescents did, and climbed the warren's latticed interior, ascending broad bone avenues to its three-thousand foot height. Like everyone else who completed the trip, she was disappointed to find the structure just as it appeared to be—a massive skeleton, picked clean of any sign of its ancient inhabitants. It was beautiful in its way, but no more beautiful than any natural feature. She had seen the ocean from its summit, and this had occupied her attention far more fixedly.

Still, she could not begrudge her new companions their interest. Prior to moving back home in her thirtieth month, many places had compelled her. The world had much appeal. As one grew older, however, one's focus shifted. She had become content to harvest and recall the violence of her youths—to listen to the breeze, take joy in the touch of her mate, and anticipate the arrival of two strangers she had known in a thousand lands, a hundred bodies.

‡

The day grew no hotter or colder, the shadows of their bodies no shorter or longer. The protracted cycle of the day aroused no urges (here, women and men ate and slept whenever they felt the need), yet hunger hit the four of them at the same moment. This was no coincidence. She and her mate stood as one, their new companions following a heartbeat later. They stretched, eliciting a few pops from their spines, and once more shaded their eyes to peer around the circumference of the shallow depression.

She winked at her mate and spoke his name, the fondness clear in her voice. He grinned, pulled her off her feet as though she weighed nothing, squeezing her tightly to his massive chest as she wrapped her pale, corded arms around his thick neck and breathed in his brassy scent. Over his shoulder, she grinned at the two new men, whose faces she had known for generations upon generations.

A slight smile pulled at the corners of the lighter-skinned one's mouth, but he said nothing.

The darker one simply stared.

They sat in the dirt and grass. From their packs came salted beef, vinegared seaweed, and raw slices of the ever-present sweetroot. It was delicious, as was nearly all food after working in the outdoors, under the sun. Under *any* sun, really.

Finished but still hungry, the darker of the the two strangers lifted one of the sweetroots he had picked. He fished a knife from the pocket of his rough cotton pants and deftly sliced the vegetable into four sections. They shared it in companionable silence.

She examined the men she knew but had not yet spoken with. Both looked much like she remembered, much as they had for uncounted ages.

The shorter and heavier of the two, the quicker to smile and laugh, had skin the color of creamed chicory broth. He stood like a man forever bent forward into the wind, with meaty shoulders hunched and chin tucked into his collar. She had never known him as a child—no, not in all the lives they had shared—but she imagined him muddling through, fighting and winning battles he had never intended to fight, simply wanting peace, a place to belong.

The second man . . . she could not help thinking of him as father to the first, though she knew this was wrong. Tall, black skinned and muscular, he held himself with a straight spine, broad shoulders thrown back, chin high. A position of habit, not true disposition. As with the other, she had only known him as a grown man. Regardless, she knew that as a child he had lorded over his peers, only with the onset of adulthood learning how not to be a tyrant, to be strong without recourse to coercion.

She liked the first immediately. In time, she knew she would grow to love the second. Just as she always had. She regretted that they chose to be alone for so much of their existence. She and her mate could stand to be apart for such a short period: they found one another readily, falling into one another as fate dictated. Even through the occasionally cloudy haze of her memory, during moments when she could not seem to differentiate one life from the next, their longing for each other was clear.

But these two?

They only came together where the need presented itself, typically in an engagement of war, of revolution. When the violence exhausted itself, when death became too much to bear, they came to her, to where she and her mate had built a small life. They carried their pain with them, bearing it on their own, remaining silent until there was something to say.

‡

What the dark one said first never varied.

"Do you recall the conditions of my death?" he asked, white eyebrows nearly meeting over his nose. He furrowed his brow. His lips quivered as he sought words for the idea he knew to be true.

"My *first* death," he clarified.

She tipped her head back and smiled into the sun.

"You're asking me to remember ancient history. But yes. I could never forget. I'd only just died, myself." She laid her hand upon her mate's knee. "You still lived, dear—remember? And yet you'd already lived such a short, eventful life."

Her mate nodded his massive head, heavy features serene.

She returned her gaze to the black-skinned man. She nodded to him, and then to the man she could not help but think of as his son. Her smile waned slightly.

"And you? Well, you'd both been alive for far too long. You were dangerous to yourselves and a greater danger to our world, threatening the existence of an entire continent of people." She clucked her tongue and shook her head. "These are simple things to say, of course, as if the millennia had turned you from men into monsters. This is nowhere near the truth."

The black-skinned man frowned. "What is the truth, then?"

She sighed. The wrinkles at the corners of her eyes deepened.

"Normal men can indeed be turned into monsters – ordinary, un-imaginative monsters. Even with their lives preserved for eons, they are of one design. But you, you were never normal men. There was something of the monster in you from the beginning, an awful poten-tial. And your children, your siblings, they too . . ."

She shrugged. Her gaze centered on an indefinite space between the two men. For a span of seconds or hours, she was not among her companions. Her name changed, and changed again. She grew taller, shorter, but no broader, no darker.

She was another time, another place. Another woman.

Telling a story, again and again.

‡

Eventually, from a great distance away, the lighter-skinned man said, "You spoke of our world, a place of origin. What was this place called?"

She blinked, struggling to hold onto the question. She had not completely returned to them, but existed in a liminal space, in the interstices between a hundred lives.

Her mate gripped her knee, causing her to sigh.

Her anchor hit soft earth again, connecting her this time, this place.

"Jeroun," she said. She repeated the word, her smile once more radiant.

CHAPTER ONE

Certain facts were indisputable, even to him, and the most basic was this:

Not long after the birth of men on Jeroun, less than a thousand years following their emergence from slumber, the god Adrash had engineered a gift for the world.

A son.

A lavender-skinned, devil-horned boy named Shavrim Thrall Coranid.

He was not born, but tipped from a jar. Nonetheless, he grew as if he were a child.

The people of Jeroun thought of him as a human boy, knowing he was not—knowing he was a unique creature only in the approximate shape of a child, composed of man, elder, and god in equal proportions, possessed of an immortal body and a vast unfilled intellect. They understood he had neither birth mother nor true father, that he had been conditioned from conception to think of Adrash as his creator, yet they persisted in thinking of him as the god's proper son.

This sentimental illusion faded as Shavrim grew into adulthood and assumed his formidable stature, and disappeared completely when Adrash took him as lover. Though the god had not announced his intention to take Shavrim into his bed, the shift from child and son,

7

to demigod and lover, happened fluidly, as though it were the only possible outcome. As though it were fated.

Men had no reason to doubt that fate and the will of Adrash were one and the same.

Shavrim had no reason yet to doubt, either.

‡

"You are mine, but I am not yours."

He had heard these words many times, always in moments of intimacy. It did not hurt to hear them. He appreciated that Adrash spoke plainly, refusing to call what they shared love. Resentment would indeed come—it could not be avoided entirely, even in one created for the role of companion—but for decades Shavrim considered the words appropriate, even comforting, a frank assurance that all continued according to a plan set out for him.

A plan he neither understood nor cared to understand.

A plan that simply *was*.

Of course, he had little enough reason to complain over his lot. The world offered him many delights beyond communion with Adrash. With the god's blessing, he took thousands of lovers. He ate countless varieties of food, drank every drink. He experienced each diversion concocted by the vibrant cultures of man, and became himself a source of fascination and joy.

Though Jeroun bore the scars of a long life, having already outlasted its first race of people, the birth of mankind had made everything new, full of light.

‡

Or rather, this was how Shavrim recalled it now, eons after Adrash abandoned the world to madness. He knew it to be comfortable fiction, a lie, a bandage over old and unhealing wounds. For certain, he misremembered the world as more beautiful, more alive than it had ever been, just as he misremembered Adrash as more cruel, more inhuman.

Sometimes, this fact made him uncomfortable.

Other times, he did not care. The events of thousands of years, stored in the branching neural tissue of his spine and limbs, collected over the course of his long, slow adolescence, could be changed if he concentrated—or simply ignored—hard enough, and as he grew older he found little reason to recall with perfect clarity events that had ceased to matter.

All pasts were versions of pasts. Thus, he interpreted whatever version he liked.

The most important of what he interpreted, however, the most impactful—these were facts.

Of this he felt sure, or at least fairly confident.

‡

And so the world had seemed new, full of light, and then it had stopped. Not all at once, true, but being that Shavrim's existence would be measured in glacial ages rather than decades, compacting normal lives into insignificance, the process could feel no way other than sudden.

It was the first morning of his four-hundredth year. He and Adrash sat on a red-tiled terrace overlooking the ocean (what island he could not now recall, and it did not matter), enjoying breakfast, talking inconsequentialities, when, as though they had been having another conversation entirely—a deeper, more cutting conversation—the god spoke eight words.

"Do you really think you are enough, Shavrim?"

Shavrim set his cup of tea, small in his outsized hands, on the table between them. Not yet worried, merely confused. "I—" He searched for the proper expression, and arrived at a smile. Despite his labyrinthine knowledge of the world and its peoples, his vast collection of experiences, his face was rather blank. Not a man's at all, but that of a child. Just as the world saw him.

"I . . . I don't know what you're asking me, Adrash."

The god smiled, beautifully. Every movement he made was beautiful, a display of perfect grace. He sat, legs crossed at the knee, naked and at ease, every muscle relaxed yet defined. Warmth radiated from his jet skin: this close, he was a source of heat as sure as the sun itself. He wore the divine armor as a skintight cap in the shape of a helm, its filigreed edges giving the odd impression of white hair on his forehead, white hair curled around his ears.

"I do not mean this to hurt you," he said, ignoring Shavrim's guffaw of contempt. "Nonetheless, it *will* hurt you. At times I feel dissatisfied with this world, with you—with me. Boredom is as good a word as any, Shavrim." He waved his right hand vaguely. "But this is not your fault. I will not blame you for being predictable as I designed."

Shavrim blinked. The skin of his face felt tight, suddenly hot.

"You are a symptom of my thinking," Adrash continued. "And my thinking on the matter of mankind has been incorrect. For five centuries I have given them too much what they want, and they are becoming complacent, unwilling to grow. I am annoyed by their lackluster art, their spineless leisurely expressions. As exhausting as mankind's displays of aggression can be, I am saddened to see the fight gone out of them." He broke Shavrims's gaze, and stared out to sea.

"I am tired of being the world's nanny, of shielding everyone from harm. Furthermore, I need other sources of companionship lest I go mad. I made a minor miscalculation with you, stretching your development unduly. That mistake must be addressed. You must stop being a child."

"Adrash," Shavrim said. "Adrash, I . . ."

The god shook his head, silencing his creation with a gesture. "I am sorry, but you have no words of relevance to this. I have decided, already, on a course of action, for you and for the people of Jeroun. I have waited to enact my plan for too long already. My evasion of the topic, I fully believe, is part of the problem." He sighed. "But enough navel gazing. Soon, within the year, you will have brothers and sisters—five companions. You six will act as mankind's inspiration, but also as its aggressors. You will spur them to grow. *You will grow up with them.*"

He stood, and walked down the steps to the beach.

Shavrim followed, massive shoulders bowed, arms hanging limp at his sides.

‡

The feeling of discontent persisted. It grew, and only rarely retreated to a comfortable distance. Surely, Shavrim had experienced moments of unhappiness before—on rare occasions, his desires had gone unfulfilled—

but these were as nothing compared to this new malaise. He absented himself from Adrash for weeks at a time, visiting the places he thought he loved and then quickly leaving, unsatiated. He found himself in new beds, but experienced nothing new.

The world had not changed, not yet.

And then, within a year, as Adrash promised, the first of five siblings was tipped from the jar: a girl, grey haired and thin-limbed, clawed at hand and foot and as pale as sun-bleached sand. Adrash passed the childlike creature to Shavrim, and Shavrim stared into her bluegreen eyes as she stared back. She did not cry, which made him resentful. He felt sure he had cried upon breathing his first breath.

"Bash Ateff," Adrash named her.

A month later, the second arrived: an unnaturally ruddy, stubby-winged boy Adrash named Orrus Dabulakm. Shavrim took to him immediately, liking the sound of his hoarse cries better than the sullen silence of the sister who had come before him.

The next month, the third—a thing of indeterminate gender, a neuter or a new sex entirely—tumbled forth and stood unaided, but did not open its eyes for twelve days. When it did, two slowly spinning wooden orbs were revealed. Adrash called this blind anomaly Sradir Ung Kim, and seemed especially fond of it.

The fourth and fifth were engineered together, a matching pair. They spilled from the jar locked together, small and hairless and pearlescent, nearly metallic, and refused to untangle from their embrace for a full day. Afterward, they became uncomfortable if separated for longer than a few minutes. Ustert and Evurt Youl, Adrash named them.

"These," Adrah said when all five were situated in their nursery high in Adrash's main keep overlooking the arid Aroonan plains, "are the bringers of a new age, Shavrim. A minor pantheon. As their elder sibling, it is your job to guarantee they keep to the path I have cut for them."

Shavrim nodded, and did not ask just what path this was. He would learn in time.

‡

"I've killed men before," Shavrim said a decade later.

He and Adrash stood on the foredeck of *The Atavast*, watching the five young demigods cavort unafraid in the shallow, glass-clear water. The sea was no place for earthbound creatures, but today the god had created a hundred-foot sphere of will around his ship, halting the dozens of streamlined serpents and fish—which had quickly been attracted by the smell of flesh—from coming any closer. The siblings dared each other to swim up to the barrier of huge, circling predators. Soon they pushed their courage even further, reaching out their hands to brush the scaled flanks, risking the loss of limbs to giant, toothy mouths.

Adrash smiled. "Adorable," he said.

Shavrim ground his teeth together. "Are you listening to me?"

"Yes, I am, Shavrim. A moment, though." Adrash opened his right hand, revealing five coins. He threw them in an arc, causing each to hit the water and fall to the sand a body's length outside his protective barrier. "We do not leave until each of you has retrieved your coin!" he called, and then turned away from the siblings' whoops and cries in response.

"I know you have killed men, Shavrim. It is a joy to watch you fight." His left hand, which he had caused to be sheathed in the featureless white of the divine armor, fell on Shavrim's right shoulder. "What I am talking about now is different. You have never killed a man for any reason other than sport—a sport whose rules both parties understood and accepted. A sacrifice. This will not be the same. You will kill for a purpose. You will kill in response to a threat."

Shavrim laughed, though it had an edge to it: it was a sound he did not enjoy hearing come from himself, a sound he would not have made a decade previously. "A threat? How many men constitute a threat against me? A hundred? Two hundred? A battalion, either way. You're joking with me, Adrash."

"I am not. Men will soon be a great deal more formidable than they are now."

"How?"

Adrash turned and leaned his forearms on the railing. Shavrim sighed and followed suit, surveying his siblings at their dangerous play. There was no real risk, he supposed: though not as sturdy as their eldest brother, each was possessed of an immensely durable body. They would never bleed out or have their heads severed from their bodies. Should they lose a limb, it would regrow. Orrus had recently lost one of his growing wings to a weapon master's blade, and already its replacement reached half the size of the original.

Sradir and Orrus, Shavrim's favorite and least favorite, had already retrieved their coins. Orrus, forever dissatisfied, plagued by voices he could not name, frowned at his accomplishment and dived under the hull—to sulk, for reasons no one but Shavrim understood. Sradir bled from a shallow wound in its side, but it stopped as Shavrim watched. It looked up at Adrash (not blind, they had discovered, yet not seeing as men saw, either), a small smile on its oddly angular, androgynous face.

It did not even glance at Shavrim.

"You said men will become stronger than they are now, Adrash. How?"

Adrash clapped as the diminutive twins shot forward and retrieved their coins, Ustert landing a stiff-fingered jab into the snout of an advancing bonefish. He laughed as Bash, who could never resist showing off, swam slowly but gracefully toward her coin, rolling away from snapping jaws effortlessly, and picked up the final coin with her mouth. Shavrim wondered if he and Adrash's conversations had always been so broken, if the god had always been so distracted. He also questioned his own moods. Had he not been happy, being Adrash's lover but not the center of his world? Had he not been content, even overjoyed, to be part of a greater plan?

Yes, he had. And no, Adrash had not always been as he was now.

"Men will discover a secret," Adrash finally said. "Something right under their nose. Tell, me, have you ever wondered why I included elder material in your makeup? Elder corpses are rare, but besides not rotting like a man's body does they are virtually useless. Correct? Was I merely being sentimental for the people this world has lost?"

Shavrim flexed his fists alternately, in time with the doubled beating of his hearts.

"I was not," Adrash said, needlessly. "There is more to elder physiology than anyone knows, a fact I have hidden from the world but will hide no longer."

"What is *more*?"

Adrash chuckled. "You are becoming irritable in your middle age, Shavrim. Good, I suppose: anger will be useful, though I would not have you unhappy every moment of the day." He smiled, white against black. When Shavrim only grunted in response, the god's smile grew. "Power is what we are discussing. Immense power, outshining even the oldest technologies that existed before your birth and only remain in memory."

"And the rarity of elder corpses?" Shavrim asked. "There's a solution for that, as well?"

"Yes. There is a graveyard—a graveyard for an entire species. You will reveal it to the world."

‡

He did so, exactly as commanded. At the foot of The Steps, the elder's greatest monument, a mountain turned mausoleum, he helped excavate the first perfectly preserved corpse.

And immediately set it aflame.

The gathered people marveled at how it burned but was not consumed. Shavrim then reconstituted its ancient blood and allowed ten men to take sips of it. They battled each other for a day, sustaining wounds that would kill normal men. Lastly, he fed every individual a small measure of the corpse's ground bone. A week later, having eaten and drunk nothing, having not slept an hour, the people stood hale.

They celebrated, and began mining their new, nearly inexhaustible resource.

Thereby, men grew into maturity—or rather, into the wielding of power. Within two generations, the world had split and its peoples had become fractious threats to each other. Their arts turned violent, viciously inventive, seasoned with elder-corpse fire and blood. They relied less and less upon what remained of their old technologies, and then proceeded to forget this inheritance completely. Manipulating their acquired magic consumed them completely. Old cities were abandoned and new cities built, spanning chasms and straddling mountaintops, each lit by the glow of thousands upon thousands of magelamps.

Adrash rejoiced in mankind's rekindled passion. He orchestrated their development, wielding Shavrim and his siblings like blades, cutting nations in two, separating culture from culture, beginning wars and stopping wars. He spoke of symbols, of the importance of identity, and using arcane means fashioned weapons unique to each of his creations:

Sroma, a long silverblack knife for Shavrim: a malevolent item, possessed of its own ill personality. It did not speak in words, but made its desires known easily enough. Shavrim cherished and despised it by turns. He tasted blood when it bit into flesh.

Jhy, a razored throwing circle for Bash, which passed through steel and rock as easily as it passed through flesh. Bash kept it close to her at all times, but always sheathed. She used it rarely, and only against the strongest mages, as if only to prove a point.

Deserest, a glass spear for Orrus—a weapon he refused to use.

Weither, an oilwood and leather sambok for Sradir. In its owner's hands, the diminutive whip became a blur, a devastating shadow that severed even the most armored men in half. Sradir never used its proper name, instead referring to it as Little Sister.

Ruin and Rust, a pair of short swords for Ustert and Evurt: blades that never grew dull and would not be tarnished. Oddly, Ustert, who seemed always on the verge of an outburst, who lived with abandon, wielded Ruin with a cold detachment, while Evurt, the quiet one, carved with Rust in wild arcs, almost as though he were trying to throw the weapon away.

Thus equipped, no army on the face of Jeroun could stand against them.

This fact ate at Shavrim. He had been warned of threats. Initially, when he spoke of his concerns to Adrash, he received smiles and hints of further developments ("Have faith in me, Shavrim. I don't labor to provide you with tools for your defense simply to watch you wave them about."), but as time passed the god's enthusiasm took on a dark, solipsist edge. Adrash spoke rarely, his moods unpredictable. He spent time away, always just out of reach, leaving the increasingly complicated task of governance to his eldest creation, often for years at a time.

Each time, coming back crueler, more inscrutable.

The thin persona of a man sloughed away, revealing the madness of divinity.

‡

Simplifying the first millennia after the introduction of elder magic, turning such a vast length of time into one color, one feeling, proved appallingly easy for one who had never been human and could only approximate the concerns of one. Surely, the change in Adrash had occurred gradually: Shavrim had known it then and certainly knew it now, yet in retrospect it was shockingly abrupt, as rapid as a droplet of ink clouding into a pail of water.

One day, he had known his creator intimately, felt the god's moods as if they were his own—or thought he did, though the distinction makes little difference. And the next, he struggled to understand the capricious demands of a stranger, an incomprehensibly powerful being who forced his creations to betray the very people they had been engineered to assist.

One day, Shavrim had been a child, trusting, and the next . . .

‡

"The world would be better without him," he said, the obvious conclusion to a hundred years of long and evasive arguments. Finally, he said it.

And then, he said even more: "He must be destroyed."

Ustert grinned, revealing her sharp teeth. She threw one shapely silver leg over her twin's and laughed. "Grief, Shavrim, that's a nice thought. But there's no chance of it happening. I don't like him any more than you do—haven't liked him since I was small enough to be mistaken for a corpse miner—but we're six against a god. Besides, he's not really *here* any longer, is he? Off on his little ship, father is, doing who knows what."

"Don't call him that," Evurt said. He sat as rigid as his twin was relaxed, a thin bronze statue of a man. "I don't like it when you call him that. He's not our father."

Ustert rubbed his cheek with the back of her hand, causing Evurt to grimace.

"So, you're not in love anymore," Bash said. She flicked at an imaginary piece of lint on her coat. "So, you've been abandoned, forced into a role you never wanted and aren't suited for." Her seawater eyes met his, and her features softened. "You used to hate me, eldest brother. I know you did. But I'd hate to think you wanted me gone from the world. Give it time. Maybe you'll feel differently. Maybe he'll feel differently."

"This isn't about love," Shavrim said.

Sradir nodded, expressionless as only it could be. "Of course it is not, Shavrim. Bash is speaking in her metaphors again."

Ustert grinned.

Shavrim looked to Orrus, who shrugged with both shoulders and wings. "I'm in," the winged demigod said in his rasp of a voice. He tapped his head and then gestured to encompass each of them. "All of us are in. We can pretend otherwise, but it's the fact."

Bash opened her mouth and then closed it.

"Yes," Evurt said, just as his twin said, "Fuck."

Sradir gazed woodenly at Shavrim. "Many will die. Even we may die. Are you that in love with mankind?" The corners of its mouth rose fractionally. "Love being a metaphor, mind."

"We aren't men, so love is not the word," Shavrim answered. "Love is never the word for us. But I won't see mankind pushed and pulled by his whims any longer, given the tools of war and domination and then crushed for their arrogance when they use them. I won't be one of those tools any longer." He stood and paced before them. "So, he's gone for a decade, two, even three. He'll be back, and who knows what he'll do then? Even absent, he exerts his influence. You can't tell me you don't all feel it. It limns our every word, or every gesture."

Silence—as close to assent as they would give. Shavrim pressed.

"We're a reflection of Adrash, and we're slowly going mad with him. We all know the result of madness on our scale, which is terrible enough, but on his? The world will be burned to a cinder, should he continue down this path. We'll be carried with him. We'll be responsible."

Bash shook her head. "But what if we're what's causing him—"

"No." Evurt stood abruptly, dislodging his twin. He made a cutting motion with his left hand. "No. We have heard this before, sister, heard it and dismissed it. The question is irrelevant because it has no answer. We may be the source of Adrash's disease—or we may not be. It does not matter. We are the cure, either way. The *only* cure."

The room grew quiet, ever the result of Evurt choosing to voice more than a brief complaint. Ustert reached forward and drew her twin back down onto the couch, wrapping her arms around him. Sradir closed its eyes, blank-faced. Bash raised her eyebrows at Orrus, and Orrus turned his intense gray gaze to Shavrim.

"We look to you," Orrus said. "Perhaps we shouldn't, but we do."

Shavrim nodded. He knew this, had relied upon it. There were advantages to the way his mind functioned, how it forced thoughts to branch out along pathways throughout his body, causing him to arrive at conclusions only after long and repetitious thought. One day he would come to feel overwhelmed by the lifetimes he had accreted in his stretched neurons, but it had not happened yet. He still possessed wisdom unique to him.

He crouched and pressed a huge palm against the sun-warmed marble floor, a floor he had slapped his bare feet upon as a child. He remembered being scolded by a tutor for running. He had scolded his siblings for doing the same when they were young.

"I won't pretend we're a family," he said. "I won't pretend we even enjoy sitting here with each other, especially not in this place. We're not saintly, by any metric, but we're not part of the disease spreading in Adrash's soul. Of this I'm sure. I think it more probable he engineered us too well to our task, and that our task was more complex than he let on. He couldn't predict what would happen to himself in time, but he knew the risk. He knew, and created us to keep himself from the void." His fingers stroked the leather sheath covering Sroma. "He even engineered us weapons for the task."

He heard an intake of breath—Bash—and held up his hand, forestalling her words of denial.

"I'm not saying he made plans for his own defeat. He will not concede to us, like a man taking medicine. He has let himself forget our full purpose, and we let him."

Sradir opened its eyes and locked stares with Shavrim.

"*We let him*," she said. The words were neither challenge nor agreement. "Well. No more of that."

‡

In the Month of Soldiers, Adrash ended his self-imposed exile of two hundred and seven years by landing *The Atavest* on the southwestern coast of Doma. Announcements, which would in time become slow and expensive, dependant upon massive reserves of elder-corpse materials, traveled quickly from Adrash's hand. Mankind—not one member of which had known their god in the flesh—rejoiced with a month-long celebration.

Despite the passage of two centuries, Shavrim's siblings required no reminding or spurring to their purpose. Indeed, time had only increased their violent resolve. They allowed the celebrations to come to an end, and then met Adrash in the scrub desert of central Gnos Min, just beyond the eastern wall of Curathe.

The god read their intention immediately. Undoubtedly, no great act of premonition: all six had been conspicuously absent from the festivities.

The battle began without a word exchanged.

‡

Thirteen hours later, four of the six siblings remained. What had been the city of Curathe ticked as it cooled before them, a vast shallow bowl of fused ceramic.

Shaky on his feet, nearing a point of exhaustion where reality blurred around the edges, Shavrim experienced a vision of what the place would become in only a few months' time. Rain, falling in the Month of Mages (not a monsoon—nothing so monumental as that—merely a few tantrums, brief reminders of a wetter time), creating a temporary lake, a waystation for migrating birds and orr-bison, a place fleetingly filled with the low-throated burp of desert toads.

One day, too soon, men would stop and wonder at it, ignorant of its origin.

"Well done," Bash said, voice heavy with sarcasm. She wiped at the blood under her nose, and spit a tooth onto the ground. "We've got him on the run."

"Shut up," Orrus said, fist tight around Deserest, the weapon he had always declined to use.

Ustert remained silent. She held her right hand out to her side, as though expecting her twin to take it.

Shavrim closed his eyes, allowing himself to be buffeted by the wind.

Adrash had taken Sradir first. A wise move, Shavrim thought: he had always suspected it was the most powerful of his siblings. Then he had chosen Evurt. Another wise move. Without her twin, who knew what Ustert would be?

One battle, and already they had lost two of their number.

Had he anticipated anything else?

"I hadn't expected it to hurt so much," he said, so softly he thought no one would notice, but he heard the rustle of Orrus's wings and knew his brother had been heard. Of course. He and Orrus had always been close. They understood one another, how deeply, Shavrim would only know in the millennia to come—alone, searching for meaning as the world spun slowly toward destruction. Searching, while he gradually succumbed to his own madness, the compounding of a thousand voices.

And yet it was Ustert who spoke in response.

"Yes, it hurts. Of course it hurts." Her voice was flat, characterless. "You always lie to yourself, eldest. You practice the worst sort of deception, hiding from what is plainly true, what is obvious to everyone but you. We were a family, or as close to family that the phrasing becomes unimportant. Whether we liked one another had no bearing on this fact. If you'd stopped, for one moment, and looked up from your worship of Adrash, your sadness over losing him, you'd have realized this sooner. Now it comes, and you think you feel pain. You feel nothing compared to me."

They waited one night to recover, sleeping on the open ground within an arm's reach of each other. Closer than they had ever been.

‡

The four moved on to Danoor, which already lay smoldering in the shadow of the Aroonan mesas. They passed through the rubbled grave of Lantern Light, turning away from the bodies that littered the brick-paved streets. Death—this they understood. An individual man's life held little importance, after all, but a city's worth? That many innocent souls possessed a weight, demanding acknowledgement even from demigods.

Adrash taunted them by being just a step ahead.

They were fast, but still crawling in comparison.

In Grass, where tradition said the first men had awakened from their ancient slumber, the god waited, hanging in the sky above the city, his aura shuddering around him in radiant golden waves. He was a man-shaped shadow at the center of a new sun, motionless. Taunting, still.

Ustert spat onto the dry earth. "Listen to me. He won't take one or two or three of us. He takes all four of us, or we kill him. This ends now."

No one responded, but all were agreed.

Shavrim peered through waves of heat into the city. From as close as a mile away, it appeared as though it had been left untouched, but as they entered its gates Shavrim saw that everyone—those visible in the streets, but the effect surely extended to those indoors—stood or sat frozen in place, either held in temporary thrall or, more likely, halted forever in the state of death. Such a thing was not beyond Adrash's power, though Shavrim imagined the act drained him considerably. A small, grisly boon to his attackers.

By unspoken agreement, a simple acknowledgement that events would unfold exactly as quickly as Adrash willed, they walked into the city. As they neared the central square, lesser buildings seemed to shuffle aside to reveal the full glory of Adrash's temple: this, the most ancient of structures, famed as the site of mankind's birth on Jeroun. Shavrim had always considered its warm sandstone edifices and encircling gardens beautiful. They remained so.

Upon their stepping into the square, Adrash commenced his descent from the sky. Slowly, maddeningly so.

Shavrim unsheathed Sroma, gooseflesh raising upon his arm at the touch of its hilt. He stretched his arms wide, muscles bunching massively in his back. He tipped his head to either side, cracking vertebrae. He touched the two small horns on his forehead.

Orrus stood, glass spear gripped in two hands before him, wings pulled in close to his back. He had never flown before the age of twenty, and then only under pressure from Shavrim. He would not fly now: it would do no good against Adrash.

Bash spun Jhy around the upraised index and middle fingers of her left hand. She also spun Weither, Sradir's recovered whip, by its lanyard. She had always been the showoff, and Shavrim admired her athleticism. He had never told her this, but surely she knew.

Ustert likewise held two weapons—her own sword, Ruin, and her twin's sword, Rust—and stood, rooted to the ground by two wide-set feet. Of the five siblings, only she had beaten Shavrim in armed combat. She had never let him forget it.

Adrash reduced the blaze of his aura as he descended. Nonetheless, by the time he landed on the steps of his temple the light from his eyes alone proved sufficient to throw acute shadows from every standing object. His four living creations squinted against the radiation, unfazed, while the people gathered in the square, struck immobile in the seconds after death, blistered from the heat.

The god stood, unmoving, encased head to toe in the flawlessly white embrace of his armor. Despite himself, as always, Shavrim admired the graceful lines of his creator's physique, its contours accentuated rather than hidden by the divine material, and felt the accompanying rush of desire. He risked a glance at Bash and confirmed the flush in her pale cheeks. She, too, could not hide her attraction, a fact which had always angered her.

It had been tens of decades since she or Shavrim had shared Adrash's bed, yet their bodies would not allow them to forget.

Orrus had not moved a muscle, revealing to Shavrim an altogether different type of strain. He had been, since birth, the least favored of Adrash—a hurt he would not allow shown on his features but still felt keenly. Ustert, conversely, had forever been a focus of the god's praise. But now, having witnessed the almost casual dismemberment of her twin, she shook with rage so thinly controlled that Shavrim feared for her. She would be a danger, very likely to herself.

Thus arrayed, they waited for the inevitable.

Hello, children, Adrash said, directly into the interiors of their skulls.

‡

The moment held, and in Shavrim's memory would forever hold— the moment separating being one of four whose souls rang in union, discordant though it was, and the next . . .

‡

It was two hours after dusk in the ransacked city of Danoor. He reclined naked on a flat clay roof, savoring the last of the day's trapped heat before it seeped out from underneath him. There was a distinct sharpness to the desert air, and he felt it—less than a man would, true, but enough to make him slightly uncomfortable. In truth, he enjoyed this unique sensation of discomfort. No matter how long-lived, one never forgot the feeling of home.

Though the city's fires had been doused, the smell of burnt timber and clay lingered.

Far off in the unlit night, beyond the border of Shavrim's orderly territory, someone screamed.

And above Shavrim—far, far above him, leagues and leagues beyond the envelope of air that surrounded the world—the heavens were shattered. What had been Adrash's greatest weapon, the ultimate symbol of his madness, a constant feature of the night sky generations of men had known as The Needle, now extended in broken orbit around the moon, each of its twenty-seven massive iron spheres spinning through the void on unplanned trajectories.

No longer in the god's control. No longer kept from falling.

Shavrim smiled, unashamed of the conflicting emotions the sight evoked. He admitted to himself that he was not quite happy, no, that in fact the sight of the world's approaching doom filled him with re-morse—but also that he felt a sense of satisfaction, of appropriateness, of *You've really done it now*. He considered with what emotion his lost siblings would have greeted the sight, and his smile widened. He said each of their names, names left unspoken for longer than he chose to remember. He spoke to them in a language the world forgot twenty-five thousand years ago.

His words were not, despite the evidence of his own eyes and hands, for the dead. He concentrated and projected them in a simple but tax-ing extension of will, broadcasting on a wavelength he alone had dis-covered, a wavelength unheard by anyone except the five ones caught in between, those unique souls who lingered in the spaces between life and death.

Souls who, for many millennia, he had believed were constructs of his own madness.

"Sisters. Brothers," he said. "This is the thing I would not admit aloud until now, but with the world on the brink of death, it seems a good time to unburden myself—of delusion, perhaps, though if I'm to be honest (and why shouldn't I be?), I know there is no perhaps, no maybe. There is no delusion, only truth. Or rather, I should say *madness* and truth. In each of the lives I live, in each of the voices of the past I let overtake me, your voices are clear. You are a constant, even in the madness I've allowed root. Your voices grow weak. They fade in and out, but they're always here."

He laid his left palm flat upon his chest. His right fist closed, and slowly his smile faded.

"You might wonder, why is it that brother has never spoken to us before—why has he not sought to make contact with us? It's a good question, for which I have no proper answer other than cowardice. I died with you, and then woke to bury you. Some contact wounds, and never heals. You may as well ask why I've avoided Adrash. Fear. Fear of what you've each become in the absence of your bodies. I know myself, even when I'm not myself, for that person is only myself in a different guise, living another life. I do this so that I avoid absolute madness.

"And yet I do not—*cannot*—know you. Not any longer. I am a body, and you are . . . I don't know what you are. Besides, it's been too long. I've forgotten too much. I've chosen to be alone, and grown used to it. Being alone is easier than having a family. When you have a family, you are responsible to each other. It's easier to navigate the world without that burden. Why should I be the one to live with it? Why must I be the eldest?"

He sighed, shook his head. That last note of petulance, he wished he could take it back, reword it. It was too late in his long life to express such things, even to the wind. Every word—he should not have spoken any of it. There was too much to say, and he was failing to communicate any of it.

A northerly wind flowed over the rooftop, and he shivered.

"Listen to me," he said, disliking the weak sound of his voice. The act of projecting, of summoning ancient words and buried sentiment, had exhausted him. And he still had not voiced the most important of what must be voiced. He disliked entreaties.

"Listen to me," he repeated, nearing a whisper now. "Look at the sky tonight, and know there is need for us yet. Yes, even as we are, mad and lost and even half rejoicing in what has occurred. We stood together once. We can do so again."

He closed his eyes, breathing deeply for the space of twenty doubled heartbeats.

"Please. Help me keep the world alive."

‡

He listened, growing colder and more convinced of his foolishness as the moon and shattered sky passed slowly overhead. Less than an hour went by, yet it felt like three. When he finally admitted defeat and stood, his joints creaked. A new weight had settled into his bones. He suffered a moment of lightheadedness and wondered—were he a normal man, if the moment would have inspired suicide. Perhaps it was the perfect time to pitch himself from the roof.

If he were a normal man, release would have been just that easy.

Not for the first time, he considered the curses placed upon him.

The first:

To be so unreasonably loyal to mankind, knowing what he knew of its members. Their pettiness and greed, their pretensions of greatness. He had suffered more of their failures and fought in more of their wars than Adrash had, yet he was the one who could not fail to sympathize with them, to want more *for* them. Oh, he had killed many of their number (just as often in joy as anger, truthfully), but this was no contradiction. Humanity existed as a mass, and only exceptionally as individuals.

And individuality? This was his second curse:

To be alone. To think on the scale of a god, and have no other gods except the ones that had abandoned you. To have known how it feels not to be alone, and to have squandered it.

He considered aloneness as he descended from the rooftop and entered the games hall from which he ran his new territory. The air was warm inside, but not uncomfortably so. Despite the number of men and women gathered in friendly competition, it was not loud. People greeted him, though not warmly. They tried—they always tried—but he was simply too intimidating, too alien, looking nearly like a man without at all being a man. Furthermore, he was their leader. He moved among them like a predator, with odd grace for such a large person.

"Shav," said Laures, his first lieutenant, a woman chosen for her intelligence, but also for the fact that she rarely spoke more than his name. It amused him slightly, the fact of her faith: she worshipped the goddess Ustert. If only she knew what kind of creature his sister had been, how dependent she had been upon her twin, perhaps she would not be so warmly inclined. Usterti believed all the wrong things about their goddess. They had robbed her of her love, made her into a solitary creature.

He nodded to her on his way out the front door.

Into the street, peaceful again. He looked either direction and set off south, intending to inspect the barricades . . .

‡

And fell to his knees.

Out in the night, closer than he could have imagined, a voice spoke— a voice he recognized instantly—a coincidence too extraordinary given where his mind had only just passed.

Vedas Tezul, it said.

Shavrim toppled onto his side and shook violently upon the ground, struggling against the shock to his body and mind. He fought to order his thoughts, to respond before the connection was severed, but before any true headway could be made a second coincidence announced itself, its voice fainter than the first but equally distinct after so many thousands of years.

Churls Casta Jons, it said.

"I . . . I . . ." Shavrim stuttered, jaws cramping and jumping. "I . . . will . . . will . . ." He bit down hard, speaking through gritted teeth. "Find . . . you."

‡

He received no confirmation that either had heard. He lay immobilized in the street until early morning, when his lieutenant Laures found him and dragged him inside. She said nothing. He stared up at her as she struggled with his awkward weight. He would not thank her, yet a portion of his mind felt gratitude, though not for her current efforts: perhaps thinking of her faith had allowed his mind to open just enough to let his sibling's voices in.

I am coming, bother, he thought. *I am coming, sister. We will be together soon. We will seal our fate, as a family.*

CHAPTER TWO

THE 10TH TO 13TH OF THE MONTH OF SECTARIANS
THE NEVAA SALT FLATS TO DANOOR, THE REPUBLIC
OF KNOS MIN

After the sun set, Churls shaved her head with his razor. She considered why she did it and arrived at no answer. She had never been one for symbols. Her hair had been short enough for the purpose, already.

Afterwards, she cut a long rectangle of fabric from a sheet and wound it around her sinuous torso, flattening her breasts before fastening on a tight, stiff leather vest and back scabbard.

Another almost unnecessary act: her breasts were small enough, as they were.

She sneered at her face in the monastery's one mirror, a vanity item she had been surprised to find in the building's cellar, and wiped at a bead of blood on her scalp.

Her reflection unnerved her. Nearly a week spent in bed recovering from from her injuries, followed by two weeks of waiting for her daughter to bring back good news from the city, had resulted in a visible change in her appearance. Her arms and thighs were thinner than she preferred. The freckles on her cheeks and shoulders, typically a near-solid mass of brownish red, had faded to a speckling.

She pulled on the pair of the rough woolen pants she had found in an alcove. They were looser than she preferred, binding in odd places. Why could men not fashion pants that fit properly?

The back of her neck began tingling.

"You can come in now, Fyra," she said.

Her daughter sharpened into existence at Churls's side, colored all in shades of white but for the pale blue of her eyes. She stood to within a few inches of her mother's shoulder, and had not been alive for well over a decade.

She screwed her features into a grimace. "It looks . . . bad. And it's bleeding in the back."

"Forgive my clumsiness," Churls said. "I had a beard when I was your age, but it fell out when I had you. As a result, I'm a bit rusty at all this." She met the girl's unimpressed gaze and fought to keep the hope from showing on her own features. "You're sure you've got a fix on them? You're sure—about all three of them?"

Fyra nodded. "For the third time, mama, yes. I'll lead you right to them. If you want, I can . . ."

Churls buckled her belt. "I don't want. To quote you: *for the third time*, no. Also, to repeat myself, we have no idea what will happen to you if you're attacked by whatever sort of mage Fesuy's hired to shield Vedas and Berun from sight." *Not to mention keeping you at a long arm's length*, she did not add. "It's enough that I let you scout. I won't risk putting you in the midst of a fight with someone that strong."

She caught the slight upturning at the corners of the girl's mouth. "And yes, that means I just admitted you're very strong. Still, you're not as strong as your mother. Not in the same way. And you're definitely not as mean. I won't hear any more about it."

Her daughter said no more. A surprise. Churls had expected a rebuttal.

She felt grateful, but also slightly awkward about the exchange. Their banter, a thing that had only started in the absence of Vedas and Berun, seemed to proceed naturally enough between them—as it should have for a mother and daughter alone, surely—yet Churls could not escape the fact of its novelty. She and Fyra had never talked that way while the girl lived. She doubted its authenticity. Furthermore, to speak so casually inspired a sense of disloyalty. She could not sustain a constant state of worry over her missing companions, but suspected she should at least make the attempt.

Fyra cleared her throat. Made a throat-clearing sound, anyway.

"You're crying, mama."

Churls wiped her eyes with a tattooed forearm. "Shit," she whispered. She breathed deeply into her stomach. "Fyra. You will not accompany me. I do this alone. Do what you like for me now, but you don't set foot beyond these walls. I need you to say you understand me."

To her credit, the child did not immediately agree. Churls approved.

"I understand, mama," Fyra said, "and I mean it this time. I won't leave. But first, you need to promise *me* something. Something big."

"What?"

"You need to keep your promise. You need to tell him about me. About *us*."

Churls tipped her head back to stare at the bare rock ceiling. The room suddenly seemed too close, crowded, as if the dead had gathered at her daughter's word. To hear Churls's answer.

"You don't know what you're asking," she said. "There's no war against Adrash. Vedas failed to rouse anything but ire and violence. His speech threw the world into discord."

She pointed heavenward, gesturing beyond the tonnage of stone separating them from the wrecked night sky. "He damned us all, and you know what, girl? I don't care, because in the end he was right. We've been living under threat for too long, cowed and in denial. If we all die in flames, we all die in flames, and there's nothing to be done. Not by you, not by me. I just want him back, and I'm going to get him back. Him *and* Berun. Beyond that? You can't make me care beyond that—not right now."

Fyra's hands tightened into fists at her hips.

"You lied to me."

Churls's head dropped. A growl built low in her throat. Suddenly, the seven-hour hike to the city seemed like an interminable delay. She wanted everything over and done. She would see everything over and done, and then she would think.

She spoke slowly, carefully. "I'm not saying I won't tell him, Fyra. I'm just saying it'll make no difference if I do." She looked up, offered the girl a weak smile neither of them believed. "Now, please, do what you're going to do to help your mother save the day, alone, and then do nothing else."

For a moment, Churls thought her daughter would refuse, but the girl merely rolled her eyes and stepped forward into Churls, filling her with warmth and light.

‡

The Nehuaa Salt Falts comprised nearly half of the area of northwestern Knos Min. The flat, featureless landscape had once been the bed of an inland sea scholars called Littleshallow, and now provided salt for an entire continent. A rainless, lifeless, maddeningly uninteresting terrain, it seemed the whole of the world when one traveled upon it. Any destination rose out of the cracked white floor as though floating, mountains and cities alike standing still in the vague distance, never growing any closer until one gratefully stumbled into them.

Twenty miles of this landscape lay between the monastery and Danoor.

Churls barely registered the distance or the time it took to cross it. She did not look behind her once to see the hills ringing the monastery fade into the night. She barely looked at the city before her. She ran, legs solid yet spring-light beneath her, losing herself easily in the rhythm of feet hitting earth. The quietly rational part of her mind worried what Fyra had done in order to allow her access to such an immense reservoir of energy—worried what the wage would be when it inevitably ran out, and whether or not she should have saved it for later—but she easily silenced it.

Too easily, she reasoned, and dismissed this too with a smile.

Her fear, a thing she had barely allowed a voice. Erased entirely.

Her annoyance at being forced into a concession, posing as a man. Gone.

Point in fact, she had not felt this good in a long time, certainly not since Vedas and Berun's abduction. In her current state, she found it surpassingly simple to absolve herself of the guilt she had given free rein for the last month.

It had not been her fault, the ambush. She could not have prevented it, given her knowledge at the time.

Her anger had fled, as well. Berun had been right to swat her across the room—an action that knocked her unconscious while simultaneously depositing her behind a row of crates. She had not appreciated how quickly the constructed man came to his conclusion and acted to keep her from being taken as well.

Of course, no one liked waking up alone, abandoned in a dangerous city with a shattered clavicle and a row of broken ribs. A twenty-mile walk back to safe shelter would not help, either.

No wonder Fyra did not like being ordered to stay away. She had sobbed (rather, made the ghost motions of sobbing) when Churls collapsed at the top of the hill overlooking the monastery. Churls had nearly killed herself by walking so far with such injuries.

"You should've called to me, Mama," the girl had said. "I would've heard. You make me so angry."

Churls grinned at the memory. Damn, but she was enjoying herself.

The euphoria lasted until the moment she entered the city's outskirts and forced herself to a walk: an act that was like stopping a massive grinding wheel with bare hands, or swimming against a swiftly-flowing river. A sense of sadness overcame her, as of an opportunity lost. She could have kept going, cutting around the city, running until exhaustion overcame her. There she would have collapsed, succumbing to sleep without worry . . .

"Stupid useless fucking . . ." she whispered, feeling like a fool.

The moon and scattered spheres of The Needle loomed full in the west, casting ample light into the deserted streets. When she had last passed through this part of the city, there were still people about, but now the buildings at the outskirts of Danoor stood abandoned—that, or the people who lived in the low, red clay residences were keeping quiet, lights out.

She kept to the shadowed side of the street, moving deeper into the city, drawn without pause toward the target Fyra had planted in her mind. She unsheathed her short, dull sword and gripped the blade near the hilt for balance.

It felt good in her hand, warming to her touch quickly, as though coming to life.

She found herself grinning again, and realized she had been humming.

"Kill Rhythm," Battle March of the Third Castan Infantry.

‡

The guard tried to scream. His tongue flicked through his teeth, pressing wet and warm against her palm. She clamped her hand tighter to his mouth as his life flowed down the front of his shirt. His struggles slowed, stopped, and she lowered him gently to the ground.

She admired the small ceramic knife in her hand—it had been the guard's only a few seconds ago, before she slipped it from his hip sheath and used it to slit his throat—and decided to keep it. She would finish Fesuy with her own sword, but the thought of using a Tomen weapon to strike the first blow struck her as poetically sound, appropriately disrespectful.

A quick circuit around the house revealed no further guards, a fact which confirmed her impression of Fesuy Amendja. The man was arrogant, stupidly so. After the risky maneuver of leaping over the heavily-sentried barricade (an act that seemed to have cost her the last of Fyra's imparted vitality), she had encountered few men and even fewer women, all but three of whom she had been able to avoid. Those three had died easily.

Though the sun still sat a half hour below the horizon, to have so few people about in a contested area seemed appallingly neglectful.

She picked the front door lock and entered the darkened two-storey building, dragging the dead guard with her.

Immediately, she felt it. The muscles of her jaw suddenly tingled, as though she had bitten into a lemon. The sensation built until it was an ache, which quickly spread throughout the bones of her skull into a steady, pounding throb. Her knees nearly gave out, but she leaned her back against the door and rode out the worst of it. Surely, whatever Fyra had done to her caused an increased sensitivity to whatever magics were in the building.

Surely, whatever Fyra had done to her would compensate to minimize the effects.

Any moment now . . . she thought. *Please* . . . But the pain persisted.

The light warned her, a second too late. An elderly Tomen woman rounded the corner, stepping down from the stairs at the end of the hallway. She jumped when she saw Churls, dropping her lantern with a glass clatter.

Churls flipped the ceramic knife. Underhanded, it was an awkward throw. The pommel glanced harmlessly off the woman's shoulder and struck the plaster behind her, but by that point Churls had already taken two steps in a run toward her target.

The woman got out one syllable of a warning or curse before Churls's forearm crushed her windpipe. Churls pinned her enemy against the wall and watched as the light fled from her eyes. For several seconds afterward, she held the woman there, heart pounding heavily enough to shake her entire body, breaths labored and painful as she struggled to keep them quiet.

Listening, over the roar of her pain.

A footstep on the landing above. The strike of a phosphor match.

Bright spots swam before Churls's eyes as she hauled the dead woman out of this new person's line of sight. The muscles of her chest and stomach had tightened with the pain, constricting her. She could not breathe in enough air, and tore at the buttons of her vest, alleviating the pressure slightly.

Above her, voices. Two men. She recognized one of their words.
Shira.

Her eyes shot to the ceramic knife, which lay on the floor at the foot of the stairs.

She did not think. Thinking would do no good in her current situation.

She rounded the corner and charged up the steps, sword in hand. Both men stood, stunned into statues by her appearance. She ran the first through his left lung and slammed into the second, carrying them both to the floor. They rolled twice before she got the upper position, and then struck him twice, open-palmed and in quick succession, forcing shards of cartilage into his brain, killing him instantly. She stood and pulled her sword free of the first, hastening his death by drowning.

The house woke up around her. From the sound of it, there were far more than a handful of men. Perhaps Fesuy had not been so incautious, after all.

She ran down the hallway, where she knew Vedas and Berun would be found.

‡

The two girls Fesuy had slept alongside—she would not think of them as women—sobbed in the corner. The man himself lay unconscious on the bed, naked, wrists and ankles tied and linked behind his back, bleeding into the sheets from a shallow cut on his temple. A heavy chair, propped against the doorknob, kept anyone from easily entering the room from the outside.

Of course, every member of the household knew Fesuy would die if they tried to enter, and this kept them out. For now. It was only a brief matter of time before they stopped caring and came in, regardless of the threat to their leader.

Churls finished her second search of the room, which every instinct told her *must* contain Vedas and Berun, and limped over to the bed. Fesuy groaned as she flipped him over. When she wound his long red hair around her hand and pulled him onto the floor, he woke and began cursing her, first in Tomen and then, when she let his head drop onto the rough wood floor, in Common.

". . . dick I'll rip out, your asshole I'll fill—with blades I'll . . ."

She knelt and slapped him, hard. "Shut the fuck up. Where are they?"

He started to speak, paused. She met his stare. When his eyes registered their recognition, she smiled. She pulled the knife he had kept in his bedside table from her boot and waved it. The pain in her jaw and temples had only increased, but she would not allow this to show on her face.

"So, you dress to look like a man," he said with a sneer. "You should not worry about that. You looked enough like one, already. In this camp, no one would have touched you. I have fifteen men in this house, all unmarried, and not one could I have convinced to lay with you."

"Thirteen," she said. "Your men are easy to kill."

She drew a shallow, straight cut on his lower stomach, and crossed it with another. He snarled and spit in her face.

"Where are they?" she asked again, pointing the tip at the X's junction.

He spit again, and she pushed the knife into him.

He screamed. Fists pounded on the door.

"Where are they?" she asked a third time, twisting the man's own blade in his guts. Not a fatal wound, not yet. He screamed again, louder, and the door jumped in its frame as his men hurled themselves against it. She stilled the knife and repeated her question, watching his face.

He tried to spit at her a yet again, and got it no farther than his own chin.

She took his face in her hands, leaving the knife sticking out of his belly. "Where, Fesuy? You have them here. Tell me where they are, and I'll leave you to your men. A good healer will have you up and about in a couple weeks."

He began cursing in Tomen again, but his eyes gave him away.

Her head whipped about to stare at the ceiling in the northwestern corner of the room. A ladder leaned against the wall underneath. It was an item she had mistaken as decoration, for which purpose they were sold throughout Danoor. She again hauled Fesuy by the hair, trailing blood behind. When the door burst open, she wanted him close at hand, but knew it would only stall the inevitable.

She needed to find Vedas and Berun. Now.

The ceiling was not high—only seven feet or so. This fact had not struck her before, but now it seemed noteworthy. Even the hallways had been a greater height, maybe nine feet. She examined the corner Fesuy had focused on, and nearly cried out in her delight. A square had been cut out of the plaster. It lay nearly flush with the rest of the ceiling, rendering it nearly invisible.

Her discovery had not been missed by Fesuy, who now began yelling instructions to his men. The door bucked harder in response.

Churls knelt, pulled the knife from Fesuy's belly, and plunged it into his chest, straight through his sternum. She screamed, pulled it out and hammered it home again—too hard: she felt something pop, something tear. She wished, for a handful of seconds while she stared at the hilt of the weapon protruding from him, gritting her teeth agony bloomed in her right shoulder, that she had been able to draw out his pain.

She recalled the earnest smile on his face, a several months ago, a lifetime ago, when he handed her a mejuan pod and they toasted it together. She recalled the smell of shit that rose from the body of the woman he killed the following morning.

The door burst open, sending the heavy chair crashing against the bed. Fesuy's men roared, and the girls in the corner screamed. Churls climbed the ladder and slammed her palm into the ceiling panel, shoulder screaming in protest.

She heard rather than felt the snap of bones in her hand. Uncaring, she hit the panel again. It levered up, and she pulled herself into the dark space beyond.

Every bone in her skull pulsed in redoubled white-hot agony. She shrugged it off as so much noise, slapped the ceiling door closed, and jammed the point of her sword into its unhinged edge. It would not hold against a concerted effort to open the panel, of course, but she hoped to have another solution soon.

She turned in a half-crouch, rapidly cataloguing the contents of the low room.

No windows. In the center, a single magelamp, set very low. A woman sitting behind it, eyes closed, legs crossed, apparently unaware of any cause for alarm. The mage.

A mountainous, man-shaped heaping of brass spheres, dimly seen in the far corner.

Beside it, a low camp bed. Upon it, a dark-clothed body.

‡

She limped over to the mage and kicked her in the stomach.

Immediately, the pain in her head ceased. She nearly fainted in relief.

The mage yelped as Churls pulled her head up by the hair. Her eyes slowly focused.

"Hello," Churls said through gritted teeth. "I'm your new boss. You do what I fucking say, immediately. Show you understand me."

The mage nodded, fear in her eyes.

Churls did not smile. "Good. There are people trying to get in here, so you have only seconds to secure this room. Fail, and I kill you."

‡

Ten seconds. Twenty. The pounding on the ceiling door continued. Thirty.

"Bitch," Churls said, tightening her grip on the mages' greasy hair. "I'd take me *very* seriously. Make this happen, *right n—*"

The pounding stopped.

"They're asleep," the mage said. "All of them."

‡

"And me?" Churls asked. "Why am I not asleep?" She needed to know what threat the mage was to her.

The woman swallowed, her eyes searching Churls's face. She was clearly Knosi, not Tomen. Potentially, a good sign: perhaps she had no loyalty to Fesuy.

"I'm not sure," she said. "Something's standing in the way. I can't touch you." Panic crossed her features. She had admitted to trying it. "Please . . . I wouldn't . . ."

Churls clapped the mage on the shoulder with her good hand. "Yes, you would. Keep them asleep, and we all live for a bit longer."

She crossed the room to her companions, bent partially over to keep from brushing the ceiling. Vedas lay immobile, sheathed completely by his black elder-cloth suit—worrying, as she had only seen him do so while conscious—but his pulse and breathing were strong. Her eyes avoided the hollow of his belly, the prominence of his ribs. His arms and shoulders were noticeably smaller. Slowly, with one and good hand and a barely functional second, she untied his wrists, which had been tightly bound with steel cord to the bed.

As for Berun, she had no way of checking on his status or removing his immense shackles, and so ignored him for now.

"Vedas," she said. She put her hand to his chest and shook him slightly. "Vedas."

No response. Churls limped back to the mage and crouched before her. The woman flinched away.

"What's wrong with them?"

The mage's confusion was obvious. "Asleep. I told you, everyone is asleep."

Churls kept herself from slapping the woman, barely. "Not them. Everyone sleeps but the people in this room. Wake them, now."

She did not wait for a reply, but went and knelt by Vedas's bedside again. She repeated his name, and waited as long as she could—perhaps thirty seconds—before turning back to the mage and gesturing her impatience. The mage, still obviously frightened, shook her head and protested ignorance.

"I don't know when they'll wake," she insisted when pressed. "They make me keep them out for most of the day. I allow the Black Suit to wake for feeding and voiding himself, but they still make me keep him in a daze. It always takes him a while to come to, longer each time. I can't force it or I risk hurting him. The construct I've only allowed to wake twice so the Titled Amendja could speak with him. He was weak, nearly insensate, both times." She pointed toward the roof, only five feet overhead. "The sun. He needs it, and I can only give him so much. Enough to keep him alive, no more."

Churls stood to examine the roof. "Increase the light," she ordered.

The magelamp brightened to a small sun, illuminating the bare room and revealing yet another ceiling panel above Vedas and Berun. Churls reached to unlatch it and paused.

"*Everyone* is asleep?" she asked.

"Yes," the mage said. "And no one is on the roof."

Churls open the panel, letting it fall back onto the roof. She looked quickly around to confirm what the mage had said, and also to determine if her assault on Fesuy's home had alerted any of the locals.

No one ran wild through the streets. She noticed a few more people about, though none seemed in any hurry. She relaxed slightly, thanking fate for thick, insulating clay walls.

The horizon glowed faintly, only forty or fifty minutes away from showing the sun. She wondered how long it would be before someone noticed the blood below the front door, noticed the missing guard, or failing either simply tried to enter the building for business. She doubted the mage could defend the entire structure from attack. Mages were specialists, after all: to become skilled in manipulating a man's consciousness took time and effort.

She checked on Vedas again, saw no change, and crossed the room again.

"Can you keep people from wanting to enter this building?" she asked the mage. "Or, better yet, can you make them disinterested in entering the building?"

"Yes. I can turn individuals and maybe small groups away from this building." The mage met Churls's stare and held it. The woman's eyes were dull and half-lidded. She had been overexerting herself or—more likely, Churls imagined—had been forced to overexert herself.

Nonetheless, there was now a note of defiance in her expression. She had realized her value to Churls.

"But I can't do it and keep everyone asleep," the mage said. "It's just too much."

Churls sat back, and for a moment refused to think.

The moment passed, and her shoulders slumped.

"Fuck," she said. "Fuck, fuck, fuck."

‡

Churls could not trust the mage not to wake everyone in the home once she was otherwise occupied. As a result, Churls brought the woman along.

Blindfolded, as she could not conceive of forcing anyone to watch her at her task.

Nonetheless, the mage understood what was occurring immediately. Even an unconscious body made noise in the process of dying. Inside the house, it was very quiet.

Thankfully, killing the two girls Fesuy had bedded proved unnecessary. They would not be able to escape the bonds and gags Churls used to restrain them. The rest, however, were clearly warriors, capable of a great deal more. She could not risk one getting loose, and so did what needed to be done. It remained a far, far from pleasant task—she had never killed an unconscious person, even an enemy—but at least, she reasoned, they were not the sort of men the world needed in greater quantities.

She breathed a sigh of relief: it seemed the only innocent death on her hands would be that of the woman she had killed upon entering the building. Then, in a small, nearly overlooked room on the first floor, she discovered two small children.

She removed the mage's blindfold and forced the woman to look.

"Dear Adrash," the mage whispered. Her eyes were wet, but her disgust with Churls was clear. "Why are you showing me this?"

Churls laughed without humor. "I'm showing you because something needs to be done. I won't kill them or tie them up, and I have no way to get them somewhere beyond these walls. There's too great a chance of our being discovered, even if I could get them to a place of relative safety. Tell me you can push yourself a bit harder."

They regarded one another. Churls anticipated the woman's refusal, and her resentment flared. The woman had allowed Fesuy to capture Vedas and Berun, an extraordinary feat considering their combined abilities. She had kept Fyra from finding them for an extended period of time. And now, now she would make an argument as to why a simple task could not be done?

Churls curled the fingers of her left hand into a fist.

"Please," she forced herself to say, voice flat.

Slowly, as if to draw out her slight success, the mage nodded. "I'll need them closer to me, however. That will make it easier."

Churls took one child in her arms, the mage took the other, and they returned to the attic.

‡

The day began, entering the room from its sharp angle to crawl slowly down the western wall. Neither Vedas nor Berun woke. Instead of watching time pass, Churls occupied herself by fetching bedding for the unconscious children and dragging bodies one-handed to the cellar. She made a good sweep of the floors, as the thought of tracking blood around the house sickened her.

When she could not rationalize avoiding it any longer, she explained the situation to the two frightened girls trussed on Fesuy's bed. They stared at her, comprehending only with repetition. Clearly, each had been sheltered and understood little of the language used beyond their country's border. Both looked horrified by the suggestion that Churls would assist them in using the toilet. They did not want her to touch them for any reason.

Churls sighed. "Fine. Piss and shit yourselves all you want. When you need water, you'll let me know in your own way."

She checked with the mage, who assured her that all was well, that she had deterred three people from approaching the house. The morning became afternoon. Her companions continued to resist waking, and so Churls took another camp bed from one of the lower rooms and placed it alongside Vedas's. She held his limp hand and did not sleep. She could not sleep, in fact—for fear of the mage trying something odd in her absence, but also, simply, because she had run out of tasks to keep her mind distracted. Even her worry over the fate of Vedas and Berun, the constant factor that had kept her from taking the broader view, was now at an end.

Whatever happened, would happen together.

This realization brought her comfort, but also consternation. She could no longer ignore the world around her—a world going mad.

A world that her lover had brought into existence.

This fact bothered her less than she would have imagined. Truthfully, it distressed her more that she could not summon the expected outrage, that she had not lied to her daughter. Vedas had been right to deliver his speech, exhorting men to stand with each other against Adrash. She approved of it, still, despite the chaos it had created. Staring at the night sky, denying or openly accepting the reality of what The Needle represented for generation after generation: neither spoke well of mankind. Both perspectives had warped the world into a place where no progress could occur.

Why labor to change anything when it might soon come to naught? *Better to stir the pot slowly, or not at all. Keep shuffling into tomorrow.*

She could no longer countenance a world like that, but berated herself for being so brutal in her assessment. How could she look at the falling sky and prefer it to an uncertain, but certainly longer, future? (A preference, she reminded herself, even Vedas did not share. He persisted in punishing himself for what he had done.) Surely, men could do nothing to stop Adrash from exerting his will.

In this light, mankind standing up for itself made no difference. Was it not a sign of their immaturity that anyone would rail against the inevitable, fighting the unstoppable?

No, she insisted, against all logic.

No more bowing, she thought. *No more accepting our fate calmly.*

‡

At the end of the world, she had begun to believe in something.

She found herself half hoping to stop.

‡

"Madam?"

Churls jumped. She had not been asleep, but she had not been properly awake, either. "Yes?" she asked, blinking away the brightness of the sky through the open ceiling panel.

"The big one—Berun. He is waking."

She rolled onto her feet and knelt near the constructed man's head, staring into the coal-black spheres of his eyes, which gradually began to glow reassuringly blue. She laid her hand on one massive, rubbled shoulder. Cold marbles under her palm.

"Berun," she said. "I'm here. It's Churls."

The mage cleared her throat. "I might not stand so close to him."

Churls grinned, and only flinched slightly when Berun shuddered and then heaved himself up from the floor, straining against the massive iron manacles bolted into the floor at his wrists and ankles, mouth opening and closing in silence. She kept her hand on his shoulder, and continued to repeat his name and tell him hers.

Just as suddenly as he had woken, he went still, falling back to the floor with a thump Churls felt through her feet. She leaned forward and shielded his brow as the glow began to fade from his eyes.

"No," she said. "No, Berun. Come back, right now."

A low sound, barely audible, came from his open mouth—the call of a bass horn from two battlefields away. Churls bent her ear to catch it.

". . . you. Safe. Vedas. Safe?"

"Yes," she said. "We're both safe, though Vedas hasn't woken yet and we're stuck in the middle of Fesuy's territory." She squinted above her head. "There's a skylight. I have as much sun coming in as possible, but I worry it's not enough. You have to be able to move, and soon. We don't have all the time in the world."

"I feel it, Churls. Thank you."

For several moments he remained silent, and Churls assumed he had said all he would.

And then:

"Two days."

‡

At midnight, the mage called from above. Churls stopped her restless pacing along the second-floor hallway and climbed the ladder to the attic.

"He's waking, but slowly," the mage said. "Don't force it."

Churls turned toward Vedas, but the mage called her back. In the magelight, the woman's reddened eyes were entirely without white. They reflected no light, as though completely dry. Blood-colored sleep granules had gathered in their corners. Her lips were cracked, around them a layer of white crust: dried spit, of course, but also a fair bit of the bonedust she had been surviving on for several days.

"I can't keep this up," she said. "I need a rest."

It was easy to believe her, yet . . . "How did you cope when Fesuy was running things?"

The mage's smile was ugly. "You killed my replacement, Shouz. He wasn't very good—he'd never been trained properly—but he serviced for a few hours every night."

"I can't think about this right now." Churls looked across the room to Vedas, bathed in moonlight, and her left foot stepped in his direction of its own accord. She paused just before reaching him, however, and cursed. Without the mage, they would be ruined. "No. Never mind. I do need you. I'll arrange something after he wakes. *After*. One more hour, you understand? Then you can rest. I promise I'll find a way."

Vedas's chest rose under her palm. He moaned. She brushed her hand along his arm, noting its thinness with sorrow, and intertwined her fingers with his. Her heart shuddered against her ribs, caused her throat to constrict with its feverish beating. She flushed, feeling the stare of the mage at her back, and nearly let go of his hand. Instead, she gripped it tighter.

"I'm right here, Vedas. Wake up. Let me know you're alive."

The black elder-cloth peeled back from his eyelids, and he turned his head toward her. His eyes vibrated visibly in their sockets as he tried to focus on her. Slowly, as if struggling to control it, he caused the elder-cloth to retreat further, revealing the gauntness of his bearded face. She kept the worry from clouding her features, or hoped she did.

"It looks good," he croaked. His hand tightened around hers. "I like it."

She smiled and shook her head. "Fuck if it does. I look like a melon."

He chuckled, which began him coughing. He let go of her hand and levered himself into a sitting position with obvious difficulty, protesting her assistance. For a moment, his entire body shook. She gave him water. He drank it slowly, displaying his rare and sometimes rather maddening capacity for self-control.

No throwing up water for Vedas Tezul. Regardless of how thirsty.

"Berun?" he asked.

"Don't answer," she answered before the constructed man had an opportunity to speak for himself. "Conserve your energy." She turned back to Vedas. "I'll sum everything up for you: It's the twelfth of Sectarians. That makes it almost three weeks that you've been kept here. It took me that much time to recover and then locate you, longer than I'd hoped. Berun tells me it'll be two days before he's ready to leave. We'll need him at full capacity."

Her voice dropped. "I don't know if we can rely on Fesuy's mage to shield us from view completely."

Vedas looked over her right shoulder, expression unreadable. "She's keeping people out? Impressive. What about Fesuy—the others? Everything's cloudy in my mind, but I seem to recall quite a few of them."

"Sixteen soldiers, including Fesuy. Plus one woman—a maid, maybe. All dead." She held his gaze until it became clear he would add nothing to this pronouncement, and pointed to the southeastern corner of the room. "I found two children on the bottom floor. The mage agreed to keep them asleep. And in Fesuy's bedroom are two girls trussed up like calves, probably shitting themselves as we speak. I think they think I'm some sort of sexless monster."

He raised his eyebrows, thoughts left unsaid.

"You're tired," he eventually said. He stared at her puffy right hand. "You're hurt."

She nodded. "My shoulder's not feeling so great, either."

He lifted his left hand and looked at it, clearly concentrating. It took several dozen heartbeats, but eventually, crawlingly, the elder-cloth retreated from the tips of his fingers, up to the second joint of each digit. The skin revealed was a markedly lighter shade of brown than that of his face and neck, the color of diluted coffee.

She closed her eyes as he ran his fingertips over her bristly scalp. He traced the seams of her skull. Gently, she pulled him toward her.

They kissed, both tasting horrible, neither caring.

‡

Vedas offered to accompany her on the roof while the mage slept, but she declined. Considering his condition, she thought it best that he raid Fesuy's icebox and fall asleep with a full stomach, which, despite his protestations to wakefulness, he did promptly upon finishing his meal.

She paced alone, a mindless circuit: Around the roof in one direction until she reached the skylight. Turn back. Around again in the opposite direction. Her mind wandered aimlessly, snapping back to task at the slightest sound or movement in the streets. Near dawn, just as she began to ask herself whether or not it was wise to be sleepwalking so close to a twenty-five-foot fall, it happened.

A shadow passed across the moon.

She crouched, peering up to see a line briefly bisecting the bone-white circle.

A tail—she knew it instantly. She had heard the rumors of the man who had once been a tamer and now controlled a significant portion of the city. They said he had brought his pet with him, though as far as she knew no one had actually seen it.

Her eyes tracked the animal's flight. Its form was difficult to determine against the night sky: gliding rapidly over the rooftops, blotting out stars as it went, the details pieced together only gradually to form an image. The gull-like wings, which appeared overlarge when compared to the thin, streamlined body at their juncture. The long, arrow-shaft-straight neck led by a smallish tapering head. Lastly, the tail, which stretched behind to nearly twice the length of the neck.

When she had turned three complete circles to follow its flight, realization struck.

It was becoming larger.

She turned toward the skylight just as the mage screamed.

Vedas had reached her by the time Churls dropped into the attic. He straddled the woman's chest as her body spasmed beneath him. Elbows locked, he pressed her head to the floor, palms tight over her eyes. Churls came to his side and immediately surmised that his efforts would fail. Blood poured from beneath his hands, pooling quickly under the mage's head. Already, her spasming was dying down.

"Leave her," Churls said. "She's dead already."

His posture did not relax. "What's happening?" he yelled.

Before she could reply, a crash sounded behind them. Berun had ripped his manacles free of the floor. He rose, each of his thousand joints creaking shrilly, standing with half of his broad torso above the skylight. Churls watched him turn a slow circle, tracking the beast on its flight.

Vedas stood beside her, bloody hands on his knees. She waited until his coughs subsided.

"Do you remember a rumor about a man with a dragon?" she asked. "A man they call the Tamer?"

‡

After several revolutions and one aborted attempt to lift himself onto the roof, Berun sagged, propping himself up against the skylight.

"It's coming down," he said, voice disconcertingly faint. "Go."

His companions refused. Vedas readied the two children as Churls climbed down to untie the girls on Fesuy's bed. She slapped them into wakefulness and led them around the room to get the blood back into their limbs. They stumbled and righted themselves, terrified of her, not wanting to be touched. Vedas pushed a screaming child into each of their chests and yelled.

"Fao! Fao!" *Go! Go!*

The girls hardly needed to be told. Both were gone without a word or backward glance. The front door slammed as they exited the house, and Churls let out a deep breath she had not realized she had been holding. She gripped Vedas's hand, tugged him weakly toward the attic.

He resisted. "Why here? Why now?"

"I don't know." She ran a shaking hand over her face. "No, I suppose I do. It makes sense. He runs part of the city. Fesuy was a rival. When I killed him and forced the mage to focus on keeping people out, the secret became plain to any mage hired to listen to the right voices. This man—The Tamer—he's come to claim Fesuy's land before someone else does."

They stared at one another. He opened his mouth, but she held up her hand. She closed her eyes tightly against the world while she worked out things she suspected would appear simple in any other state of mind.

"No, you're right," she said. "He could've attacked Fesuy any time he liked." She nodded upward. "There's a dead woman there to prove it. Not only that. He has a wyrm. Why hasn't he used it before now?"

She did not wait for his answer. It would not have mattered, she supposed: they were not leaving Berun alone, frozen into place where he stood, an easy target for the wyrm's grasping claws. She climbed to the attic, Vedas at her heels. They squeezed around the inert form of the constructed man and stood on the rooftop, searching the sky.

Vedas gasped. Churls followed his gaze and only just kept from following suit. She had been looking high, hardly expecting the animal to have banked so sharply into a descent—to be so near. Instead of measuring its body against the stars, she now tracked its movement relative to the vertical wall of Usveet Mesa. Moonlight played along metallic purple-black scales, shifting focus from one wing to the other as the animal altered course to keep its lower wingtip from brushing the occasional three- or four-storey building.

"Orrus Dabil Alachum," he swore. "It's huge. I heard the stories, but I never imagined . . . It's going to collapse the entire building when it lands."

Churls smiled grimly in agreement and sat. She patted the rooftop next to her. "Nothing we can do then, is there? Besides, it's better to be on top of a falling house than inside it. Sit with me, Vedas."

He stared down at her, clearly at a loss. She sympathized.

"Is that you, Churls?" he asked. "Churli Casta Jons does not—"

"Churli Casta Jons is injured and exhausted," she said. She patted the rooftop again.

He sat, and together they waited.

‡

The pressure of the wyrm's downbeating wings pressed them flat, driving the air out of their lungs. The gale ripped tears from Churls's eyes, but she refused to look away as the sky above her was eclipsed, becoming a massive, heaving reptilian belly. The beast fell and seemed to continue falling until surely she must be crushed. Vedas gripped her hand tightly enough to grind her knucklebones together, but she barely felt it. Her mind had become a howling cacophony. She anticipated nothing, patient while her lungs burned for air, lost in wonderment and terror.

Huge, carriage-sized talons spread to grip either side of the rooftop, causing the entire clay structure to groan like a living thing and crack like falling timber. Even when the wyrm settled itself and the pressure in here ears finally let up, noise enveloped her. A massive sound, as though a thousand bellows were being compressed simultaneously, came from above.

Breathing. The expansion and contraction of lungs larger than herself.

The spell broke, and she remembered her own body's need. She inhaled, far too fast. Pain stabbed through her chest and she rolled onto her side, shaking as her lungs seized inside her. She thought with a clarity that surprised her . . .

Hypnotized by a bloody big lizard. What an idiot thing to happen.

She finally regained control of herself and pushed up into a crouch, holding out a steadying hand to Vedas as he got shakily to his feet beside her.

The wyrm's belly heaved above them, a smoothly muscular wall of alien flesh. When the animal breathed in, its scales lowered near enough to touch. The house continued to groan under Churls and Vedas, quaking alarmingly with every shift of the wyrm's wings—wings that extended over several nearby buildings, shielding the sky from view entirely. It was said by men who made their livings along the deeper shorelines of Knoori that oceanic creatures could reach an enormous span, but without water to support a body, how could it possibly . . . much less fly . . .

Churls and Vedas exchanged a wide-eyed look, and she surprised herself by recalling a moment when, as a child, she and a neighbor boy had nearly been trampled by a draft horse that reared before them. They had shared the same stunned expression of horror and amazement.

"The head," Berun said, voice almost unheard over the sound of the wyrm's breathing. His next words were lost, merely a fading brassy undertone.

The head. Churls and Vedas turned to watch it swing in toward them upon its long neck, its perpetually grinning visage growing and taking on definition. It was a great, predatory wedge, bony and sinewy and blunt, filled with recurved teeth that hung down from its upper jaw even with its mouth closed tight. Its eyes burned with a visible amethyst light and smoke poured from its nostrils. Long past the point where Churls thought it would stop growing, it grew, until it was before her—massive, an entire creature of its own. Able, should it choose to, swallow her whole without pausing to chew.

A man sat upon it. He slid down its side and dropped onto the roof.

It took several seconds for Churls to see him as anything other than a small thing standing next to the wyrm's gigantic head. She blinked, and the image reoriented itself.

He was not a small creature, except by comparison to his pet. Though not unusually tall (she marked him at a little over six feet in height), he was immensely broad through the shoulders, chest, and thighs. In loose-fitting garments, he might fool someone into believing him fat, but his tight, sleeveless vest clearly strained against slabs of muscle. She knew his belly, ample though it was, would be a solid drum if collided with it. It would be ridged with muscle, a steel washboard.

This was a man not easily knocked down, or even swayed from side to side.

He wore a leather cap and a pair of smokeglass goggles. She could not yet tell the color of his skin or determine a likely nationality.

"You are Churls and Vedas," he said. He spoke softly in a baritone rumble, yet it carried easily over the sound of the wyrm's bellows-breathing. He looked down at the constructed man near Churls's feet, torso half-in, half-out of the skylight. "And this, I assume, is Berun."

"Well done," Churls said. "You know our names and you ride a dragon, and I bet they call you the Tamer for fairly obvious reasons. What do you want?"

To her annoyance, he chuckled. He took a step forward, and she tensed. Vedas did not move perceptibly, but the elder-cloth closed around his features. She wondered why he had not done this earlier—it would have helped him breathe as the wyrm came down—and realized he had likely decided not to on account of her. She could not be shielded from it, and so neither could he.

She clenched her teeth and put her hand on the pommel of her sword. She was not as good with her left arm, and the weight of her gimp right shoulder would throw her off. Still, her opponent stood unarmed.

Next to a dragon, she reminded herself.

The Tamer stopped after two steps, smile in place. He held up a broad, placating hand.

"To talk to you," he said. "That's what I want, and all I expect. If, afterwards, you decide to accompany me, so much the better."

"Accompany you?" Vedas asked. He exchanged a glance with Churls. "That won't be happening."

"So certain," the Tamer said. He lifted his goggles, turned on his heel, and walked to the edge of the roof. "I'd not speak so hastily." He waved them forward over one shoulder, not looking to see if they came. "Fesuy had a sizable population of dangerous men under his control—warriors with considerable martial skill, Tomen mages with less, and even a few rented mages of other nationality. A few of these last possess considerable talent, enough to do damage to anyone left on this roof. They're waking up along with the rest."

He turned back, seemingly unsurprised that neither Churls nor Vedas had moved. He patted the side of the wyrm's head. The animal did not react: it was a stone fallen from the sky, still smoldering.

"Try as she might, Sapes can never keep from causing a stir when she lands. This time, we even lost the element of surprise. I went out of my way to alert you to our arrival. I assumed you wouldn't run, and I was right." His smile returned. Despite herself, Churls noted that while he was not attractive, he had a distinct charisma. "I mean it as a gesture of trust between us. I'm dealing with you openly, making my intentions obvious."

Churls heard shouts from the streets below. "Make them more obvious," she said.

The Tamer nodded. "I'm no friend to Adrash. Neither are the three of you." His eyes locked on Vedas. "I believe your words were, *Our fellow man is not the enemy. Adrash is the enemy.* They're words I agree with exactly, words that seem to have sparked a reaction in the heavens.

You've been blamed for beginning the end of the world. You no doubt believe yourself responsible."

Vedas remained silent. He could have denied it, Churls reasoned, but anyone would have pegged it as a lie. He had delivered his speech, whereupon the whole of Danoor had witnessed the rise of the fractured Needle. There was no one else to blame.

She expressed as much.

"Attaching blame doesn't solve every mystery," the Tamer said. "There are times when events coincide in such a way that the answer seems obvious, but is in fact a greater mystery. This is such a time. I know the only man who could be responsible. He is an elderman by the name of Pol Tanz et Som—a mortal creature like you, now likely dead."

Vedas made a sound halfway between sigh and groan. "And? Get to the point."

The Tamer quirked an eyebrow. "I thought the news would be welcome. You are absolved of guilt."

"A name is all you've given us, and a name is useless. The situation is unchanged. Offer us something, or leave."

A shout sounded from the street. Very close. Fear of the wyrm would keep Fesuy's people away for a few minutes yet, Churls guessed, but it was only a matter of time before the line broke. She did not want to go with the Tamer, but he had forced their hands by killing the mage. He held every advantage. They were treed prey, and he knew it. Whether or not he minded drawing the moment out, however, resulting in the injury or death of one of them—this remained to be seen.

Her gaze fell upon Berun, inert and vulnerable.

"The Tamer won't leave us here," she said to Vedas. "One way or the other, we're going. It might as well be now."

Vedas shook his head in disagreement.

Churls resisted the urge to swear. "Quickly, then, both of you. Come to some kind of terms."

The Tamer removed his goggles and leather cap, revealing two tiny horns that sprouted from his forehead, mirror-images of the ones Black Suits such as Vedas wore on the hoods of their elder-cloth suits. He dipped his head at Vedas, as if to acknowledge this fact.

"I offer this: an opportunity to change the world. To free men of tyranny." He lifted both hands to the sky. "The proof is above us, Vedas Tezul. Adrash's will is not total. Tell me this displeases you. Tell me, and I'll go away."

Vedas said nothing.

The Tamer did not press his advantage by raising his voice in encouragement. He did not proselytize obviously. Instead, his voice dropped nearly to a whisper.

"Come with me," he said, "and I'll show you how to make good on your word. I'll show you a way to stop hating yourself for what you *think* you've done."

‡

It was this last statement, Churls knew, that decided him. Without a path to redemption, a man would watch the world burn. With a measure of hope, the same man . . .

Well. He would not be the same man, would he?

CHAPTER THREE

After they arrived in the Tamer's quarter of the city, she waited long enough to confirm that Berun remained undamaged from the flight (a handful of minutes exposed to the slanted morning sunlight allowed him enough energy to utter three words: "Go, Churls. Rest.") before she collapsed onto the bed in the room provided for her and Vedas.

Exhaustion should have taken her immediately. When it did not, she lay perfectly still, pretending at sleep. She listened to Vedas as he paced, sat for minutes in heavy silence, and got up again. He held his breath and let it out explosively. Finally, at the point where words seemed ready to erupt from him—at the point where she nearly gave up, herself, and admitted to being awake—he exited the room.

She sighed in relief, and rearranged herself into a more comfortable position.

No, she did not want to talk yet about what had happened. She felt, in fact, that the issue need not be confronted at all. Vedas could feel betrayed by her insistence that he come to a resolution with the Tamer for as long as he needed: eventually, he would admit the situation atop Fesuy's roof had been unworkable. To take the stand that he had in delaying an inevitable decision, letting pride cloud fact for even a moment, had revealed more about himself than she considered wise.

They had already given up something by trusting the Tamer. Vedas need not volunteer more by making his fears so apparent.

He had not needed more information atop the roof. He had needed to be convinced to step off the roof.

Sleep came halfway. She lay awake but dreaming, reliving the flight from Fesuy's territory: the exhilarating drop of her gut as the wyrm rose in mammoth surges, its wings snapping like ship sails—the spaceless, agreeably nauseating moment of freefall during each upthrust—the wind warm but cutting over her scalp, in her eyes, pushing her first one way in the saddle and then the other, now and then slamming into her as though trying to toss her out into space—and over it all, the sound of breathing, titanic and utterly inhuman. No shift from inhalation to exhalation, just one long sustained howl of air sucked into the creature's cavernous lungs, a roar that filled every open space in Churls's body, forcing the awareness of her own fragility.

She had loved every horrifying second, and loved every second again, momentarily safe and warm, bathed in sunlight from the open window. The waking dream hardly needed improving the third and fourth time around, yet she managed it: instead of gripping the handles of the saddle, Vedas wrapped his arms around her stomach, pressing his chest against her back, his rough cheek against hers. She gripped the hard cords of his forearms, laughing at his childlike fear, careless in a way the world never seemed to allow. When the wyrm suddenly dropped toward an open area of ground at the northern tip of the city, he squeezed the air from her lungs.

They landed, and entered a bedroom filled with morning light. She took him on the floor, roughly, and then let herself be taken on the bed.

She woke fully and masturbated while her arousal remained, before Vedas returned. Using her left hand, it took longer than usual.

The act left her with the vague feeling of guilt, a feeling she expected and dismissed with a small measure of difficulty. She would not be celibate with herself, not in her fourth decade and certainly not with the world in the state it was, yet she also comprehended how little experience Vedas had with intimacy. Unjust though he undoubtedly knew it was, he would be hurt to discover her pleasuring herself. He understood the baser needs of a person only in theory.

Denial had long since become his way of life.

While she could respect this measure of discipline in a man, she regretted the ways in which it made him inflexible, unwilling to give himself over to joy. Vedas had taken to physical intimacy with an intensity, single-mindedness, and talent she had anticipated, enjoyed, and lamented. She wanted him to stop thinking for one damn minute of his life, yet knew he would not. Not now, having had a hand in plunging the world into madness.

She growled into her pillow. It tired her to think of him any longer, to consider her prize, and how it was not perfect. He had given more of himself than she had ever believed he could.

Her own selfishness gnawed at her, and eventually carried her into dreamless sleep.

‡

Someone called her name. She came out of sleep with the back of her neck tingling.

Instinctively, she knew it was well past midnight, into yet another day, and that she was alone. Vedas had chosen a bed in another room. She thought it likely he had not done it out of spite, but kindness—to allow her uninterrupted rest. It was exactly the kind of decision he would make.

"When are you going to learn?" she mumbled, then: "You can come in, Fyra."

Her daughter materialized at the foot of the bed. Churls resented the smirk, but said nothing.

"You're hurt," the shade of a girl said.

Churls held up her puffy right hand. "I am."

"Your shoulder too, and your left ankle. I can fix them."

"I know."

"But I'm not going to, am I?"

Churls let the question hang between them. The girl sought only to help, and it cost Churls nothing to accept. It would make them both happier. Churls tried to remember what her own mother had denied her. Less than she had shared, surely. The woman had allowed far too much, making it easy for Churls to disappear into the ranks of the infantry, ducking her responsibility to Fyra.

Mother and daughter stared at one another, the bed an ocean separating them. Churls considered how maddening it was, having a child. It had always seemed to consist of such awkward moments, where an errant word could tear everything apart.

"Fyra," she said. "I'd like to stop having the same conversations. How about you?"

The girl squinted, skeptical. "Sure," she said.

"Good. Then we'll start right here." Churls patted the bed before her, and forced an approving smile when the girl sat. She held out her broken hand, wincing at the twinge in her shoulder. "Encourage it on its way, Fyra. Don't fix it completely—just do enough to make it heal faster. No, I don't want to go over why. You know why, because I've said it over and over again. When I'm ready to reveal you to Vedas, I will. Nothing you can say will make it go faster, so just leave off it. Either that, or do it yourself. I can't stop you talking to him."

"No," the girl said. "I'm not going to do that, even though he should know about me. He already guesses something. He saw you *glowing*, Mama."

She had a point, one Churls had been studiously avoiding thinking about for months now. On their journey to Danoor, their ship had breached in the shallows of Tan-Ten, and only Fyra's assumption of Churls's body had saved them. It was madness to deny this event, yet Vedas seemed equally intent on letting it pass out of memory, or at least conversation.

Though grateful for this unexpected pass, their willingness to hide from one another saddened her. He had seen her naked many times— had seen her womb-birth scar, as obvious as a tattoo.

Instead of arguing the point, Churls simply nodded. "Then why not tell him? It should be easy for you. You're not bound by all of these—" She waved her good hand around. "—rules, are you? You don't have to pay attention to me. You can do whatever you want."

Fyra shrugged. "What I want to do is keep my promises." She poked her index finger into the flesh of her mother's palm.

Warmth radiated into Churls, ceasing her aches. She closed her eyes and sighed in pleasure. If she had access to Fyra's abilities, she would never have to worry about money again. No drug had ever worked so quickly. It loosened her tongue.

"You were always too serious, daughter. Promises are for adults to try to keep. When you're young, you lie, and you get away with it because you're young. Be young—you might like it." She opened one eye to look at the girl. "Besides, you never told me you wouldn't tell him."

Fyra shrugged. "I can make a promise to myself."

Churls chuckled. "Thank you."

"You're welcome."

The oddly companionable silence stretched. Churls enjoyed it, keenly aware of how imperfect the world was. How imperfect it had always been. Men deluded themselves when they believed in *better days*, some bygone era when the sun shone brighter. Better days had never existed. Joy had always been stolen, and sweeter because of that fact.

It ended when Fyra removed her finger from Churls's palm, forcing unclouded awareness once again.

"How did you know it was safe to come?" Churls asked.

"It wasn't easy," Fyra said. "You told me I couldn't leave to look for you, so I had to get someone else to do it. Her name was Elya. She died in the city a few months ago, when the riots started. She didn't want to do anything for me at first, but I was nice to her. I showed her how to do some things, and so she found you."

Churls was tempted to ask Fyra to clarify further, but resisted. She had no clear idea how the dead communicated or what their existence looked like, only that her daughter was unique among them, better at interacting with the material world. There were factions, some of which had aligned themselves with Fyra—and, by extension, Churls and Vedas. They wanted to be of some assistance in the war they imagined Vedas had begun.

"And now that you're here," Churls said, "I imagine you have an opinion on the Tamer?"

The girl's features twisted in annoyance. The light she radiated grew into a small blaze before dying down again. "You know how upset I get when I can't figure things out, Mama."

Churls waited for more. She grew impatient and gestured for Fyra to continue.

"There's nothing else," the girl finally answered. "He's like looking at a black rock. I know there's something inside him, but I can't see it. He shouldn't be able to do that. Even the mage who hid Vedas and Berun, I could see her, just not what she was doing. It was like she put a big blanket over what I wanted to see. But the Tamer? I don't think he's a mage. I don't think he's human. I think he's something nobody's ever seen."

‡

He cooked breakfast himself, a thing that struck Churls as odd. It was not that he was a man, or even that he was the man who had a day ago stolen them from atop Fesuy's stronghold—no, it was simply that he seemed so at ease, as though acting out a morning ritual with family. He radiated good will, putting her in an agreeable mood despite her sizable reservations.

Vedas worked at glowering, and more than once opened his mouth to speak, but she recognize how forced the performance was: he, too, could not resist being swayed by their host's inexplicable mood.

It did not hurt when the meal turned out to be delicious. Churls had been eating dried stocks for well over two months. She had nearly forgotten about food, and took to eating like a person starved. For once, Vedas was not shy in his expression of enjoyment, and ate three full plates. The Tamer, not to be outdone, matched both of them.

Churls watched their host without trying to shield the fact. He seemed not to mind, meeting her eyes now and then with a frank smile before returning to his food.

Without doubt, the Tamer was one of the most compelling men she had ever seen. Though his skin was a lighter shade of eggplant and his broad build was the polar opposite of a true hybrid's, much about him reminded her of the eldermen she had known. (A quarterbreed, she had heard him called, a mythical creature that could not, should not, exist, an impossible mating of elderman and human.) He possessed the same amber-colored eyes, the same black pelt over his scalp. A similar sort of sinuousness defined his face, as if every muscle were larger and closer to his skin than a man's.

Muscle, in fact, would quickly become an overused word if she were forced to describe him. A fighter by trade, she had surrounded herself with soldiers and athletes for most of her adult life, and even among their number the Tamer's physical development was a spectacular oddity. Lions and draft horses were adequate comparisons, not men.

More remarkably, she knew, unreasonably yet with certainty, that what she saw was no product of training: he emanated good health in a way she had never before encountered, more like a fixture of existence than a fleeting portion of it.

Vedas, while far more attractive to her, nonetheless appeared somewhat brittle in comparison. It was as if, all at once, her eyes had been forced to recognize what lay inside him, waiting and always growing— a feature obvious but until now overlooked.

Death. Now acknowledged, it could not be unseen.

She looked at her own freckled forearms and saw it in herself. It struck her, how little it mattered, to suddenly discover something one had always known. She squeezed Vedas's hand under the table.

"What a strange mood this is," she said. "It's not what I'd expected upon waking. I'm not angry or nervous. In fact, I'm not even suspicious, and that makes me very suspicious." She met the Tamer's open gaze again. "Let's start at the beginning. You're not what you appear to be, are you?"

He nodded. "Likely not. What do I appear to be, Churls?"

"A man, more or less." She paused, considering her words. "Though I doubt it's less."

The Tamer laughed and slapped the table, causing their plates and silver to jump.

"Clever. And right to the point." He folded his napkin expertly and placed it beside his empty plate. He touched two thick fingertips to his stubby horns, both of which were slightly darker than his skin, appearing in texture like a fingernail. "I'm not less than a man. In truth, I'm further from a man than your friend Berun is from a stone sculpture. I won't demure in that regard. I—" His head tilted to the side, eyes staring over Churls's shoulder. "Speak of the creature itself, and it arrives."

A creak made her turn. Berun slowly made his way down the stairs leading into the kitchen. For a moment, she fought the urge to offer him assistance, and then gave up. She stood and went to him, wrapping her good arm around his massive right one. His craggy, outsized features drew into a smile as he looked down at her.

"Berun," Vedas said. "Vedas," the constructed man returned. The words were spoken with little obvious feeling, but Churls recognized their hard-won affection.

"Welcome again, Berun," the Tamer said. "You need no food I can provide, clearly, but if there's something else I can do, please ask."

Berun stared at their host in silence, and then rumbled, "I've been left alone to recover for one day and an evening, and now part of the next morning. My ears have been open the entire time. You could have visited with me and explained yourself. Vedas woke from his rest briefly to lay upon the roof with me. He said that we're being encouraged by your men on the lower floor to stay here, to continue resting, that all will be explained. And so . . ." He made fists and rested them upon the table. Not quite, but almost, a threat. "I need nothing but for you to explain yourself."

The Tamer's smiled disappeared. He nodded, stood, and took their plates.

When he turned around, a fractured expression had altered his features markedly. A new man stood before them, one who appeared neither friendly nor particularly sane. His left eye rolled up into his head, and the other twitched madly as it settled briefly on each of them.

Churls fought the nearly overwhelming urge to send her chair skittering across the floor behind her, to place distance between herself and him. Vedas slowly lifted his hands to the table's edge, likely to prepare himself for upending it. Berun's eyes flared briefly, two magnesium-blue flares.

The Tamer made a series of gutteral utterances while his lips moved, neither sound nor movement appearing in concert. Slowly, however, his throat managed to catch up with his mouth, and an alien vocabulary emerged, veering between utterly indecipherable and disturbingly familiar, putting Churls in mind of every time she had heard spats through thin tenement walls or from across a collection of tents. The odd word caught and guessed at.

She spared a glance at Vedas. His brow furrowed as he sought to comprehend something that clearly continued to slip away.

‡

Finally, the Tamer's alien words ground to a halt. His left eye rolled back into place and his features evened out, solidifying into a glare he shared with each of them in turn.

"Shavrim Coranid." he said in a strained whisper.

Churls raised her eyebrows.

"Shavrim Coranid," the Tamer repeated. He repeated them a second time, and slapped the table. Color bloomed in his cheeks. He closed his eyes and bowed his head, breathing audibly through his nose, struggling, obviously, to contain his anger. When he spoke again, it was with a voice shaking in rage, struggling to not become a shout.

"I am Shavrim Coranid." He looked from Churls to Vedas, brows raised. "Shavrim Coranid. *Shavrim. Coranid.* This . . . This name means . . . This name means *nothing to you?*"

His gaze settled fixedly upon Vedas. Churls looked from the Tamer to her lover—the former, shaking from head to toe, and the latter, unnaturally still—and imagined that if she passed a hand between them it would encounter resistance. She opened her mouth to speak, and found, quizzically, that any question would be unnecessary.

She anticipated Vedas's nod a heartbeat before it came. When it did, she shadowed it. Berun stood immobile, a question creasing his features.

Vedas nodded. Churls nodded.

And then they both, at the same moment, said yes. Yes, the name meant something to them.

‡

"A name, once heard, cannot be forgotten," she had once overheard a Bashest priestess tell a practitioner. The words possessed a ring of truth to them, though Churls's mind had never been particularly suited to remembering. Faces, names, dates, she could not recall them beyond their moments of relevance, yet she knew with a peculiar certainty that she had never forgotten a single thing. Once acquainted with a place or person, even the most dim memories could be summoned again to help navigate oddly familiar streets, to understand a near-stranger.

As a small child she had taken ill with bone featherings, forcing her mother to visit a sawmage: not even someone who worked on livestock, no, but a local man who healed pit-dogs and other fighting animals. (They could not have afforded someone who worked on livestock.) When her mother mentioned his name a decade later, Churls did not associate it with the event she remembered only fuzzily.

She did, however, experience a surge of discomfort upon hearing it. The sawmage's name, which, of course, she could not now recall, was *ugly*, even offensive. It seemed wrong that it had come from her mother's mouth.

Had hearing it actually caused her to rub the long, jagged scar the man had left upon her right thigh? She recalled doing so, but it hardly mattered. The rush of emotion that had accompanied two small words—a name, surely, she had only heard a smattering of times as a sick-unto-delirious child—had not been an imagined thing. She had not created it out of nothing. It existed, a permanent connection to a place and time.

Likewise, she could not dismiss her reaction upon hearing the Tamer's true name. It had not been immediate, no: it had built slowly within her, an increasingly undeniable pressure between her ears each time the man spoke.

Shavrim Coranid, SHAVrim Coranid, SHAVrim CORanid.

When it finally registered, when she could not discount her reaction as an ordinary response to the man's anger, it was as though it had always been a part of her, this name, and attendant to this name a weight, a collection of impressions beyond the scope of recollection, pressing upon her without discomfort, welcomed without conscious volition—as if a door had been opened into a previously undiscovered room, admitting a stream of vaguely familiar people who spoke in nearly-recognizable languages, who told tales of places she could almost picture.

All of this, at once. In a flash of awareness, her skull had become pregnant with associations she could not yet contextualize. She admitted the possibility of it being the product of enchantment, but it hardly mattered. If Shavrim Coranid were powerful enough to place such a complex sense of recognition within her mind, then all things in his presence were suspect.

‡

He collapsed after hearing their affirmations. Berun lifted him easily and took him upstairs. In Shavrim's room, the three of them stood silently around his bed for several minutes, staring at his motionless body as though it were a fascinating vista, a landscape they had seen a lifetime ago, perhaps, or had heard described by a relative. Churls spared a look at her companions, just in time to see them doing the same. They avoided meeting each other's eyes.

Without a word, Berun turned and ascended to the rooftop.

Similarly content not to speak, Churls and Vedas returned to their room, where, after a long period of examining the floor between them (she, feeling not the slightest trace of awkwardness, but instead a mounting sense of purpose, of waiting for the exact moment to move), they embraced. Slowly, they undressed one another—she completely, he as far as he would allow her to peel back his suit. She pressed her fingernails into the elder-cloth and carefully expanded holes that he allowed to form in the material, slowly revealing his chest, belly, upper and lower back, and buttocks.

She stopped before going lower, her hands playing over his rawboned torso. Inexplicably, sadness no longer gnawed at her to see how wasted he had become. For a fleeting moment, his frailty seemed appropriate, even beautiful. Its impermanence appealed to her, as did his atypically casual reaction to it. He had always been so worried over his body, touching it as though he thought it would suddenly fail him. As if, having lost something, it could never be regained.

It was a preoccupation born of privilege. He had always had enough to eat, enough spare time to train. A man like him had no reason to worry, and so he did.

"You just needed to lack for something," she whispered to herself, slipping her hands around his ribs and squeezing him to her, possessively, protectively. His fingertips ran lightly up her back. Gripping her head in his hands, he kissed her, tongue flicking over her teeth. When he pulled away, his arms fell around her shoulders and he buried his face in her neck. She shuddered at the scrape of his beard. Gooseflesh rose, covering her from head to toe.

They pulled each other onto the bed.

Immediately, she knew it would not be as it had been before. Unclothed, Vedas had always possessed a hint of nervousness about him, a feature now entirely absent. He moved as he had always done in his element: she thought of the sparring they had done, the times she had seen him confront an opponent, reacting fluidly, refusing to be rushed yet without an ounce of hesitation. At times, he became animated in a manner she had not yet seen, eyes wide or eyes shut, grimacing and smiling, abandoning himself to his sensations. He did not hide himself from her, or worse, try to impress her by taking control, but instead responded to her naturally, like it had always been a familiar thing between them.

"You're *here*," she breathed when they surfaced for air.

"I am," he said, and surprised her by returning a knowing smile.

She buried her fingertips in the thick nap of his hair and pushed him downward.

Afterward, they lay together, spent, touching only at the hands and crossed ankles, comfortable on a level she had rarely felt in the previous year of traveling and fighting and worrying. Of course, now that she acknowledged it, it began to fade. She fought to keep it from going away, and failed.

She frowned, her suspicions finally demanding full attention.

Somehow, he precipitated her words. She felt it in the air a moment before he let go of her hand.

"Vedas," she said. "We need to question this. All of it. Even if we don't want to."

Out of the corner of her eye, she saw him turn away from her. "I know," he said.

"It feels this good to you, too, doesn't it, what we just did, how we are now? It feels right, but you and I aren't . . . I mean, we haven't . . ."

"I know."

She squeezed his hand, grateful he had filled in the blanks. "It's not just that. There's also this feeling of . . . knowing? Shavrim, that name, it . . ." Again, she searched for words." It means something to us. I could feel the moment when we realized it, together—both of us. Just like here, now, it feels real, *full*, like something obvious I'd forgotten."

"Like a dream," he said, "one you only recall later, because of a smell or a series of words. It didn't exist, and then—" he snapped his fingers "—it does."

She nodded. "Yes. Exactly. But we don't wake up from life, Vedas. We're not dreaming."

"You know there's more to the world than we see," he said. "I may be opposed to Adrash, Churls, but I'm not blind to the way forces other than he have bent creation. Miracles occur, beyond our reckoning. I'm not saying I'm convinced, but who's to say Shavrim Coranid isn't revealing something to us that we should know, something greater than ourselves?"

"Something greater, Vedas? No. The world has been shaped by many hands, but what of it? The events that appear as miracles, then and now, are exercises in power vastly greater than we can summon. They're impressive, no doubt, but they're also normal, completely of this world. Inexplicable things don't happen." She closed her eyes. "Nothing I've experienced would lead me to believe there's anything more than this, right here, this moment with you—"

Her last word ended in a croak.

The quality of the air had changed. Concentrating against the hammering of her heart, she realized that Vedas's breathing was no longer audible. His thumb, which had been rubbing at the back of her hand, had stilled.

She had been about to lie. Not to keep silent about Fyra, but to actively mislead.

Vedas released her hand and sat up. His suit slowly began to mend, circles closing to cover the areas of his back and upper buttocks he had allowed her to unveil. She pinched the bridge of her nose, grimacing, then swung her legs over the side of the bed and quickly pulled her clothes on. She allowed one glance to confirm that his nakedness had been covered completely.

"Fyra," she said. "Fyra, it's time."

‡

They stared at one another. The girl defiantly, chin up. The man expressionlessly.

"Fyra," Vedas said, voice flat. "You're the daughter."

The girl looked to Churls, who shrugged.

Fyra nodded. "Yes."

Vedas gestured for more. When neither mother nor daughter spoke, he sighed. He met Churls's gaze levelly, eyebrows raised.

"*Nothing you've experienced would lead you to think there's anything more than this, here?*" He pointed at Fyra, a clear indictment. He smiled, utterly humorless. "A bit of an untruth, isn't it, Churls?" The smile vanished, replaced again with a blank expression. He turned back to Fyra. "Please. Explain to me what your mother couldn't, or wouldn't."

Fyra surprised Churls by sneering at him. "Don't act like that," the girl said. "Mama made some mistakes. I wanted her to tell you, and that made me angry. But you . . ." She pointed at him, returning his earlier gesture. "You could have asked her after Tan-Ten. You didn't, so don't blame her for just now getting around to it."

After a brief pause, Vedas dipped his head in acknowledgement of her point.

They waited, Churls resolved not to speak. Finally, the girl caved.

"Ten years," she said. "I've been dead for ten years. Almost eleven. I wasn't always around. For a while, I don't think I thought anything at all. I was sleeping, I guess."

Vedas appeared to accept this without difficulty. "And now you're present—all the time? Hiding? Watching?"

The girl blushed a warm pink. Churls had never seen it happen before, not in life and certainly not after death. She had thought the girl's ethereal form incapable of generating color other than the blue of her eyes. Seeing it affected Churls in a way she could not have imagined.

It hurt, seeing it. Color in her daughter's cheeks.

She turned toward the window to hide the expression on her face.

"No," Fyra said. "Not always. I can't be here all the time. Even when I really want to be, it can be hard. The dead call me back. Not everyone wants me here."

Vedas shifted on the bed. Churls sensed his eyes on her, but did not turn back. She had invited Fyra into the room: the two of them could do the rest. She would not influence what information they did or did not share with each other.

"Why?" he eventually asked.

"I saved you and Mama on Tan-Ten, and then I fixed her shoulder after you hurt it. Don't say it. I know you didn't mean to, but you did. There are ways for the dead to be part of the world, to help the living, but most of them are afraid of doing it. They don't want to attract anyone's attention, especially Adrash's. That, or they're not good at crossing over."

"But you are?"

"Yes. Yes, I am. Better than anybody, ever."

Churls heard the smile in her daughter's voice, and grinned in response.

The expression fled upon hearing what Vedas said next.

"And Berun—does he know about you?"

The question hung in the air. Churls fidgeted with her belt buckle, and made herself stop. Now that the issue had been broached, it seemed pure, embarrassing foolishness that she had avoided it. And yet, so much had been successfully avoided for so long, what did one more avoidance matter?

Just after rescuing Churls and Vedas in the shallows of Tan-Ten, Fyra had indeed appeared to Berun, leading him to shore, saving him from a slow death of light-suffocation under Lake Ten. Days after Vedas's speech, she had almost certainly helped Berun find Churls in Danoor, though neither the constructed man nor Fyra admitted to it. What Churls had never ascertained was whether or not Fyra had revealed her identity to Berun.

"I think so. I helped him," the girl said. She glanced at Churls. "Twice. But I can't be sure if he knows exactly who I am."

"Well, then," Vedas said. He swung his legs over the side of the bed and stood. "There's an easy way to be sure."

He opened the door and left without a glance back.

"That went well," Fyra said.

Churls sighed. "You have an interesting definition of *well*, daughter." She gestured Fyra toward the door.

"Not yet," the girl said. "They can wait. Give me your hand. There's no reason not to fix it now, right, Mama?"

Churls thought of arguing, but saw little point. Berun was patient, and Vedas could stand to pace through a minor delay.

As radiance flooded her body, touching every nerve and rendering it liquid, Churls reflected not on the violence or the tension of the last several days, but on all the talk. There had been too much. She could not fight the sinking feeling that like Vedas she had given too much away, that she had been careless in her words and revealed something she would regret. Of course, filled with Fyra's soft healing fire, she could not put her finger on just what she had lost—or if, indeed, anything had been lost. Perhaps it was mere paranoia, the result of having talked herself into a corner. She had never liked ceding control.

"Fyra," she said. "Why didn't you tell him? About . . . about . . ."

The girl smiled. "Yes, mama? Tell him about what?"

Churls's head swam. Her tongue was thick, heavy in her mouth, and then it seemed as if it had fled her body entirely. She blew air out between her lips, causing them to flap. She laughed, though she saw no humor in the situation.

Her lips worked at the words before they came out:

"The . . . dead. How they want to . . . help us. A war. *The war*. Why not?"

"Be calm, Mama," Fyra said. "I'm trying to do something. You're more than hurt. There's something else, something I couldn't see before, when you wouldn't let me in. Let me figure it out." She flickered, growing in brilliance and then subsiding. One moment, she seemed of normal size, and the next she was a toy in Churls's outstretched hand.

"Fyra," Churls said. "I'm more than . . . hurt? Fyra?"

She fell back onto the bed. Her eyelids fluttered, vision losing focus. She labored to roll her eyes downward, to locate her daughter. Her limbs shook, no longer under her command. Gradually, the room grew dark, fading into black around the corners of her eyes. Closing in upon her.

Sleep, Fyra said.

‡

She woke, and immediately sat upright. The room possessed a startling clarity around her, a sharpness that cut through her disorientation. The blanket under her hand, the reflection of the mirror . . . every object she saw seemed suffused of its own light. Less than a handful of minutes had passed, she knew immediately, yet a longer span of time had passed inside the confines of her skull.

Fyra materialized before her, unusually faint.

"Mama," she said in a voice that sounded as though it came from another room. Worry made her look decades older. "Mama?" she repeated, squinting as though she were having trouble making out the woman sitting before her.

"Yes, Fyra?" Churls asked. Her voice, richer than she remembered, fuller in her throat and ears. She reached out with a steady hand, marveling at the texture of her skin, its smoothness and inexplicable, almost metallic sheen. Her fingertips stopped a mere hairsbreadth from her daughter's cheek. "Fyra, what is it? What's wrong?"

The girl's eyes widened, and she shrunk back. Her form wavered like a guttering candle.

"Mama? You're not alone," she said, and disappeared.

‡

Churls's brow furrowed in confusion.

"Fyra?" she asked. "Where did you . . .? What did you . . .?"

She blinked, and the world turned gray.

No, it did not turn gray. It grew dim. It was as if a shadow suddenly passed over the building. She stood and crossed to the window, leaning out to squint at the sun.

The sky stretched overhead, a clear bowl of blue, yet to her eyes it seemed drained of its vibrancy, filmed over with a layer of grit. As her gaze descended, the world darkened until the street below appeared shrouded in fog. She looked at her hands, and there it was again, clear in the calloused, labor-worn flesh of her palm:

Death. Once acknowledged, it could not be unseen.

Alone, without someone equally fragile with which to share her realization, it pained her to see. It was like an unhealing wound, a cancer. The vision of her mother, laid out in her aunt's threadbare bedroom, came to her. It had only been three years ago, but she still dreamt often of the wake. A fully-grown adult, inured to death—an experienced soldier, no less—her heart had nonetheless pounded as she took her mother's hand, finding it cold, its skin a parchment stretched over bird-thin bones.

She retreated from the window, hugging herself against a coldness rooted deep in her marrow.

"Fyra?" she asked. "What's happening, girl? Come back."

A painful knot formed in her throat. She had never seen her daughter's remains. She had been away, avoiding home and every responsibility home meant. Her mother had buried Fyra a month before Churls returned. Churls had not been there when her mother died, either—had missed it by days.

The world operated in cycles: one got what they deserved, in the end.

Churls would die—alone, she knew.

She retreated further until her backside hit the bed. She flinched, and reached back with shaking fingers to uncover the mattress. Her eyes never left the open window, as though she expected the arrival of death itself. The sheets still smelled of Vedas, yet another kind of longing.

"Fyra?" she repeated, knowing the girl had gone back to the dead and would not return for some time. Her daughter had discovered something, and taxed herself in the process.

Churls cursed. The world never stopped moving underneath her.

Though the temptation existed, she did not give in to irrational self-pity. She did not say her mother's name, or Vedas's. There would be no use, she reasoned, of wishing for comfort from either of them. Her mother had surely passed out of existence upon death. She had known her own strength, had come to terms with her place in the world in a way Churls could barely conceive. Inys Casta Jons had accumulated no soul-debt, no unfinished business, and would not have stuck around to watch over anyone. She had been ready for death.

And Vedas?

Churls shook her head. She did not close her eyes, did not sleep. She stared at the window until the sun passed directly overhead, until its direct rays no longer entered the room, and then she went downstairs to get drunk.

‡

She saw Vedas leave. He met her eye briefly as he passed through the games hall that made up the first floor of Shavrim's headquarters, but his expression gave nothing away. She watched the flow of muscle under his suit as he walked out the door, aware of her sad desire but unable to do anything about it. She sniffed at her fingertips, which still bore a trace of them both.

"Another," she told the bartender.

Five ales in, she ordered a sixth and then a seventh. An eighth and a ninth. She reached the point where she not so much thought about anything as let thoughts revolve around her, touching her awareness only briefly. Muddy-headed, she came to two swift, resigned conclusions she would not have been able to arrive at sober:

Vedas's anger—there was nothing she could do about it. There never had been anything she could do. They were, the two of them, too wounded to be anything other than a mess, moving from one feeling to the next without any means of control. Had she the ability to do it all over, she likely would make the same mistakes. Different words, same foolish sentiments.

What Fyra had said—it made no sense, and would make no sense until the girl returned, so why consider it any more than she had to? Fyra would not allow harm to come to her mother, if it were within her power to prevent it. And if she could not prevent it?

Churls ordered her tenth ale, scowling at the bartender when the woman raised her eyebrows.

There was, of course, a third issue that could not be completely ignored. She raised her eyes to the ceiling and winced.

Berun.

Berun, with whom she had shared so much—with whom she, in some ways, felt a deeper sense of connection than Vedas. He had listened without judgment, an immediate sympathy between them from the beginning. He had never asked anything of her, had expected only . . .

"Shit," she said to herself. What had he expected?

Trust. To be treated like any friend should be treated.

She ordered her eleventh ale.

"Fuck," she muttered after three sips, and rose unsteadily from her stool.

She ascended to the roof of Shavrim's base of operations, pausing before taking the final step onto the still warm clay surface, peering around until she located the mountain of rubble that was Berun's cross-legged form. His gaze, she could see, was directed away from her, toward the sporadically lit city. She felt the chilly mass of Usveet Mesa, looming behind her.

She shivered, and opened her mouth to speak. She closed it again when words, even his name alone, failed to come.

Her fingers curled into fists. Her cheeks flushed. Impotent, she pivoted clumsily to leave.

"Churls," the constructed man rumbled, drawing the sound of her name out.

"Yes," she whispered, and took the final step onto the roof. She crossed to where he sat and stared down at him for a moment, unsure of her next move. He turned his craggy head up to her, the glow of his eyes intensely blue, a searing radiance in the darkness that made her blink. She swayed in place, and his massive hand came up to the small of her back, steadying her. She reached back, her own hand covering only a portion of his.

It struck her for only the second time since they had known one another: he radiated heat. Far less than a man, but it was something. It made him more human, though he might take offense with that summary.

What had he said when she noticed it, that first time? She could not recall. She wondered if it would come to her later. She hoped it would.

"I'm sorry," she said.

He laughed, a deep metallic tolling from within his great chest. "Sorry?" he asked. "Sorry for what, Churls?"

She broke his gaze. "Fyra. I should have told you."

A slight pressure upon her back. "Sit," he said.

She sat. His arm remained behind her, close but not touching. A minute passed, and then two. She finally rolled her eyes at her own foolishness (what would a constructed man care?), and leaned over onto his shoulder. His arm moved to support her back. She felt subtle shifts in the way he held himself as he accommodated to make her more comfortable against him—a thing, she imagined, he would not have known to do before meeting her.

"I need no apology, Churls," he said. "I *want* no apology. I told you, when we came into the city for you, I recognized her. I wasn't mad at you then. I'm not mad now. You have your secrets. From Vedas, you've kept secrets. Apologize to him, if you must apologize to someone."

She smiled grimly. "He and I may be past the point where apologies mean anything." She gestured out across the city. "He's out there now, and not here. I think I may have broken everything."

He shook his head. She saw it in her peripheral vision, and felt it through his body, the slide of his component spheres over each other.

"No. You've broken nothing. You give Vedas too little credit. Once, he wouldn't have thought about his anger. Not long ago, he couldn't see out from under his guilt, the hate he directed at himself. But now? Now, he's a different man. You're the first thing in his mind. If you can't see that, you're a fool. A friend, but still a fool."

He smiled down at her. "I almost think we've discussed these things before."

She remained silent.

"You'll see," he said. "The world is on the edge of death. Even as I am, not a man, I can see how wrong it would be to witness everything die without knowing who truly cares for you. You care for me. We share a bond." He tipped his head, touching his forehead to hers. "Again, even as I am, I can see this."

She nodded, not trusting herself to speak.

"And Fyra?" he asked. "She's still away, among the dead?"

She wiped at her eyes, though they were dry. "She's gone. Off to wherever she goes. Beyond where the world can touch her, beyond even Adrash."

She looked to the sky, where the broken Needle spanned. Drunk, it no longer filled her with the same fear. She was, however, suddenly aware of her anger. How dare the world be kept on a tether, threatened so? Who gave Adrash the right to hold the world in a thrall?

It was an idiot question, of course. Strength gave him the right.

And now—who but the dead could oppose him? She thought, for the thousandth time, of what it could mean to accept Fyra at her word. To accept her and her companions' help, to wage a war upon Jeroun's one true god.

As though his thoughts had strayed to a similar place, Berun spoke.

"And what of our captor's claims, Churls? Do you really believe our captor has a way to make good on Vedas's speech, to wage war upon

Adrash? I saw what passed between you and Vedas. You recognized Shavrim. His words mean something to you."

She nodded, her eyes riveted on the chaotic view overhead. "I did recognize him. As did Vedas. I assumed you did, too." When he said nothing, she knew her assumption had been wrong. "But beyond the sense that I remember him? There's a void. No context, no specific memory. It's like it's been removed from my mind." Her voice dropped to a whisper. "Or maybe we're being manipulated. Of course we are. How could both Vedas and I both remember him? How could I know anything about the man's claims?"

"You're asking me?" Berun asked, amusement clear in his voice. "You, who are haunted by the spirit of your daughter, are asking me, a constructed man who has been assisted by that same spirit, what is possible? You're asking a half-broken creature, only recently freed from the bonds of his creator, for advice on the workings of gods and men?"

"I am," she said, finally lowering her eyes from the sky, meeting his bright gaze, holding the connection.

Searching.

"Fate help both of us, Berun, but I am."

CHAPTER FOUR

THE 16TH TO 18TH OF THE MONTH OF SECTARIANS DANOOR TO MAREPT, THE REPUBLIC OF KNOS MIN

For the third night in a row, Vedas dreamt of the silver woman, cold and desirous of his warmth, a perfect complement to him: a needle of cold light, a finely focused lance of pain in the center of his being. They made love, quickly to suit her and then slowly to suit him, trading aggressions and tendernesses, moving as one mind. Knowing one another, as intimately as siblings. They referred to each other so, in fact—*sister, brother*—yet the words were puzzlingly alien, familiar and unfamiliar at once, altered to suit minds approaching but ultimately eclipsing human.

For the third time, the experience confounded him. He had never dreamt, aware of the dream. He had only ever been an unwilling participant, a mere inhabitant of his own body, forced to act and to believe wholeheartedly in the reality of his mind's illusion. Now, however, he knew himself as Vedas, the Vedas of the waking world, *here*, aware, alone, of one mind . . .

Yet not alone. Of two minds. Himself, and another.

Another, whose body and thoughts were as intimately recognizable as his own.

In his first and second dream, this had been the extent of it: the deep awareness of himself as someone else, less an occupation than a transformation.

In this, his third dream, however, he became aware of a new aspect, a pressure within his body, a looming awareness in both minds. As of an oncoming storm, or the tingling sensation of knowing someone is about to enter one's room.

Within the dream, dawn came to an end. The sun peeked above the belly of the world, instantly igniting the interior of the vast golden room in which the two made love, piercing through the amber lenses of his eyes, causing him to pause, mid-thrust.

He—the one who was and was not Vedas—quirked his head to one side, listening. His companion lifted her silver head and peered over her shoulder at him.

"Brother," she said. "We're not done."

"I know, sister," he responded. "A moment. First, say my name. I need you to say it."

She smiled, showing two rows of sharp white teeth. "Say please."

"Please," he said.

She spoke his name. He sighed in realization, and spoke hers.

‡

His eyes snapped open. He was alone, he knew instantly. Nonetheless, he rose and searched the room thoroughly. The crawling sensation of being watched persisted, just as it had on the previous two evenings after he woke from the dream. If anything, it had increased.

Sleep was a shore too far, and a new question had arisen.

He would seek answers, once more.

He descended to the first floor, into the games hall. Walking the room counterclockwise, he made himself meet the frank stares of Shavrim Coranid's men. Most were Knosi, openly curious about one of their cousins in a way he was only slowly becoming accustomed to. The assumption that, as countrymen, they had something in common, appealed and repelled in equal measure.

A few black-suited individuals smiled, offering him spots at their tables. He declined each with a polite wave of his hands, a gesture he had acquired from observation.

Undoubtedly, everyone in the hall knew who he was. What he had done.

They were allies, presumably, yet some among them—the paler-skinned Castans and Stoli, in particular—appeared discomfited by his arrival, shuffling their seats closer to their tables, shutting him out. He smiled at this, sadly amused without really understanding why.

Upon sight of his target, he became self-conscious. He straightened his already rigid spine, painfully aware of the thinness of his arms and legs, the hollows in his torso.

Laures, Shavrim's first lieutenant, stood where she had the two nights before, leaning against the wall with her arms crossed beneath her breasts. Unlike any Black Suit he had ever seen, her hands and forearms were bare, unprotected by the elder-cloth. Oddly again, though not entirely unknown in his experience, she wore clothes over her suit: a thin hempen vest and loose pants of the same material. Both were dyed the red-black color of dried blood.

"It's for the Mother," she had told him during their first conversation. "It symbolizes what she left after birthing the world."

He stared, uncomprehending.

"I'm Usterti," she said, as if that were sufficient explanation.

The name had communicated nothing singular to him, then. He pretended to understand what she had said, knowing it would not fool her. He knew what an Usterti was, of course. In theory, he knew a great deal about the religion, but theory carried him only so far. People did not act as books had led him to believe they would. They did not talk in straight, easily-comprehended narratives. Appallingly often, they did not even slightly resemble the pictures he had painted of them. He had heard all Mother-worshippers were witches or pornographers, ugly inside and out.

Laures was beautiful, long-limbed and athletically proportioned, clear-skinned, darker even than he. She wore her hair short, woven in tight, ordered rows upon her scalp. He thought it strange, how attractive he could acknowledge her to be, yet how little her form appealed to him. It seemed wrong that he should view her as more of an object, an abstraction worthy of admiration but not lust. Reason argued that if he had he spent his life among his own people they would not appear so coldly uniform, like a series of glazed statues.

"Vedas," she said, the trace of a smile on her lips.

"Laures," he said, leaning against the wall at her side, affecting her casualness.

"Here again," she said. "You shouldn't be. The morning will come sooner than you think, and Osa's no small trip." Her eyes traveled up and down his body appraisingly. "You're not the Vedas Tezul I heard described as the winner of the tournament. You have no fat, and precious little muscle, to burn up. Go to sleep. Recover as much as your body will allow."

He only just kept from wincing, and shook his head. "I can't sleep. I have another questions."

She laughed. "I already told you all I know about Shav last night. What little there is to know, you know. Trust me."

"No. It's not him I want to talk about." He made himself meet her stare, fighting the impulse to keep what secrets he had. If she had any loyalty to Shavrim (and he had no reason to believe she did not), she would tell him everything Vedas said. Perhaps, to Shavrim, the words would mean something. Perhaps he would be able to fill in the holes before Vedas could, using it to his advantage, manipulating them even further. With truth or with lies: it made no difference.

Vedas saw no other option, however. Without an answer to this newest question, sleep would continue to elude him.

"The Mother you spoke of," he said. "Ustert. There are things I seem to recall about her."

Her eyebrows rose fractionally, half her mouth moving with them. Regardless, he noted the way her posture stiffened. The fingers of her right hand twitched on her left bicep.

"You knew her then, did you?"

He kept his expression sober. "I remember reading a series of stories about her—stories from before the world was born."

She dropped all pretense of joviality. "Stories? Lies, you mean."

"They were not written by your sisters, obviously. They were written by men, trying to understand." He ignored her chuckle of contempt. "I don't mean to offend you by talking about them. I'm not insulting you, nor am I trying to get at secrets you don't want to reveal. All I'm asking for is confirmation that such tales exist."

She shrugged. "Ask."

Men are not a thing one talks about with an Usterti, he had been informed.

"I could be wrong, but in one of them . . ."

Out with it, he told himself.

"In one of them, Ustert had a twin. A man, or maybe a boy."

After a moment, she nodded.

"Do you know his name?" he asked. "Will you tell me?"

‡

She had an answer for him. It showed on her face, yet for the space of many heartbeats she visibly fought with herself over whether to voice what she knew. Perhaps it would be a breach of her faith to utter the name.

Just as he was about to tell her not to worry, to absent himself and make another attempt at sleep, she spoke.

"Evurt," she said. "His name was Evurt."

He shuddered as something within him stirred.

‡

He turned to look back at the city. Only eight miles out, and already it had become a vague spread of dirty, jumbled earth. Behind it, the vertical wall of Usveet Mesa stood, shutting out half the day, cutting off any view to the west. Distance had only served to make it larger: as the mountain's true scope became apparent, it began to loom even more, to oppress.

He wondered what kind of people would settle at the base of such a monolith. Had his ancestors longed to be humbled, every day—to be reminded how meager their efforts were? They could not hope to outlast the mountain. It would continue to stand, inviolate, exerting no effort while they struggled, generation after generation, to etch their names in shifting sand.

It had outlasted one species, already.

Human beings are fools, he thought. *And the ones who came before them were fools.*

This thought sat cold within him.

Shielding his eyes, he surveyed the cloudless sky until he located the winged shape of the creature guarding their exit from the city:

Shavrim's pet Sapes, itself an hybrid of wyrm and elder, a living link to that superseded species. He lifted his right hand, spreading his fingers wide, sliding his palm smoothly over the atrophied muscle of his chest. Not even true contact, but feeling transmitted through two layers of cloth composed in part of elder skin.

"And what if you die within it?" Churls had once asked. He recalled the feeling of her fingertips, brushing over the edge of a hole he had caused to open in his suit. Back and forth over his right hipbone, from bare skin to covered skin. It surprised him to realize he could not tell where one ended and the other began.

"I'll rot," he replied. "Someone else will use my suit."

"And if you die alone, at the bottom of a crevice?"

"I'll rot," he had repeated, suddenly and profoundly uncomfortable.

Sapes' form disappeared against the sheer black wall of Usveet Mesa. Vedas dropped his hand and turned back to his companions. Churls had stopped to watch him, concern written on her features. He met her stare for a moment, expressionless, allowing nothing to pass between them, and then shifted his gaze to Berun, Shavrim, and Laures.

To his annoyance, they too now stopped to regard him.

"I'm fine," he said. "Keep walking."

He waited for them to move before resuming his own progress. He stared at their backs, lingering on the broad form of Shavrim for several heartbeats, struggling to understand how he had ever allowed the man to convince them to abandon the city. How, despite the madness of the man's words—the very idea that a means to defeat Adrash existed, that anything other than the entire mass of humanity could stand against Jeroun's only god!—traveling to Osa had come to seem the right choice. The only choice.

He struggled against this increasing sense of surety, if for no other reason than one among them needed to. Churls and Berun, the two voices who had long argued against Vedas's own certainty, had agreed to Shavrim's goal surprisingly quickly. Perhaps they had not required as much time to come to terms with the situation (a situation, he reminded himself, that amounted to sitting and waiting for the world to collapse) and simply accepted Shavrim at his unlikely word, yet this sounded an unpleasant chord within him.

A thing was either true, or it was not. One did not arrive at truth by wishing it were so. From the moment they met Shavrim, they had been pressed against the wall by circumstance. This was not a position from which a wise choice could be made.

Feeling helpless was its own form of tyranny. He knew this. He knew it better than most. He had lived most of his life oppressed by a false truth.

‡

They stopped out of the way of the wind, in a dry stream-bed where the skeletons of cottonwoods arced overhead. He did not attempt to conceal his exhaustion, but waved away their protests when he offered to gather firewood, just as he had when they told him he need not carry any of their supplies. He climbed the sandy bluff and returned with armloads of fuel—first kindling, which he found scattered at the feet of the dead trees, and then larger branches, which snapped like bones in his shaking hands, covering him in dust, making him sneeze.

On his fourth trip, he walked a handful of paces away from the trees and stood motionless in the spare, cold light of the desert, breathing heavily, savoring the brief moment of solitude. Looking into the sky, he counted the scattered spheres of the Needle: seven, eight, nine . . . and then a tenth rising above the horizon. He resisted the urge to touch his fingertips to the horns of his suit, cursing Adrash with a gesture. A small gesture of defiance, fighting reflex.

His lips moved. Again and again, he formed the name—*Evurt*—but did not say it aloud. A simple act, giving voice to thought, yet it struck him as more than a mere word. A name was a summons to its owner. He wondered if Churls had felt the same when she realized her daughter had returned from the dead, as if every moment alone were pregnant, existing always on the verge of saying it. *Fyra. Fyra. Fyra.* Drawing the girl into reality.

He wondered if Churls knew yet another name, now.
Ustert.

He shook his head, seeking and failing to clear it. There was no reason to assume Churls had experienced anything like his dream. He had never taken a lover before her, and suspected his inexperience was leading him to false conclusions.

As always, logic failed to alleviate his worry.

Upon returning to the camp for the seventh time, he realized he had gathered far more fuel than necessary. He stared at the pile of wood he had created, brow creased. Waiting. Berun, Laures, and Shavrim had left for a perimeter check, leaving Churls alone to set up the tent. He felt her gaze at his back, or he thought he did: when he finally turned, her attention was fixed on her task.

He pretended to concentrate on building the fire, longing to bridge the silence between them but suspecting he should preserve it for as long as possible. She was stronger than him, more practical and persuasive. A lifetime outside an abbey's walls, making due alone, had made her capable of discerning judgment, while he, he was no judge at all.

If he opened himself up to her, she would sway him away from doubt. For two days, he had restricted himself with her, engaging in only the briefest of exchanges.

He knew himself to be a fool, or perhaps he was a coward: it made no difference. A part of him remained in Danoor, struggling to make sense of what had occurred there. An even greater part of him remained in Golna—would always remain in Golna, unchanging.

His fist tightened around a wrist-thick branch until it cracked. Behind him, Churls paused in her work. She had heard something, in that sound alone.

"It's how often I wasn't in control," he said. He swallowed, cleared his throat. He opened his mouth and then closed it. The quiet stretched.

"What did you say?" she eventually asked.

He shook his head and returned his attention to the fire.

Berun, Shavrim, and Laures returned. The constructed man settled down, his dusty spheres squeaking like damp cloth to brass fixtures. His eyes were dimmer than Vedas recalled seeing in some time. Clearly, he was tired, or as close to tired as his body could become. Vedas had never determined what, if anything, Berun felt. Surely, he was not as mighty as he had once been: an injury suffered during their journey to Danoor (an injury Vedas still did not understand) had resulted in him being unable to alter his form or rotate the spheres that made up his body, severely restricting the amount of sunlight he could receive as nourishment.

They nodded to one another.

Shavrim spoke quietly to Churls. She shook her head and he laughed, clapped her on the back, and put a hand on her shoulder to steer her over to the fire. He met Vedas's stare with no trace of animosity: in fact, he smiled openly as he sat, as though they had shared a joke.

Vedas felt no anger. This *did* anger him.

Churls spared no glance at him as she crouched to warm her hands. He stared at her bare head, his desire undeniable and frustrating.

Laures, observant, looked from her to Vedas, and gave him a small, sad smile.

Shavrim cleared his throat.

"Weapons, Vedas. We should talk about weapons. When you lived in the abbey of the Thirteenth Order, I assume you trained with many different kinds?"

The question took him by surprise. It should not have. They had left the city for a reason. A mad reason, of course, but Shavrim had at least been forthcoming about just *how mad*. They were to retrieve weapons Adrash had left on the domed island of Osa—weapons the white god had hidden for fear their existence would threaten his own.

"Ah," Vedas said. "Weapons. I'd forgotten for a moment." He stopped himself, just in time, from allowing sarcasm to creep into his voice. He had agreed to their course of action. No one had put a knife to his throat.

He opened his hands, as if to accept a gift. "Yes, I am familiar with most weapons."

"Familiar? How familiar?"

"Familiar enough," Vedas repeated.

Shavrim laughed. "Modesty doesn't suit you. Would you show me?"

Vedas stood, swaying slightly. His suit hardened subtly along the back of his legs, assisting him without his consciously willing it so.

"I don't think . . ." Churls began.

He looked down at her, daring her to finish the thought.

She opened her mouth, and then promptly shut it.

This too made him angry.

‡

Shavrim selected a pair of short swords for the two of them, both similar to Churls's vazhe yet certainly sharper. Before giving his even an exploratory swing, Vedas weighed it in both hands, examining the scrollwork on the pommel, identifying a northern Tomen hand. He possessed extensive knowledge of blades, though they had never been his favorite sort of tool. He preferred striking surfaces, concussive edges.

He walked a few paces from the fire and turned. Shavrim lifted his shirt over his head, threw it to the dirt, and followed. The sword appeared comically small in his massive fist.

Not for the first time, Vedas appraised the man as an opponent.

Thickly built, he mused, *would be an understatement.*

Had Vedas been at peak condition, Shavrim would still have outmassed him by a factor of two. They stood at roughly the same height, both rather taller than average, but only one needed to turn sideways to make it through doorways. Typically, this would not have caused Vedas more than a few moments of calculation. He had faced much larger combatants, both suited and unsuited, and knew best how to use their size against them.

But Shavrim did not move like a man weighed down by muscle. Though he hid it rather well by moving slowly, Vedas recognized the grace in his movements for what it was: a deeply ingrained sense of *place* within the world—a proprioception far beyond what training could produce. It was as if he were a fixture, a center upon which everyone around him spun. With a slight twitch of muscle, he would send an opponent flying. Vedas excelled in fighting because he possessed such a center. He recognized this in Shavrim, and felt sure his was recognized in turn.

As Vedas pulled the hood of his suit over his head, his gaze lingered on the two small horns on Shavrim's broad forehead. They sprouted seamlessly from his flesh several inches directly above his eyes, darkening slightly as they neared a point.

No casual observer would fail to notice the similarity between the hood of the elder-cloth suit Vedas wore and the head of Shavrim Coranid.

Like all things about the man they had once called The Tamer, this made Vedas suspicious. It seemed too great a coincidence. Beyond this, it caused a small, superstitious part of Vedas to wonder if the man were possessed of some arcane fighting ability. He feared it, and he feared very little when it came to violence.

He had known only one other man who roused the same emotion. Abse, the abbey master of The Thirteenth Order of Black suits—the man who had identified in Vedas the potential to become a great fighter . . .

Abse would not flinch away from a man because of a coincidence, a vague feeling of unease.

Vedas took a ready stance, arms loose, legs set wide, the tip of his blade wavering slightly, purposefully, the head of a snake. The elder-cloth flowed to cover his face. It constricted around him, wonderfully alive and responsive, hardening to cup his genitals, becoming shields over his kidneys and vulnerable clusters of nerves. All traces of fatigue fled his system. He stood, sheathed completely. By comparison to his opponent, he was only a thin black shade.

From the corner of his eye, he saw Churls and Laures stand.

Shavrim moved, just as quickly as Vedas suspected he would. Sword low, rigid. Vedas waited until the last moment, anticipating the other's move correctly: as Shavrim's blade came up toward his wrist, Vedas flicked it aside and turned, stepping laterally, allowing the larger man to step past him. Having confirmed his opponent's speed, working on instinct, he immediately ducked. Shavrim's blade severed air as it passed inches above Vedas's head, creating a sound like tearing paper.

Vedas cut diagonally, aiming for the other's midsection.

. . . and stopped at the merest contact.

Shavrim froze. Vedas pressed his blade to the flesh just below the man's ribs. His right arm was a rod of steel, welded to the weapon in his hand.

"Familiar enough," he said.

After several heartbeats of silence, Berun burst out laughing, a huge joyous bell of a sound.

The tension fled from Vedas. His arm fell, and he started shaking. To his surprise, he did not have to force a smile at Shavrim, who clapped him on the back hard enough to rattle his teeth. A spell had been broken, he sensed—not a great thing, no, but it was a relief to feel an easing of his animosity. He and Shavrim returned to the others, where he expected to be received with the same lightheartedness.

Churls stared into the fire, unwilling to meet his gaze.

Laures simply looked from one to another, and offered him another sad smile.

"What?" he asked. He waited until Churls peered up. When she did, he could read nothing in her expression. "What?" he asked again, raising his voice. He looked around at his companions. The mood had turned, clearly, in the space of seconds.

"Is there something I don't know?"

"No," Churls said. "They're responding to me. My mother always said no one could be happy when I'm in a bad mood."

She stood. "Now would be a good time to talk."

‡

They stood just out of earshot of the others, awkwardly distant from each other. For Vedas, who had made a habit of not touching others beyond training and fighting, the realization of their physical separation came as a shock. To not touch Churls, even simply to take her hand, took a physical effort—an effort he had been making for some time, in truth before their failed attempt to capture Fesuy and hold him accountable for the murder of a stranger.

During his captivity, Vedas had never dreamt. Fesuy's mage kept him deep, deep below the level of recall. A blackness, a void, was all that remained. Even when they woke him, to allow him to eat and relieve himself, his mind was a smoked lens. And yet, in those blurred moments, he thought of her, regretting his inability to connect, chastising himself for being intimidated by urges that (for all other men, he imagined) came naturally. He had anticipated his own death, knowing he had not lived a single moment of truly forgetting himself, of *letting go*.

He took a step forward. The muscles in his shoulder jumped as he began to reach for her.

"Vedas," she said. "I'm worried. I'm worried, and I'm angry." She held up a hand to stop him from speaking. "We'll start with the worry."

He nodded, feeling like a child.

"What you just did with Shavrim . . ." She jerked her chin in the direction of the fire. "I've trained with you for months now, and you've never shown me anything like that. Either you've been lying to me about your skill, which I think is unlikely, or there's something happening here we need to acknowledge and try to understand."

He opened his mouth to deny it, and thought otherwise. "Are you sure?"

"You're not?" she said, squinting at him as though trying to determine if he were serious. Her features softened. "Vedas, I *know* you. Even at your peak level, you couldn't have deflected that first strike, dodged the second, or much less finished with your own. The first technique is simply too precise a technique for you, and the rest, well . . ." She shook her head. "He moved faster than I've ever seen you move, which means you moved faster than you should be able to move. In your condition, this is obviously—"

"Understood," he said, fighting the nonsensical urge to defend himself. He tipped his head back to look at the chaotic sky, fixing his gaze on the closest madly-spinning sphere. "You do realize, of course, this is one among many strange occurrences, Churls? I gave a speech, and on that very night the world proceeded to fly apart. The world blames me, and then Shavrim tells me it's not my fault—and furthermore, that something can be done about it. By *us*. And now look where we are."

He leveled his gaze at her. "Oh, and then the other interesting bit. I've recently learned something new about you, haven't I? A daughter—and not any ordinary daughter. In light of all this, it hardly seems the time to start questioning something as benign as my sword-arm suddenly becoming quicker."

She closed her eyes and breathed deeply. Vedas stared at her freckled face, thinner than he had ever seen it. Not beautiful, no: she would not be described as beautiful by most. She had told him that, as a child, she had often been mistaken for a boy.

He took her hand. "I'm sorry," he said.

Without opening her eyes, she smiled, lips parted slightly to reveal the gap in her two front teeth. "It wasn't right of me, but I didn't know how, Vedas. I was never . . . good . . . at being a mother. I don't know how to talk about Fyra, or *to* Fyra, much less deal with the questions

I have about her existence. She wants to help us, she and other dead who feel as she does. And now . . ." She opened her eyes. "As you said, *look where we are*. What are we doing?"

He squeezed her hand, and she squeezed back, lightly at first, and then harder, until they were both gripping with fierce intensity. He eased up, and eventually she followed.

"Will you sleep next to me tonight?" she said. "Or do you want to be alone for whatever's coming our way? I don't want to be alone."

"I will. I don't want to be alone, either."

She kissed him, lightly. She smelled strongly of the road, of dust and sweat. Like him. He dropped his head so that it rested against her sandpaper scalp.

"And the risk? The reason you've been keeping me at arm's length, Vedas?" She shook her head slightly, scratching against his forehead. "Don't deny it. I know there's more to your avoidance than just being upset at me for keeping secrets. You think I'll convince you what we're doing is right. You don't see that I have every bit as much doubt as you."

"Then why? Why are we here? I want an answer for this."

She slid her hands under his arms and embraced him. He returned it, no longer reluctant.

He felt, rather than heard, her chuckle.

"Haven't you learned yet?" she said. "Living life with the expectation that you'll always have an answer when you want it—that is the surest recipe for unhappiness. Answers come only in time. And right now, with the world on the verge of death, time is the one thing we don't have."

"So, it really is just that, following a madman or nothing?"

"I think so, Vedas. We've reached the end of the road. That, and that alone, is why we're here."

‡

He went to bed with her beside him and did not dream. He slept as if dead, like he had under the mage's spell. He woke and, though not whole, felt a great deal better.

The same could not be said of her, he saw immediately. Her eyes were red-rimmed and watery, and she flinched at his first touch. They worked in silence with the others, taking down the camp.

"Dreams kept you awake?' he finally said, as casually as he could.

Her fingers worked at a knot in the tent lines, and then stilled. She did not answer, pretending, perhaps, that she had not heard. Slight thought the movement was, he caught the small, quick turn of her head in Laures' direction.

‡

Three thousand years previously, the Summer Wars had cut a vicious swath through eastern Knos Min, resulting in the destruction of seven cities. Marept, the most northerly and least populous, was burnt nearly to cinders by the invading Tomen—a bedraggled contingent of several hundred men and women, all of whom had smelled defeat on the wind and chose to imbibe the fire spells their leaders created for just such an occasion, creating a miniature organic sun in the city center.

Alone of the seven cities, Marept had never been rebuilt. The wind would not even deign to bury it, and so its bones were left to bleach. Of course, legend told that it had begun to die well before the Summer Wars, that the River Sullen had spurned the city for dumping tannery toxins in its once-clean waters. Certainly, some event had caused the waterway to change course, for it ran now nearly two miles west of the city it had once run through.

The people of northern Knosi felt deeply about their rivers, having so few of them. They attributed personalities to each, talking as though about distant relatives. A river like Sullen, though rarely navigated, was known to every schoolchild. Even Vedas, who had spent the vast majority of his life away from the country of his birth, who had avoided his people whenever he could—even he remembered his mother's tale of Sullen's anger toward the people of Marept.

Staring at the river's surface now, he felt his mother had spoken truer than she could have known. Surely, she had never stood where he stood, thirty miles south of the only bridge to even bother crossing the river, nearly a stone's throw from a once-great city the world had been content to let slowly crumble into the desert.

"Sullen," Churls said at his left. "That's a good name for it. I hardly even want to fill our bags with it."

He grunted, tipping his head back to stare into the chalky, overcast sky. He reached and let his fingers graze hers. She took his hand, and all at once he wanted to be far away, ignorant of the world. In a place where no one dreamt of dead gods.

No, he did not want to ask her what had kept her awake.

Laures walked to the water's edge and spit. "My mother said any river east of Danoor was haunted."

"That would make nearly every river on the continent haunted," Churls said.

Laures turned to her with a smile. "My mother was a fool."

Berun shrugged with a shrill sound and waded into the river, trawling two huge water bags in his left fist, holding their comestible supplies high in the other. Most of his body disappeared, invisible below the surface, until only the top of his head showed at the halfway mark. Here he stopped, lifted the hand bearing the water bags and crooked a finger, urging them forward.

Shavrim followed first, chuckling. Vedas and Churls entered the piss-warm, sluggish current together.

Just before his feet left the sandy bottom and he began his first stroke, Vedas looked back to see Laures still standing on the bank, head turned as though she were listening for something. She bit her lip—an expression of anxiety on her face so out of character that he stopped for a moment to stare.

He nearly called to her.

And then a dark line bisected her forehead, accompanied by the sound of a honeydew being rapped sharply with a knuckle. A smattering of dark spots bloomed in a circle at the center of her face.

Vedas tipped his head to the side for perspective, and felt his testicles rise.

An arrow bolt protruded between her eyes.

Laures took one unsteady step toward the river and collapsed into it.

A cloud of dust rose in the distance beyond where she had stood.

‡

Shoulder to shoulder, they raced toward the dead city. The earth shuddered under their feet, out of time with their steps: Berun kept close at their heels, arms wide as he ran, offering as much cover as his massive body could provide. Now and then, an arrow clattered against his brass spheres or hit the ground to either side, yet the bowmen were clearly only harrying their quarry, conserving their missiles until a clearer shot presented itself.

Vedas sprinted ahead of the others and reached the first fallen column of Marept, taking a defensive position and surveying their pursuers. An arrow shattered on the stone before him, but he paid it no mind. It would hurt to be struck, undoubtedly, and might even break bone, but his suit had tightened around him. It would minimize any impact while preventing the point from entering his flesh.

He counted. *Twelve . . . No . . . Fourteen.*

All mounted on horseback. Stiff red-haired, clearly Tomen.

Six of the men held staffs that glowed with greenish magefire at their tips. Vedas had been surrounded by such mages on one or two occasions when Fesuy woke him enough to fully comprehend his surroundings. They were immensely dangerous—he had sensed this before, and knew it in his gut now. Even under the watch of Shavrim's wyrm, they had found a way out of the city.

"Fesuy's men," Vedas said when Churls and Shavrim were safely beside him, blocked once again by Berun, who stood, facing the approaching men, undoubtedly aware of the threat they posed even to one such as he.

"How do you know?" Churls said, squinting around the constructed man. "And besides, how could they have left Dan—"

"He's right," Shavrim interrupted. "And how it was done hardly matters. Sapes can only do so much to suppress magic, and her eyes can be blinded by someone with enough skill and alchemicals." Frowning, he looked from side to side. "We can do nothing from this position except die. We should get deeper into the city."

They moved rapidly, Berun clearing a path before them, lifting and heaving huge blocks of masonry out of the fractured roadway and throwing them behind his companions to block their pursuers. Though Vedas had seen Berun perform extraordinary acts of strength before, the display of force shocked him. Several days of receiving direct sunlight had clearly invigorated the constructed man, but the wage for doing so would be monstrous.

Once they reached a defensible position, Vedas predicted, there would only be three to stand against the coming storm.

No conversation would be heard over the sound of crashing masonry and Berun's thunderous steps, yet a quick glance confirmed to Vedas that both of his companions had come to similar conclusions. He met Churls's grim expression, and wondered how much of his own concern could be read under the mask of his suit.

"There!" he only just heard Shavrim shout.

A stone building lay directly ahead, alone amid the rubble. Standing, more or less, open to the sky but with all four walls intact. Vedas scanned it and thanked fate that Shavrim was no fool. It would be fairly defensible. Having stood for ages, it likely would not collapse upon them.

Berun lifted a massive fallen pillar that blocked the entrance, and roared as it slipped from his hands to fracture at his feet. He backed up and then took two steps toward the wide doorway, dropping his shoulders and ramming a broken section of the pillar, skidding with it into the interior of the building. His foot hit the left side of the doorframe, causing fragment of stone to rain down.

Vedas winced, but the walls failed to even shudder with the impact.

Berun remained inert as Shavrim leapt over him. Vedas pushed Churls forward, and then offered cover as best he could as she knelt to check on the constructed man.

"—am . . . fine," Berun said, his voice a faint brass rumble. "Defend . . . selves."

Churls nodded, tight-lipped, and moved into the shadowed security of the walls.

Outside, it was utterly silent. Undoubtedly, Fesuy's men had ditched their mounts to navigate the rubble Berun had left in their path, and were now advancing on silent feet toward their holed-in targets. They would be unafraid, utterly sure of themselves. They had little reason not to be. Perhaps, this would play to Vedas and his companion's benefit.

Vedas immediately quashed this brief optimism. Any advantage would be fleeting, ultimately meaningless. He smiled cheerlessly at Churls.

She read the expression, even under the elder-cloth, and rolled her eyes. "The fun never ends, does it? It won't be long now."

He nodded. "No, it won't."

Turning full circle, he examined the large, open space of the ancient building, knowing without a doubt that they stood within one of the more important buildings of Marept. A temple, perhaps, or a civic structure. The walls extended nearly thirty feet overhead: they were thick, ably hewn without mortar, simple stones cut and fit precisely into place. It was no surprise that it still stood. For a moment, he wondered about the people who had labored to build it, and felt keenly the injustice of it all.

To have built such a place, so cunningly, and have it abandoned to this appallingly slow decay. It must aggravate the dead, he reasoned.

"Better it were destroyed," he muttered.

"What?" Churls said.

He rubbed at his eyes. "Nothing." He peered over his shoulder at Shavrim, who stood stock-still at the door, surveying the scene outside. He lowered his voice to a whisper. "This will go very badly, likely very quickly. What of Fyra? She could help us."

Churls crossed her arms, features carefully composed. "She'd be here, Vedas, if she could. I don't want her badly hurt—if she *can* be badly hurt, that is—but I'm no idiot. I realize the straits we're in. I've been calling to her as best I can since we left the river."

"What could be keeping her away? Has something taxed her unduly?"

"Does it matter? She's not here."

The muscles of his jaw jumped. He considered challenging her, demanding an answer to the question she had clearly avoided. Instead, he turned away to join Shavrim across the body-length span of the doorway. Rubble crunched softly under Churls's feet as she came up behind Vedas and crouched. She placed her hand on his back, and it surprised him, how welcome she felt touching him, and what effect it had. His annoyance was not so much forgotten as immediately put into context.

She had secrets, and they hardly mattered now.

Outside, all was still. And then a crow cawed just to the left of the entranceway.

Vedas caught Shavrim's wry glance, and raised an eyebrow in return. It had been an extremely clumsy signal from the Tomen's point man.

Six lights briefly flared, several hundred feet directly before them. The two men turned away from each other, ducking inside the shelter of the doorframe.

Vedas wrapped his arms around Churls just before a beam of sizzling radiance shot through the entrance, punching a hole through the building's rear wall. Even with his eyes tightly closed, the magefire's brilliance shone through bone to light up the interior of his skull. He felt the heat of it even through his suit, bathing his back in flames. His pain increased, doubling and then tripling. Rather than fighting it, he focused upon it until it suffused him, smoldering everywhere within him without ever igniting.

Churls, however, had not even the protection of a suit. She screamed, and it was the sound of an animal being torn limb from limb. As though in response to her agony, the elder-cloth tightened and jerked spasmodically upon Vedas's frame, threatening to tear his arms free from her, yet he only tightened his hold, shielding her as best he could.

She continued screaming, one long, raw, sustained note of torture. It went on and on, until it was a finely focused lance of pain in the center of his being.

‡

Once again, something within him stirred. It more than stirred. It opened its mouth within him and roared to match her pain.

The roar became a word. A *name*. Its utterance was a declaration of outrage and conquest. Vedas was overwhelmed in an instant, shoved to the side of his own consciousness, a mere watcher. A tamed beast, ridden.

‡

He stood up and walked into the magefire coursing through the door.

He walked into brilliance, glancing down only briefly at the prone silver figure of his lover.

His *lover* and *sister* . . . but these two words were insufficient.

He smiled. Words used to describe what they were had only ever been the tools of men. Like men, words soon faded into nothing.

But a name? *Her* name?

Ustert.

This name would not fade.

This name meant more than all the souls of mankind combined.

‡

Evurt walked out of the temple and extended his right arm. The fallen column of flame his enemies had summoned flowed around his taut bronze form, quickly thinning behind him into a river, a stream, before withering altogether. His palm now pressed against a solid wall of shifting light, he began walking forward, pushing the magefire back toward its source—back toward the men who had the gall to attack him and Ustert.

A man came at him from the left, leaping over a low wall. Evurt turned his head only slightly, taking in the form of his attacker calculatingly: tall, ruddy, robed, a stiff crown of hair wound around his scalp. A curved sword held in both hands, close to his ribs.

Evurt waited until the man was nearly upon him, anticipating exactly how the cut would arc up from the hip, before casually slapping the blade, breaking the steel in two and shattering every bone in the man's hands.

Evurt heard this last fact, in perfect detail, as the snapping of twigs under one's foot.

He reached out toward the man and snapped his neck.

Two more men came in swift succession, from the right and the left. Instead of encountering either physically, Evurt took two swift steps backward at the last possible moment, spreading his palms as though parting a double swinging door, causing the tunnel of magefire to bulge, engulfing both off-balance attackers. They opened their mouths in silent screams, their skin crackling and blackening instantly. In seconds, they were ash under his feet as he continued forward.

Abruptly, the magefire died.

Evurt did not stumble or blink in surprise. The expression on his angular, hairless face remained neutral until six men rose from kneeling positions behind their upraised staffs, five archers with drawn bows at either side. At this point, he smiled across the hundred-foot span separating him from them, revealing small, sharp, even teeth.

"Hello, corpses," he said in a long-extinct language.

Three arrows shattered into splinters upon his chest without rocking him back an inch. The fourth and fifth he caught and threw back faster than human eyes could register, with such force that they nearly disintegrated on their flight back to their targets. Regardless, both mages were killed instantly from the force, thrown off their feet to land some distance behind their startled companions.

He walked toward them slowly, smile unwavering. He opened his arms and let their arrows die upon him, their spells sizzle and fade into nothingness over his sculpted body. He felt no more than a slight tickle, occasionally, only at the fringes of an attack displaying true talent.

But what was the talent of a man? Nothing, compared to him.

As he neared them, he switched between languages, all dead, repeating the same phrase:

"These are the wages of arrogance," he said as he turned back an arrow—as he redirected the flow of two spells and with them bore holes through the chests of the ones who had sent them—as he reversed the charge of another and turned its caster to ice . . .

As he, with a twitch of his fingers, fused the feet of the remaining five men to the ground.

They tried to pull free, but quickly realize their struggles were useless. The bowmen dropped their bows and reached for their swords. The remaining mage stopped his efforts entirely and raised his chin in defiance. Evurt crossed the remaining distance to them, swatted two of the warriors' blades away, and took the third. Decapitating all three with such skill that each toppled gracefully sideways, he caused the mage to be drenched in blood.

He reached out and slowly, inexorably, pried the staff from the mage's hands. He broke the weapon over his knee, causing a brief flare of sparks to erupt from its lit end.

The mage spit upon Evurt's chest.

Evurt recognized the curse the man spoke next, and knew something of his parentage.

"This is the wage of arrogance," Evurt said in archaically-accented Tomen.

He thrust the jagged ends of the mage's own staff into the meat below the man's clavicles, carrying him to the ground to the sound of both ankles snapping, impaling his shuddering body upon the sun-baked dirt. The mage screamed until his voice ran out, and then screamed some more.

Evurt cocked his head almost curiously, and then tore the man's lower jaw off, silencing the cries to a bubbling exhalation.

‡

Behind him, a voice called his name. It was not his sister's. Nonetheless, he recognized it, let it resound within him.

He turned, slowly, unafraid but not without a measure of caution.

Shavrim stood in the temple's open doorway, hands open at his hips.

Evurt's brow creased in confusion. The temple . . . he knew it from the frieze above its door, had been received by its priests on several occasions—Ustert, standing at his side in the courtyard, impatient as he was with their lengthy prostrations and rituals . . .

Better it were destroyed, he had whispered. *Then we'd never have to be this bored again* . . .

The smell of orange blossoms . . .

Agolet was its name. *Agolet, Twin Temple of Marept.*

But it was not at all as he remembered. He looked from side to side, his consternation growing.

This was a graveyard, forgotten, its tombstones toppled.

Marept—what had become of the city?

"Evurt," Shavrim repeated. "Brother, it's been too long."

"Don't use that word," Evurt said, but quietly. Shavrim would still hear it, he felt sure. It would hurt him, possibly. He had always liked the idea of family. He was often more like a child than man, as a result always on the verge of offense. Evurt had no small affection for the horned fool, and certainly respected his power, but he could rarely resist taking advantage of his brother's lamentable sensitivity.

When had they last spoken? What of the others? What of . . . what of Adrash?

Evurt shook his head, grimacing, suddenly frightened of his own dimwittedness. He had never liked asking for clarification, always preferring the answers he found for himself.

"What is this?" he said through clenched teeth.

Shavrim began walking toward him, steps measured, open hands lifted to either side, presenting no threat.

"You called to me, Evurt. Look at yourself."

"Called?" Evurt echoed. "When?" He looked down at his torso, running his hands over the muscular ridges of his belly, noting their odd softness and texture. His hands—he lifted them, turning them over, wondering at their appearance. They were . . . thicker? Yes. Thicker. He stared, and they seemed to shift in color, becoming a darker bronze, nearly black, losing their metallic sheen.

For a moment, he even saw the suggestion of veins on their backs, an imperfection, a marring upon his flawless skin. He turned his head to stare at his shoulders, which, again, seemed broader than he remembered. He lifted a leg, horrified to find this outsized, as well, a pillar of animal gristle.

All at once, his vision shifted. The world darkened, losing focus and vibrancy. He blinked, trying to clear away the film before his eyes, but the effect remained. The strength fled from his limbs and he slumped, as though lead had flooded his veins. He took two faltering steps backward, uncomfortably aware of wanting to run, to flee.

His foot caught on a rock, and he stumbled.

He did not fall, however. He was caught. Shavrim stood before him, gripping him tightly below the underarms, holding him easily at arms length.

"Brother," Shavrim said. He pulled Evurt into a crushing embrace. "You are not you. You cannot sustain this kind of activity. Rest, and then we'll see each other again."

To his horror, Evurt discovered that he was nodding—that he had lifted his arms to embrace Shavrim.

Clearly, he was not himself.

The world shuddered around him, in time with the jagged hammering of his heart. Blackness encroached at the edges of his existence.

He closed his eyes, allowing darkness to overtake him.

CHAPTER FIVE

THE 20TH TO 25TH OF THE MONTH OF SECTARIANS MAREPT, THE REPUBLIC OF KNOS MIN, TO UAL

Someone held his right hand in a firm grip. It took him several minutes of concentrating on his fingers and palm (disturbingly, they were naked) to realize this fact, yet upon confirming it he did not move or alter his position in the slightest for fear of revealing that he had woken. Instinctually, he remained motionless, and the rationale for this too took him several minutes to work out.

He knew no one with so small a hand.

"I know you're awake," the girl said. He knew the voice instantly.

"I am," he said, suddenly, intensely present within his body, as if her voice had made him aware of every sensation. His palm started sweating. Wanting to pull his hand away from hers, he nonetheless resisted, maintaining his meditative stillness—for reasons that, even upon examination, became no clearer. In the space of a few breaths, the urge itself faded.

"Your mother," he said. "She's . . .?"

She squeezed his hand even tighter, flooding him with warth. "She's fine. Angry and confused, but fine. You, though, you're still not right inside. I'm working on it."

Working on it. "How long have I been asleep?"

"Three days. You'll need two more before you can travel. Are you in any pain?"

Again, he felt an urge—to shake his head—and did not act on it. He had not opened his eyes. Oddly, he felt no desire to. He wanted to know if they were still in Marept, if Shavrim and Berun had been injured. He wanted to know what he had done, but could summon neither the memories nor the curiosity.

He felt *good*. *Protected*. As though it were all in someone else's hands.

"No," he said. "No pain, Fyra. Whatever it is you're doing, keep doing it." His brow furrowed. "How are you holding my hand? How can I feel it?"

She laughed, and he smiled, feeling lightheaded, carefree.

"Oh, I'm doing so much more than making you feel like I'm holding your hand, Vedas. What I'm doing right now is mostly keeping you from making stupid decisions, like getting up before you're ready. Influencing you is hard because you're so stubborn about being upset all the time. I probably should have just kept you asleep, but there's something I need to tell you. *Before* everyone else knows you're awake. I want you to take this with you, back into sleep. When you wake up, it will be important. Do you understand?"

"Yes." Yes, he did. How could he forget this feeling?

"Good," she said. Her grip lessened, and it was like being doused in cold water. A great portion of his serenity immediately fled, allowing worries a voice. When he truly woke, what would he recall from before his injuries? Would he hate himself for not forcing Fyra to let him speak to the others?

The girl sighed loudly. She said his name in a tone mothers used toward their children. "Stay focused on right here, right now. I told you, my mother's safe. So are Berun and Shavrim. The world hasn't ended. But you *do need to pay attention*. Promise me you won't forget what I say next. Tell me you can keep a promise."

He frowned, worrying at her intensity. "I won't. I can. I promise."

He did not hear her moving. Perhaps she made no sound. He sensed, however, that she had leaned toward him, placing her mouth close to his ear.

"Someone's trying to keep me away," she whispered, "and that someone is *inside you*. I don't know what he is or what he wants. He's too powerful. I'm scared of him." She made a sound, a soft, distressed cry. "It gets worse. You're not alone in this: there's also someone—a soul, a personality—inside my mother. I knew it the other day, after we first talked. I saw her there, seeing out from behind my mother's eyes. Maybe the same has happened to Berun, too, but it's harder to tell with him."

The words resounded in his head. *Someone. Inside you. Inside my mother.*

The muscles of his belly twitched as he thought to sit up, to do anything but allow the situation Fyra described from continuing. His neck flexed twice, convulsively, lifting his head a few inches before it smacked back against the pillow. Each movement, accompanied by sharp flashes of pain referring throughout his body.

"Stop!" Fyra hissed. She gripped his hand tighter once more, saturating him in bliss so rapidly that he giggled. "Don't try to move. You can't do anything about this in your condition. Besides, he's not with you now. All of this will make more sense when you're recovered. For now, you just need to know about it, and know who's behind it."

Through the haze of contentment, his terror was an abstract thing.

Incurious, he asked, "Who?"

"Shavrim," she answered.

He thought, unconcernedly, *Of course.*

His eyes shot open, through no effort of his own. Fyra's coldly radiant head was poised above his, her pale hair hanging down around both of their faces, linking them, enclosing them in their own private space. He stared at the off-white freckles patterning her nose and cheeks, struck by how like her mother she was.

When she smiled, she revealed a gap between her two front teeth.

"I know you're a good man, Vedas Tezul," she said. "Keep your promise. Remember—"

"I'm not," he interrupted. "I'm not . . . good." He chuckled, not caring what he said. It struck him, suddenly—it was *wonderful* to not care. He had always felt guilty unburdening himself of anything, as though he were tying stones around his listener's neck, so he had rarely done it. "I've watched children die, Fyra. I've trained them, knowing they might die. I lived with this awareness, that it could happen, and still did it. I was punished for this long before it ever happened. Some people are cursed. When I was a child, like you, there was a man—"

"Shut up," she interrupted in turn, squeezing his hand again to fill him with her warmth. She shushed him. "Quiet, Vedas. I've seen what happened to you. Don't make that face. I'm not a child, and no one is cursed. Now, you have to listen to me. You have to keep your promise: remember what I've said. Carry it with you into your dreams. And when you wake, healed and back to your normal, angry self, do something useful with it. Don't let me down."

He smiled, shuffling his awkward admissions of guilt to the side as easily as he had voiced them.

He promised he would not let her down.

‡

An hour before sunset, Shavrim returned from hunting, three large desert hares dangling from his meaty fist. Vedas rose and began preparing the fire. Churls looked up from cleaning the first of the hares, exchanged a quick glance with Shavrim, but said nothing.

"I'm fine," Vedas said. "Stop worrying over me."

A private smile tugged at the corners of his mouth. He had said such words to her on far too many occasions. In truth, he felt more than fine—incredible, as though he had woken from the soundest sleep of his life. Constraining the energy in his limbs, hiding the effects of what Fyra had done from Shavrim, was far more a danger than overexerting himself.

Of course, it was not only Shavrim he kept the secret from. He doubted Churls knew what her daughter had done, though her quizzical glances revealed a good measure of suspicion.

She would know soon enough, of course.

Thinking on this, he came to a decision. All at once, there seemed no reason to wait.

He winked at Berun across the fire. The constructed man's features broke into a frown, followed quickly by a smile. His eyes flared briefly.

"Vedas," he said. "You are in unusual spirits."

"I am, Berun," Vedas said, voice low, not bothering to broadcast his words. They would hear him just fine. "I'm refreshed and full of new thoughts. There are things I need to consider. Did you know, for instance, that Usterti believe in more than their goddess?"

"I did not," Berun said.

Shavrim raised his eyebrows, expression open. Vedas admired his acting.

Churls did not so much as pause in her preparations. She angled her face, which still bore the tight redness of what appeared to be (but he knew was not) a sunburn, down toward her task. She, too, knew how to hide, though not as well.

Vedas nodded, and spit upon the firestarter in his hands. It flared to life as he reached forward to place it amid the kindling. He grinned. Unusual spirits, indeed. He felt incautious, even mischievous, as if Fyra had infected him with a portion of childhood.

Or, he reasoned, he might be feeling the influence of the one Fyra had warned him about. This did not strike him as likely, though: the dreams he had experienced, both before and after he had spoken with the girl, did not lead him to see Evurt as the frivolous sort.

Regardless, his smile vanished. Even thinking of the name was enough to constrict his throat.

Nothing for it, he thought. He would make himself speak it. He would make it real.

"Oh, it's true," he said. "In the abbey, I studied the witches' sect. They're not fond of talking about anything other than the Goddess, I gather. I asked Laures about it before we left, and I thought she might attack me for having the gall. She did confirm what I'd been taught, however." He blew into the kindling, watching it catch, and then sat back. "A few of their stories tell of Ustert's brother—her twin—a figure who died or merely passed into oblivion."

"Fuck!" Churls yelled, dropping her knife to grip her left hand. "Cut myself." She stood, glaring at Vedas. "What in the hell are you talking about?"

"Ustert," he said. He swallowed, took two quick breaths. "Evurt."

She flinched.

Berun's head swiveled from one companion to another, one shelf-like brow raised questioningly. "These names," he rumbled, "They mean nothing to me."

Shavrim chuckled. "It's a miracle they survived unscathed, those names. There's something to them, I suppose, an indelible quality. Even the pronunciation—it's been much the same throughout Knoori for, oh . . . well, it's been millennia." He spread his heavy arms. "You want to hear what happened, Vedas? You want to know what it means?"

Vedas nodded.

Shavrim returned the gesture, and then looked up at Churls. "We'll wait while you clean and bandage the hand, though I doubt you'll need to. Ustert Youl would hardly let you die from such a minor scratch. Even in your body, in her doubtlessly confused state, she'd not suffer that kind of indignity."

‡

As Shavrim talked, the memory roused itself from the back of Vedas's mind. He easily recalled the heat of the magefire, and wrapping himself around Churls in an attempt to protect her.

The . . . *assumption*, he began to think of it—this came to him in fragments, like a puzzle being assembled before his eyes, accompanied by sensations that pricked at the nerves embedded in his muscle, skin, and bone. He clenched his fists and released them, twitched his shoulders and fought the urge to stand and act out what he knew his body had done. Impossible things.

Thoughts and emotions flooded his mind, disturbing in their alien intensity. Arrogance beyond human reason. Anger, cold and fathomless. Confusion upon the discovery that he, Evurt, stood in another's skin. And attendant to the confusion, disgust. Vedas's body, even the way the world appeared dim through his feeble human eyes, had repulsed Evurt.

This, most of all, chilled Vedas to the marrow.

He knew, now, how a god looked at humankind. The disdain, he had expected. Even the humblest merchant, risen to enough influence, soon became a master of contempt. Power begat this perspective, Vedas knew, and men could not entirely resist thinking of their neighbors as less than human: at various points in the history of the world, peoples had been enslaved and even made extinct. The cousin of such violence existed in every man. He could know that hate more intimately if he allowed himself to blame others for his ills.

It was appallingly easy to create divisions, to build walls instead of bridges.

The scorn of Evurt served to render all of his thoughts on the subject irrelevant, as if all of history had been as meaningless as children arguing over the rules of a game.

As if failure were an inescapable taint, written into the very flesh and soul of mankind.

‡

Vedas wanted nothing to do with gods. He never had, even when he believed all but one to be mere fictions, remnants of a long and deluded past.

And now, sitting before him, yet a third god made real.

That is, if Shavrim were to be believed. Vedas wanted to disbelieve him, but could not.

"Why us?" was his first question.

"I don't have that answer, Vedas," Shavrim said. "It's not as if I can ask my brother now, is it? He has retreated, or you've pushed him to the back of your mind. But, at a guess? You're strong, and you were in the right place at the right time, openly opposing Adrash on the world's largest stage."

He dipped his head to Churls. "You were equally strong, if not in many ways stronger, and you'd fallen in love with him. You must have been a tempting pair, a lodestone for Evurt and Ustert."

Vedas neither accepted nor rejected this, though he allowed himself a measure of relief. How might he have reacted, had Shavrim claimed a god had inhabited him since birth—directing his every move, placing him strategically at this exact point and time?

"Why are they here at all?" was his second question.

Shavrim gripped his crossed ankles and rocked back, angling his face toward the open sky framed by the four walls of the ancient temple. Vedas followed his gaze, letting the pause stretch for several minutes before impatience compelled him to break the silence.

He opened his mouth—and promptly shut it.

The spheres of The Needle had been rearranged slightly. The two that had appeared closest to Jeroun were noticeably smaller. Both spun at a much-reduced rate. In addition, four of the smallest had been clustered together near the moon.

Surely, he reasoned, an encouraging sign, yet he could not feel hope.

"Consider your past," Shavrim finally said. "Three score years and some, correct? The Needle has appeared the same, throughout. It has been a fixed thing. But three scores and some is no time at all. Still, it feels like something, no? You feel older, seasoned. Consider how alien former versions of yourself are to the man you have become. How few choices he made that you would make. How much of a fool he was, Vedas. Hold that awareness in your mind. Truly feel it, the regret and anger at your own stupidity, your cowardice and impotence.

"Now, consider what you would do if you had even more time, perhaps millennia, to meditate on the actions or inactions of that fool. Would you not grow to hate yourself as no man has hated himself? Would you not wish to die, knowing you could never right your mistakes? Tell me that would not be the inevitable outcome of a life that long."

Vedas fixed him with a cold stare. "You wish to die? Somehow, I think you're not trying hard enough."

Berun looked from Vedas to Shavrim. "Agreed. You tell us of your relationship to these—" he grunted "—gods. You tell us you are one of their number. Now you want death, perhaps the easiest thing for a man to achieve. No wonder you talk of fools."

Shavrim smiled, unwilling to take offense. "Wishing to die and dying are two separate things. I continue breathing not for lack of trying to quit. On occasion, that is: I've come to embrace my immortality. But this is not my point."

"Get to it, then," Churls said. Without glancing up from her work—which she had continued, despite her wound—she gestured at Vedas with her skinning knife. "He asked a question, Shavrim."

"Which I was attempting to answer. Forgive me. I've spent many lifetimes *not* revealing what I am. I've had no practice at it, yet I'd prefer for you not to fly into a rage when I tell you this is all my doing. But that is not within my control, is it?"

When no one answered, Shavrim's smile dipped but did not disappear. He pointed to the moon, sighting along his thick forearm with a squint.

"For most of my life, I've had Adrash over my head and five siblings buried under me. Humanity is the bridge between those two worlds. Though your expressions, and those of your creations—" he nodded at Berun "—are not my own, I'm fairly fond of you. My family and I once fought on your behalf, when we first identified the madness in our creator. Twenty thousand years later, when I felt the presence of Evurt and Ustert again in the world, I decided I must persuade them to help me."

Vedas stood, restless with questions yet unable to decide upon the most pressing. He massaged his temples and cracked his neck, trying to ease the tension that suddenly seemed bent on crippling him. Since Churls had rescued him, he had swung from one reaction to the next, one extreme giving way to another with no time to adjust. The earth was unstable beneath his feet.

Fortunately, Berun had not been similarly affected.

In addition, the constructed man had learned the art of sarcasm: "You *felt* the presence of Evurt and Ustert? And this simply *happened* to coincide with Adrash destroying The Needle?"

"No. It wasn't a coincidence. I told you the name of the elderman responsible. Pol Tanz et Som incited this. There is no other explanation."

"And how did he do that?" Churls said. "You're telling us Adrash couldn't simply swat him away? Who is this elderman, that he should inspire such world-shattering rage?" She stood, circled the fire and crouched, one bloody hand on Shavrim's shoulder, face only inches from his. She spoke through a tight jaw. Spittle flew from her mouth. "Is he another god, then, or is he merely . . . *ridden*, like me? Or Vedas? Will we wake up tomorrow and find Berun taken, too?"

She slapped him, her right arm a silver blur.

The sound of the impact, the crack of timber.

Shavrim's head whipped to one side and he threw out an arm to steady himself.

‡

Vedas tensed. It took him several heartbeats to realize just why he had done so, beyond the clear threat of Shavrim reacting to the blow.

He stared at Churls's bare arm, upraised and rigid, every muscle limned with tension.

Sun-red, freckled skin. The faded markings of tattoos. Nothing more.

And yet, his eyes had not deceived him.

She had struck with the arm of the Goddess.

‡

Shavrim chuckled.

A handprint of hare blood was now emblazoned across his left cheek. His own blood welled at the left corner of his mouth. He licked his bruising lips and nodded.

"Well delivered," he said. "When you are as I am, Churls, you learn to appreciate anger that cuts to the point. At the same time, you avoid what is necessary to speed the process up. Don't let my age fool you—there are things that frighten me. I have abilities beyond merely remaining alive, but they are a threat if allowed too deeply. I've not lived so long without . . . sequestering my existence, without forming identities that were thereafter abandoned. Within me are all the lives I've lived, a smattering of which possessed unusual insight. A few of these former Shavrims are anxious to return."

He stood and retrieved one of his packs. He removed a bundle of thin steel chain and threw it to Churls.

"Wrists and ankles, as tight as you're able," he said, presenting his back to her and kneeling.

"A chain?" Berun said. He got to his feet, his thousand ball joints sighing. "I can hold you tighter than any chain."

"You cannot," Shavrim countered. "This is no ordinary chain, and I'm no ordinary man. No disrespect intended, Berun, but the one I'm summoning would have no problem proving just how greatly your strength is outclassed."

Berun crossed his immense arms. "You are bleeding. From a slap."

"Indeed," Shavrim said. "But it wasn't Churls who slapped me, not entirely—just as it won't be me before you in a few moments. It'll be a wilder, more brutal creature, kept in check only through the will of the man I am now, a small voice of reason attempting to quiet a storm."

Berun grunted, and turned away.

Churls stared at the chains in her hands. For a mad moment, Vedas imagined she would strangle Shavrim with them.

She began binding his wrists. "Who is this former self, this wild creature?"

"A seven-thousand-year-old relic," Shavrim replied. "A fool and a mass murderer. On occasion, I've given in to self-pity, allowing my hatred for Adrash to cloud my mind. During one such period, I traveled to the southern Tomen coast. I persuaded the locals there to accept my presence by telling their fortunes and fighting in their border skirmishes. I've always been good at the latter, but the former? Somehow, possibly by way of the madness I'd allowed to creep into my soul, I tapped into a potential I'd never known I had. I listened, and for the first time truly heard the dead."

Churls paused in her task. She could not avoid a quick glance in Vedas's direction.

"The dead?" she said. "What do you mean?"

"I mean those souls still lingering near the living, unable or unwilling to leave the material world behind. They have much to say. Some are able to read the future—or predict it well enough to appear to read it. They have access to every moment of their lives. They observe us without our knowing. Because of the threat inherent in rousing my former self, I'd hoped to wait until proof presented itself concerning Pol Tanz et Som, who I believe to be dead. He was powerful, yes, and uniquely tempting for me: he inspired me, on many occasions, to bring my own former selves to the fore. Certainly, he was fated to madness because of what he'd done to himself, yet I don't believe he was inhabited by one of my siblings.

"As for Berun, I feel quite sure that he . . . I think I would have recognized . . ."

He shook his head and lowered himself onto his side, allowing Churls to bind his ankles to his wrists.

"No," he said. "Enough waiting. This is wiser. It's better to know for certain, now."

Vedas caught the man's expression. It could not be mistaken for anything but fear.

Shavrim met Vedas's stare and lifted his chin, gesturing to their packs. "Hold a blade to my neck and remain ready. If I appear about to break my bonds, or if my state persists past the point where I've confirmed or denied our suspicions, slit my throat. I'll bleed, but I won't die, and it will weaken my body enough for me to reassert control of myself. In that case, leave me here and continue on. I'll meet you in Ual, eventually."

Without waiting to see if his order was followed, he closed his eyes and took four immense breaths, the last of which he held still within him long enough to make Vedas concerned.

He took a step toward Shavrim just as a great shudder ran through the horned man's trussed body. Shavrim groaned, varying in pitch as the air—more air than lungs should hold, surely—passed out of him, finally winding down to a grating wheeze. The skin of his face, neck, and upper chest darkened, exactly as though he were choking. With a mighty gasp, he breathed in again. In, fully, and out, fully, the process resumed. Each time the cycle completed, the shuddering became more violent.

Churls backed away. Vedas put the point of his sword to Shavrim's throat, maintaining pressure upon it throughout the paroxysms. Berun continued to stand silent, arms crossed, glowering at the scene.

‡

The shuddering stopped. Shavrim's left eye opened, revealing a madly vibrating pupil. Gradually, it stilled and focused on Vedas, who pressed the tip of his blade more firmly to the man's throat.

A smile slowly pulled at the corners of Shavrim's mouth. The right eye slowly opened.

The huge, bunched muscles of his shoulders swelled as he tested his bonds.

He grunted, and his smile grew wider.

When he spoke, his voice was an octave lower—so low and accented that several seconds passed before Vedas realized the words were intelligible.

"—that limp-pricked fool," he said. "Friend to ghosts, fucker of men."

"Are you talking to me?" Vedas said.

Shavrim regarded him silently. To a casual observer, he may have appeared still, yet Vedas noticed the subtle muscular contractions in his thighs, belly, and upper arms that gave him away. Shavrim was testing the chains, methodically, searching for a weakness, determining where best to apply his strength in order to escape.

"No," he finally answered. "I'm not speaking to you. I'm speaking to the faggot I've turned out to be." He raised his head and inclined it quizzically, as though listening. He sniffed and sneered. "Or perhaps I'm wrong. You've the stink of one who's been buggered, and also of the dead. Of course, you *are* going to die. All humans smell of the dead. I may be getting confused."

"I have questions for you."

A nearly sub-audible laugh. "Of course you do. It's not as if I don't know why I'm here. The world is at its end, and all of you . . ." He lifted his head and winked at Churls. He whistled at Berun. Vedas kept his blade steady. ". . . believe you can do something about it. Pissing idiot idea. Adrash was more than a match for the six of us gods, and now you . . ."

All at once, his body went rigid. Vedas readied himself, but the man did not attempt to break free. In fact, after only a moment Shavrim dropped his head onto the ground and let it roll back, causing Vedas's blade to etch a fine line of blood on the man's throat.

"Ah," Shavrim said. "Ah-ha, ah-ha. Now I see. It took me a moment, but there it is. Hello, brother! Hello, sister! Can you hear me?" He looked up at Vedas, one eyebrow raised. "Are you in there, Evurt? Come out, come out!"

Vedas allowed himself several heartbeats of reflection, shining a torch around the interior of his skull, searching for the interloper he knew to be hiding there, before answering. He increased the pressure on Shavrim's neck, forcing the man to rest his head upon the ground or have his throat slit.

"It's only me," Vedas said. "And I have questions that need answering."

Shavrim's amused expression did not fade. "Oh, ask, Vedas Tezul. Ask away."

"You know of the elderman Pol Tanz et Som?"

A slow nod. "Yes. Another buggering, presumptuous little shit." Shavrim raised his chin to the night sky. "Still, he did accomplish this, more than most of you mortals ever will."

"Is he alive?"

No hesitation. "Yes."

"Where is he?"

"Don't know. Don't care." He flexed at his bonds, no longer attempting to hide the fact.

"Is he like us?" Vedas gestured to Churls. "*Inhabited?*"

The chain rustled as it shifted on Shavrim's wrist. "Like you two, you mean . . ." His eyes widened, and his voice lowered to a whisper. "Oh, good. Oh, very good." He smiled, and his voice rose. "Pol, I have no idea. He has talent, and not a tiny bit of madness. But the bloody big man made of balls, there, behind me?"

Berun uncrossed his arms.

"Yes! You!" Shavrim called over his shoulder. "The fool I've become didn't see it, right before his eyes, but I do. Hello, neither brother nor sister! Come out and play with us!"

The constructed man took two steps toward Shavrim and halted, stock-still, as though both feet had become rooted to the ground. A whisper-soft sound of metal rubbing metal cut through the air: the closing and opening of his great fists.

"The name, then," he said. "Speak it."

"Sradir Ung Kim," Shavrim said.

Berun's head swiveled from Vedas to Churls. "The names he spoke to you meant something. They stirred you. But there is nothing in this name, Sradir Ung Kim. I feel nothing. He is wrong."

"I'm not," Shavrim said. "You're merely thick. Sradir is within you, and it will come out. Soon, if I am any judge. It was always an odd one, choosing its odd moments." He grinned at Vedas. "You'll enjoy when it when it shows itself. Sradir was—*is*, I suppose—an unusual creature. It never seemed to get humans, the way the rest of us did. A wooden heart, that one."

He flexed at the chains once more, swelling his chest and heaving with every muscle. The chain groaned, and Vedas prepared to do what was necessary.

Fortunately, the links held. Shavrim simply grunted and rested his head upon the ground.

"Shavrim?" Churls said. Her voice made it clear which iteration of the man she had spoken to. "Shavrim? We have our answers, or as good as we're going to get. Come back now."

Shavrim laughed. "Oh, he'll not be coming back. And you haven't all your answers. I have more to say about the dead. There's another that hovers around Berun, and he means the world no good. He'd see a blanket of ash covering everything. Why? Who knows?" He shrugged, flexing once more at the creaking chains before subsiding with a contented smile. "And then there's the little thing my weak heir hasn't quite worked out. I'd particularly like to talk about her, as she seems to have a legion at her command."

"The little one?" Churls said.

"Yes. The one standing behind you."

Churls turned, and Vedas looked up.

But Fyra had already disappeared. A second later, she reappeared at Shavrim's back. After a brief pause, she closed her eyes tightly and thrust her ghostly hands into his shoulder.

Shavrim gasped and the girl cried out. Screams ripped from both of their chests, creating a disharmony that grated awfully upon the ears.

‡

They struggled: he, away from her, and she, away from him. Her arm seemed stuck inside the man's flesh, though such a thing was clearly impossible in her insubstantial state. The screaming continued, unabated—Fyra continuously, a siren screech unhindered by lungs, Shavrim pausing only for harsh gasps of air—while both sought to undo what had occurred.

Vedas kept his blade pressed to the flesh of Shavrim's quivering throat, not in the least dismayed by the cut he created there. He had never slit a throat, but he knew the difference between a shallow wound and a killing wound. He knew it by feel.

"What's happening?" he shouted to Churls. Berun closed around Shavrim and held him down, avoiding contact with where he and Fyra were fused.

"No idea!" she answered, taking one step in his direction, only to take one step back. "Fyra! What are you doing? How can I help you?"

The girl brought her teeth together, altering the pitch of her agony without lowering the volume. Her voice resounded inside Vedas, settling in the pit of his gut, in his bones. His temples throbbed. It took a will to stand: he fought the temptation to simply let his knees fail beneath him.

Shavrim's voice grew hoarse. He coughed between breaths, flecking the ground with blood.

Churls's indecision had come to an end. She ran forward and knelt at her daughter's back, thrusting her hands through the immaterial body, placing her palms flat upon Shavrim's shoulder, just where the girl's wrists entered. She leaned her head forward—*into* Fyra's own, creating the illusion that they shared a skull. Churls shook as she pushed, clenching her jaw against the vicious rattling of her teeth. Her breathing came in quick, shallow bursts.

She closed her eyes, and the girl's opened. White smoke poured out, evaporating above Fyra's head. The girl's lips came together, shutting off her scream so suddenly that Vedas flinched. Still, a humming issued from within her: the sound of her pain continuing behind her sealed lips, building up within her small form. She rocked back and forth in time with Churls, and gradually, hairsbreadth by hairsbreadth, more and more of her wrists came free.

Shavrim's screaming intensified with each pull, raw like a wound ground in glass.

Berun kept his broad hands on the man's upper arm and thigh, holding him down. Vedas thanked fate for it, too: without the constructed man's help, Shavrim's seizures would surely have prevented Churls from assisting Fyra. The girl would have been thrown around like a ragdoll.

Vedas kept the blade to Shavrim's neck while circling around his head, coming to Churls's side. He reached for her, intent on helping in any way he could. By pulling with her or merely laying a hand on her shoulder. If power could be transmitted through Churls to Fyra, then surely . . .

"No!" mother and daughter yelled in unison, halting their movements. Fyra's radiance doubled, tripled. A metallic sheen fell over Churls, as though she were reflected in a silvered mirror.

Vedas reached forward again, only to be stopped as Churls's head snapped up. Her face had taken on a harsh angularity. Her eyes were two golden slivers of light.

"No, brother," she said. "Let us do this work. Afterwards, you do yours."

She turned back to her task, the appearance of the goddess fading.

Fyra and Churls began moving once more, a moan escaping their lips, increasing in volume until it was an oddly-pitched chorus, as of a hundred voices howling—

—and, for a moment, appearing at their backs, disappearing through the temple's back wall, rank upon increasing rank—

—kneeling, hands upon each others' shoulders—

—rocking back and forth, in time with Churls and Fyra, adding weight to their struggle—

The dead, coming to aid one of their own.

Vedas blinked and they disappeared, leaving the afterimage tattooed upon his eyelids.

Below him, Shavrim cried out again and again, a series of hoarse, surely agonizing coughs. Fyra had managed to pull nearly half of her hand free.

"Hold steady, Vedas," Berun cautioned.

Vedas looked down to see the tip of his sword in the dirt. He pressed it home once more.

Churls's movements became increasingly jerky. Now, her elbows were locked. Only her neck and shoulders moved back and forth.

Nonetheless, it was enough. Finally, it was enough.

With a gasp from both parties, they fell back—Churls onto the ground, Fyra partway submerged in the ground at her side, half-in, half-out as though she were floating on her back on the surface of a salt lake.

Shavrim gave one last gasp and went slack, head lolling on the ground.

Vedas dropped his sword and knelt at Churls's side. Her pulse was strong but irregular. Her breathing came in jerky inhalations and shuddering exhalations, in through the nose and out through barely parted lips. Under her eyelids, her eyes swam in twitchy patterns. He watched her for the space of a dozen breaths and then willed his suit to unmask his face. Mind struck unfathomably blank, a sound in his skull like the hiss of calm waves, he bent to kiss her.

"Vedas." Berun's voice seemed to arrive from a great distance away, his methodical, accented speech tinny in Vedas's ears. "What are you doing?"

"This," Vedas answered. He pressed his lips to hers, and the world dissolved.

‡

The sun hung directly before him, though he did not shield his eyes. He stared at it directly for an indeterminate time, several heartbeats or the better part of an hour, wondering at its appearance. He had never before noticed, but it was not a stable, unvarying thing. The sun pulsed, expanding and contracting slightly. It breathed, varying its light in intensity from one moment to the next.

Someone squeezed his hand.

He shook his head, and finally registered his surroundings

He stood on a vast, red-soiled plain carpeted in white and yellow flowers that swayed in the breeze, moving like the surface of the sea. The horizon was close, a knife's edge or a table-end. It smelled as it always did on the outskirts of Danoor, away from cooking fires, inefficient plumbing, and the press of bodies.

He breathed in the ancient, baked dust smell of the desert, and knew.

The plains of the Aroonan mesas were a holy place. None but the Aroya people and their closest descendents were allowed to walk on the heights. This restriction was one of the oldest and most binding rules of the Knosi people.

He could not bring himself to care about trespassing. His mind moved glacially, catching up to his curiosity slowly.

Someone squeezed his hand, and he turned.

Churls stood at his side, the fingers of her left hand entwined in his right. His *naked* right hand, he noted by feel.

He looked down. His suit had retreated far up his arms and legs. The borderline between skin and suit was chaotic, appearing almost like the torn edges of multiple strips of fabric. Centered upon his chest was a perfect circle of flesh. Small holes in the elder-cloth peppered out from it, forming a five-limbed swirling pattern that extended onto his shoulders and arms. He had never chosen to make such designs upon his suit. Point in fact, he doubted he possessed the skill necessary to make such a thing occur.

Examining the design, he registered a second shock.

Where exposed, his skin reflected the slanting sunlight as though it had been flecked in metallic dust—as though he had been at work at a grinding wheel, honing the edge of a tool. He scratched at the portion of his exposed chest, and then stared at his upraised hand. He made a fist, and the skin of his knuckles did not pale slightly as it stretched over the bone underneath: instead, each knuckle warmed in color, glowing bronze under his nearly black skin.

He looked at Churls again. Her skin had once again taken on a metallic aspect to match his own. Silver to his bronze. Vaguely, muzzy-head, he recognized the significance of this.

She smiled at him oddly. The lines of her face were subtly wrong. No, even its structure was wrong, marked by higher cheekbones and a thinner jaw. The skin of her face seemed too tight, stretched taut and glistening over the bones of her skull.

His lips formed two names, but he spoke neither.

Churls. Ustert.

Her smile widened, revealing two rows of small, perfectly straight teeth, lacking any gap between her two incisors. His cock stirred, and he grimaced, tightening his suit around his genitals, clamping down physically on his arousal. Without taking his eyes off Churls, he rubbed at his jawline, finding it smooth, as hairless as that of a child's. His scalp, too, was without a hint of budding hair. His hands felt oddly outsized, palm too broad over his mouth, fingers extending too far around his cranium.

He searched for words to express his concern. He wondered if it would even be wise to do so. He did not want to reveal more of his own ignorance, having revealed enough ignorance to account for several lifetimes.

"Quit worrying," a voice said. "You're safe here."

Fyra stood before them, her expression calm. Unlike when they had met, she was now painted in the shades of life. Her pale, freckled skin shone with an inner light. Her eyes were liquid, the color of seawater. When she grinned at him, he returned the expression automatically, unselfconsciously. He had once, as a child, smiled that way. He drew strength from the solidity of her presence.

"You're not completely you, Vedas," she said. "Neither is Mama. I couldn't prevent bringing something of them here with you. They wanted to see this, I think."

"What?" he asked. "Wanted what?"

"Vedas," Churls said. "Do you know where we are?"

He shook his head.

"We're in the land of the dead. A vision, sustained by those who have passed."

He tore his eyes away from Fyra, though breaking the contact between them took a physical effort.

"How do you know this?" he asked. "This is all your doing, the two of you?"

Churls nodded to Fyra with an expression of unclouded affection Vedas had never before seen. "A lot can be passed between a mother and daughter, in the moments where they struggle together. We know each other better now—far, far better than in life, undoubtedly. And it's not our vision completely, Vedas. We're not alone."

Between heartbeats, an army of thousands grew behind Fyra, silent and arrayed in every style of dress the world knew. Vedas's gaze passed over those closest to him. The sun shone through a few of their bodies as though they were formed from glass. Most did not visibly breathe, for why should they? Some were stiff and gray, granite statues rather than men. Many were strangely flat, an image on a canvas. Not one appeared as substantial, as concrete, as Fyra.

He recalled her claiming to be *better than anybody, ever*, and he no longer doubted it.

The girl stepped forward, taking his left hand. Together, they faced the dead.

‡

For a time, nothing moved, and Vedas became aware of a sound.

A low thrum.

The first hint of the ocean lapping upon the shore.

Thunder, so faint that it could have been imagined.

It was all of these sounds, but it was also a symphony of voices. He knew this, and did not know how he knew it.

The dead could not hide their thoughts, not completely. They wanted to be heard.

"Magess Um," Fyra said. "Tell him what you told me."

One among the assembled ranks stepped forward. Skeletally thin and nearly translucent, she was a mere whisper of a person, wrinkled and wrapped in dun robes. Despite her worn and watered appearance, she held her chin up, holding Vedas's stare. She did not stoop, and stood only an inch or two shorter than him. She could have been his grandmother, such was the similar hue of her skin, the nap of her hair, and the straight breadth of her shoulders.

"This is Jojore Um, former Magess of the Knosi Kingdom under Queen Medn," Fyra whispered. Vedas looked down at her, surprised by the note of respect in her voice. "She is the oldest of us, much older than I knew any of us were. She has experience no one else has, by thousands of years. It is an honor to talk to her. Listen."

Jojore did not smile. She did not even open her mouth.

Vedas Tezul, weak-blooded cousin, she said directly into his mind. Hers was a flat, haughty rasp of a voice, heavily accented though comprehensible. *I am not pleased to meet you. Nor am I impressed by what I see. Regardless, you are standing here before me. You are at a crossroads, with the fate of all life drifting in the wind. Wish that it were otherwise, it matters not at all. You will have to do.*

Vedas frowned, but not at her words, insulting thought they were. A series of nearly colorless slowly-moving images of himself accompanied her speech, forming in his mind and quickly collapsing, as though she were shuffling through a bystander's memories of him.

. . . ten or eleven years old, running along an avenue in Golna, carefree. . . . older, into his early twenties, thinner and likely stronger than he was now, lifting an opponent amid the chaos of a street battle. . . . holding the body of Sara Jol. . . . and only days past, atop Fesuy Amendja's stronghold, facing the man he had then known as The Tamer.

Yes. Him, Jojore said. *You are not to doubt this man, Shavrim Coranid. And yet you are not to trust him. He is legion inside himself, and there are worse than the one the girl just saved you from. There are worse than even the being Shavrim is now suspects. He has forgotten much that is a danger to you, to himself.*

"How do you know this?" he asked. "Why should we trust you?"

Fyra dropped her head and groaned.

Jojore's expression hardened. *You will address me by my title. You will call me Magess Um. I am doing you a favor, never forget it nor doubt me. I know these truths because I know the relic Shavrim claims to have been.*

She sneered, and an image came to Vedas of Shavrim, naked, painted in swirling patterns from head to toe. He stood on a battlefield, alone, breathing heavily and surrounded by corpses. *I was one among the dead who helped him see likely paths to the future. I would not discuss with him the fates of goat herders or fisherman. I would only speak to him matters of importance, of life and death. I grew to know him. I heard him when he came back into the world, just as I hear whenever he takes that aspect.*

"You know who he really is—who he claims to be?" he asked. She scowled, and he forced himself to add her title.

I do. And he more than claims. He is what he says he is. I am not blind, as you clearly are. I know his nature just as I know your own, beyond the thin shield of your mind, your fragile skin and bone. She turned her head to Churls. *As I know who you are. You are both ridden, hosts to souls older and more powerful than any in the history of the world excepting Adrash and Shavrim. They should not be here, but it is beyond our will to keep them out entirely.*

Vedas winced as two blinding images of Ustert and Evurt seared into his mind's eye.

. . . the two of them, svelte and severe as knifeblades, silver and bronze, locked in a violently passionate embrace on a massive bed, in the very room he recognized from his own dreams. . . . and then, both standing, hand in hand, alongside four others, Shavrim among them.

The image passed too quickly to gather much detail beyond this, but Vedas imagined that one among them possessed wings.

Jojore nodded. *The pretty one. His name was Orrus Dabulakm. He was Shavrim's favorite. And this one . . .*

The image returned, held. It shifted suddenly, and he stared directly at the tallest of the six figures. She—or he: Vedas could not tell—seemed to stare directly at him with dull, featureless eyes. Thorns grew from her shoulders, elbows, and knees. She held in her hand a short whip.

. . . is Sradir Ung Kim.

Her sneer returned. *Yes, the . . . artificial man . . . he too is ridden, as the relic Shavrim claims. He is not his own creature.* She looked pointedly at Fyra, then at Churls. *But he has never been his own creature, has he?*

Churls shifted her weight from one foot to the other, clearly uncomfortable. "That's not my secret to tell," she said. She opened her mouth to speak again, and then closed it. She angled her head forward to peer at Fyra. "Why did she look at you?"

Jojore made a cutting motion with her left hand before Fyra could respond. *Enough, you foolish people. Enough secrets. Time is not infinite.* She met Vedas's gaze again. *There will be a reckoning for the one called Berun. It will come from two directions: from Sradir Ung Kim, and from his creator Ortur Omali. Sradir will act as it will—no, I cannot read its intention—but Omali is known to us, to many of the dead. He cast an immense shadow in life and is still felt here from his place in limbo. He is wounded, but still the most powerful agent of those who would see the Needle fall and rupture the crust of Jeroun, extinguishing life's fire.*

"Churls," Vedas said quietly. "You knew of this . . . possession?"

"Yes," she said. "It wasn't my secret to t—"

"Shut up," he said. He shook his head, marveling at everything that had been kept from him, all that would continue to be kept from him if he did not insist on being enlightened fully. Keenly aware of his anger, he nonetheless understood it as an unproductive emotion, a petty thing that could not be allowed to last: Churls had had her reasons for keeping him in the dark, as had Berun. He would not blame them, no, yet he would not remain in ignorance.

Their hesitation could not be allowed to shape events.

He released Churls's and Fyra's hands. The world dimmed perceptibly—perhaps, he reasoned, because he could not exist alone in the world of the dead. He likely did not possess the understanding or will sufficient to sustain the link.

As if to confirm his suspicion, Churls reached for his hand.

He stepped forward, out of her reach, and gripped Jojore Um's upper arm.

The texture of her skin, like volcanic glass. The widening and narrowing of her dark eyes. During several long seconds, he seemed to stare at her through a darkening tunnel, the bright dream of the dead fading around him in increasingly constricting waves.

"I am not your weak-blooded cousin," he said, hearing his words through a wool sheet, a thin wall. He did not yell, but increased the volume of his voice with each sentence. "I am full-blooded Knosi, son to full-blooded Knosi. I am Vedas Tezul, the man who declared war on Adrash. I am ridden by a god, and still live and speak in my own voice. I will not be talked to as if I were a child. I will not be told what to do, kept in the dark, or moved about like a game piece—by you, by Evurt, by anyone." He smiled tightly. "You will acknowledge this."

For a moment, she looked as though she would reject his assertion. Slowly, however, one corner of her mouth turned up. She nodded, and the daylit mesa snapped back into focus.

Finally, she said. *A reason to hope in you. No cousin of mine comes crawling.*

He leaned into their embrace, and whispered in her ear.

"Don't tell me anything more. Show me. Show me everything."

‡

Shavrim lagged behind them for the two days it took to reach the docktown of Ual. He waved them forward when any member of the party slowed to accommodate his pace. He kept his features carefully composed, though now and then he huffed in annoyance.

Vedas could not resist making the comparison to himself. On the trip to Danoor, he too had been injured and labored to keep up with Churls and Berun. He too had refused to accept any concession to his condition. Watching Shavrim struggle, Vedas fought to reconcile his distrust with a newfound sympathy. When night came, he stared across the fire at his clearly exhausted companion, trying to piece together what Jojore had revealed to him about the man.

(No, despite what he had learned, he could not bring himself to think of Shavrim as a *god*. The world already possessed one too many deities. Vedas denied the label, as though denying it would do a damn thing.)

The weight of time: this, Vedas could not easily comprehend. How could a being exist in a body so clogged with lives, the identities and recollections of millennia? Thanks to Jojore, he now understood Shavrim had been made, in the much same way Berun had been made—that the man had been designed from the outset to withstand the physical and intellectual rigors of immortality. Whereas Vedas possessed one mind housed in the fragile confines of his skull, Shavrim's mind branched and divided throughout his body, compartmentalizing his ponderous existence, allowing him to close and open doors to all but forgotten memories.

And yet, even with this knowledge, Vedas could not conceive of the pressure upon the man's shoulders. Though aware of the limitations of his own knowledge, as well as the impossibility of any true comparison to mortal men, he could not prevent himself from reading much in Shavrim's defeated expression.

What occurred in Marept had broken him in some fundamental way.

To his surprise, Vedas found himself warming to the man. Shavrim had never acted on Vedas or his companions' behalf, but he had also never lied. He would see his family returned to him, and this stirred buried recollections within Vedas. Had he not wanted a family, a place to belong? Had he not tried, for most of his life, to achieve some sense of peace and justice?

He did not hate understanding how he and Shavrim Coranid were alike.

In truth, since communing with Jojore, he had discovered an untapped reserve of compassion for both Churls and Berun. He felt warmly inclined toward Fyra, protective, affectionate in a way he had never before allowed himself around children. The urge to chastise himself emerged, for it was as though he had forgotten a thing so obvious he should never have been able to forget it.

Churls. She had lived with a burden far heavier than his own—far heavier than anyone could be expected to endure. As the trainer of recruits for the Thirteenth Order of Black Suits, he had seen children die, knowing himself to be responsible, or at the very least complicit. But Churls? His knees grew weak every time he contemplated the bleak weight, the overwhelming guilt, of losing a child rarely seen and never truly comprehended. Churls had willfully neglected her daughter, choosing wrongly each and every day she spent far from home.

She had not deceived herself in anything. She had known she was running.

Not for the first time since leaving Golna, Vedas appreciate the power of experiencing unclouded vision. He had once considered himself a man of insight, aware of what moved those whose lives intersected briefly with his own, but to truly comprehend what another felt, the total acknowledgement of their mistakes, their joys and failures and boredoms . . .

Oh, yes, he loved her.

He would use this word, *love*. He would mean it for the first time since childhood, when love was an automatic function of living, of being dependent upon someone. Committing to it, as they traveled through the desert toward a seemingly impossible goal, ridden by forces they could not as mortals grasp, struck him as appropriate.

The mortal mind could be illuminated. Even someone as crippled by doubt, as awkward from self-imposed isolation, as he could experience a communion with others. There was considerable risk, but he now understood the risk must be taken if one were to make it to death a complete man.

Of course, *man* could mean so many things. Berun, too, suffered in ways Vedas could sympathize with. Vedas recalled all the ways in which he himself had been manipulated since the death of his parents, first by one and then another abbey master. They continued to exert their pull, even from death and across the continent, telling him that he had lost his way, that he had betrayed his order and the oaths taken there.

Of course, as with Churls, what he knew of suffering in this regard paled in comparison to Berun, who had never had room enough to call himself his own creature—who had at every step been under another's thumb.

Haunted, the three of them. He, Churls, and Berun shared this bond. His friends had known this intuitively and supported him, well before he knew himself.

Friends. Yes. In addition to love, he would use that word. It brought a smile to his face.

And Fyra?

Fyra. To whom they owed their lives. For which she continued to exhaust herself, asking nothing in return. She possessed an unquestionable loyalty to her mother, and, for reasons Vedas could not fathom, a growing sense of attachment to her lover and Berun. She had become invested in their combined fate, to the point of acting as emissary, rousing the dead from their fear, convincing them to risk their own existence to oppose Adrash.

Ostensibly to oppose Adrash, he reminded himself. Everything beyond helping her mother was secondary. She was still a child, for all her power—a child who did not know the wage of her offer.

Jojore knew, however.

We could help you, and stand a chance of surviving, the dead magess had said as they stood and surveyed a blasted, permanently twilit plain—an outcome, one of many, in which Adrash let the Needle fall to earth. *The girl, however? She will die a death beyond death. She will pass out of existence. I am not always able to read the wind, but this much is clear. Know the wage of choosing to accept our help.* Her expression grew hard. *It is a small wage, cousin. She is just one girl. Powerful, yes, but still just one girl.*

He had nodded, but only in confirmation of the conclusion he had already reached. Churls would not lose her daughter a second time.

‡

The nations of Knoori could not easily be linked, one with another. The magic needed to communicate over vast distances existed, but the expenditure was too great for the commoner. As a result, news traveled glacially.

Having no family to speak of, Vedas had never given this fact of existence much thought, yet traveling to Danoor had altered his perspective slightly: he had often longed to communicate with Abse, seeking counsel over the long journey.

Of course, had he received such counsel, he might well have delivered the speech the abbey master had written—a document that sought only to cement the power of the Black Suits, altering the dynamic not at all, keeping warring parties in their old positions. Had he listened to Abse, he would never have allowed his doubt to take such firm root, or his desire for Churls to bloom. He would not have become something other than Vedas Tezul of Golna, a child in a man's body, a mind bound by the cords of dogma. He would not have a hundred new doubts, or a sense of purpose despite the doubts.

Certainly, he would not be staring at a statue of himself, at a crossroads far from Danoor.

He looked away, horrified. The smell of saltwater filled his head, though the ocean could not yet be seen. Over the flat northeastern horizon, he could make out a gleaming arc of reflected light, an incomprehensibly huge bubble stretched over a vast portion of the earth's belly: Osa, or at least the top of the immense crystal dome that covered their eventual destination.

He concentrated on it intensely, as if by doing so he could convince the others to turn their gazes away from the embarrassing object before them.

"Well, this is odd," Churls said.

Shavrim grunted. After a moment, Berun began laughing. Heat rose in Vedas's cheeks.

The statue stood, propped in the sand two miles west of Ual. It was a crude, half-sized thing with exaggerated musculature and even more exaggerated genitalia, painted black from head to toe. In one hand it held a roll of paper. His victory speech.

A sign hung from its neck.

UAL IS LOYAL TO THE PROPHET VEDAS TEZUL
IF YOUR ALLEGIANCE LIES ELSEWHERE
LEAVE OR BE DROWNED IN OUR SEA

Churls resisted laughing, but could not hide the amusement in her voice. "It's really quite flattering, Vedas. You're a hero."

She frowned exaggeratedly at his expression, and squeezed his hand.

"Come now. We'll be welcomed like royals. After Danoor, shouldn't we thank fate for anyone kindly disposed toward us? We could have walked into a town overrun by Adrashi."

He met her stare and she sighed.

"Fine," she said, and pressed her palm flat against the statue's forehead. She walked forward, toppling it easily to the ground. Over her shoulder, she smiled at him. "What? They're about to meet the real thing, anyway, so what's the harm in a little sacrilege?"

He tried to see the humor in it. He did. She raised her eyebrows. He admitted defeat, and smiled at her. It was a forced reaction, but to his astonishment it helped: as he passed the downed statue, the situation suddenly struck him as comical. He experienced the increasingly familiar suspicion that, should he choose to view the world differently, the world would indeed appear differently. Was it necessary to view events through such an uncharitable lens? What, he asked, did it profit him to greet each day with a wary eye? He had always been dying. The world had always been dying. It would all end one day, and what would be left of Vedas Tezul?

He stopped in his tracks, turned back, and stooped to shoulder his wooden likeness. Shavrim watched him. He nodded, expression unreadable, when Vedas stood.

Berun looked from one to the other. "What are you doing?" he asked.

Vedas shook his head, not entirely sure, but suspecting he would know in time.

‡

The residents of Ual had little to spare, but they spared all of it to accommodate their prophet. He balked at their generosity, but in the end relented.

They slaughtered a ewe within a half hour of his arrival, prepared and set dinner for twelve men between the three of them, and made up he and Churls's room in the town's one inn as if hosting (just as she had predicted) a king and queen. Joyful and embarrassed at all the attention, full to the point of bellyache and more than a little drunk, they fell asleep before the thought of making love occurred to either of them.

At two hours past midnight, he rose and left her. His movements were silent, even to his own ears. He had felt sluggish upon entering the room, but he felt light and strong upon leaving it, filled with a purpose he did not need to question. Following the compulsion, he smiled tightly in anticipation, his jaw clenched and his fingers balled into fists.

He would go, but he would not be corralled.

His brother waited for him in the town square, arms crossed, under the broken sky. This word—*brother*—formed on Vedas's lips, but he suppressed the urge to speak it. He clamped down upon the sense of familiarity that threatened to dictate the conversation before it had even begun. A door closed in his mind: he locked Evurt as best he could behind it.

"Shavrim," he said.

The man canted his head forward, causing the moonlight to catch oddly on the stubby horns sprouting from his forehead. For a handful of seconds, they appeared larger than they had before, sharpened into vicious points. Stretching, reaching . . .

Vedas kept himself, barely, from taking a step back.

Shavrim's left eyebrow lifted and he raised his chin, breaking the illusion. He smiled—a touch sadly, Vedas estimated. Vedas had seen the same expression on Abse's face many times. When the abbey master's most gifted disciple had not reached the correct conclusion. When events did not turn out as the abbey master planned.

Abse had been able to recognize immediately, the moment when Vedas's sympathy shifted away from him.

"Vedas," Shavrim said. There was no question in it.

"Yes. That is my name."

Shavrim nodded, eyes bright, intent. "It is. It is. And yet you're here, where I expected Evurt to be." He sat, cross-legged on the ground. He gestured that his visitor sit. "I won't pretend this pleases me, Vedas, but there's little I can do. You're surprised that I tell you this? Let me ask—do you think I've been honest with you? Have I been forthright?"

"You have," Vedas said immediately, and then discovered room to doubt his surety. He considered several responses, and then shrugged before sitting across from Shavrim.

An odd decisiveness had settled upon him: he would allow the man to lead, to either tell the truth or implicate himself. He would trust himself to tell the difference between the two.

Behind the closed door in his mind, he felt a force push back against this resolution. Evurt did not want to wait, yet Vedas found it easy to dismiss his impatience. Each inhalation seemed to anchor him more firmly to the earth. Even his newfound affection for Shavrim did not fade. In fact, it was if they stood upon equal ground for the first time.

They stared at one another, silent.

Shavrim broke first. He laughed suddenly, as though Vedas had told an amusing joke.

"You're an interesting man, Vedas Tezul. When we met upon Fesuy Amendja's roof, I told you I could show you a way to stop hating yourself, never imagining you might come to terms with yourself alone. Every rumor I'd heard had led me to imagine you as the most inflexible sort."

Vedas said nothing.

"To be clear, mine was a genuine offer. Adrash is not invincible. He can be wounded. He might even die. What I did not share then, but shared soon after, was the way in which you'd be able to make good on your word—not through your own efforts, but through my brother's."

He sighed, and his sad smile returned. "Yes. I had hoped to see Evurt again, to fight alongside him, despite what damage it might do to you. I thought he and Ustert were the world's best chance. I still worry that they are, that we have missed an opportunity at an entire world's expense. Their assumption of you and Churls may still happen, of course. I won't lie and say it wouldn't please me. Regardless, there's substantial doubt in my mind. Perhaps they chose vessels less wisely than they could have. Perhaps you are too strong to be taken and used in the manner they intend."

Vedas said nothing. He closed his eyes as the pressure behind the closed door intensified.

After a long pause, Shavrim said, "Perhaps this is a good thing, however."

The pressure doubled, tripled. Vedas considered clamping down upon it entirely, grinding Evurt's influence to a halt before it became overwhelming, but did not. Shavrim would not stop attempting to rouse his brother. He would test Vedas, again and again.

Might as well have it out now, Vedas thought.

Evurt did not deign to respond.

"Perhaps you are what the world needs," Shavrim said. "Two mortals. After all, if Evurt's strength is insufficient to overcome you, what use could he be against our father?"

The pressure increased until Vedas's skull creaked with it, bathing him from crown to chin in pain so intense he struggled to loosen his jaw to scream, yet loosen his jaw to scream he did. He opened his eyes, and a golden light poured forth from them, fractionally easing the weight pressed against both temples. The colors of the night bloomed around him suddenly and Evurt's consciousness, menacingly alien and disdainful, flooded his own. He rocked from side to side dizzyinglly, as though his body, his mind and soul, were being pulled from either direction.

As though he were scales, measuring shifting weights.

"Shavrim," he said in one croak of a voice while another, steadier voice spoke simultaneously, saying the word he had not wanted to say.

"Brother," Evurt said.

In this one word, Vedas heard the god's satisfaction, the arrogant presumption, and his anger flared in response.

Losing to Evurt was not an option.

Thus, he would not lose: it was this simple. His teeth snapped closed and he growled, like a mutt cornered in an alley. His eyes closed, like shutters on the invading sun. His hands rose to his head, and gradually he stopped rocking. Then, after an infinity of fearing his skull would collapse upon itself, of holding back the raging divine tide within him, he found control once more.

The light slowly faded from his eyes. Evurt howled from behind the closed door.

"Shavrim" Vedas said. In one voice. His own voice. "You can stop trying." He shrugged. "Or don't. I can't summon the interest to care, either way. I know what you're doing, and Evurt won't be coaxed that easily from where I've put him." He stood, pain a forgotten memory, smiling down at Shavrim without an ounce of anger. It was easy to simply choose a mood. He wondered why he had decided, on so many occasions, to be angry or fearful. He questioned why he had let himself be pushed from one period of uncertainty to another for so long.

"Try again and again, but I know you better than you know me. Knowing you, I know something of your sibling. He has immense power, but he's caged where I can see him. I will instruct Churls and Berun how to feel their presence, and how to stop them. If they want to assist our efforts, we will allow them. We. Mortal men and women."

Shavrim's brow furrowed. Vedas imagined he saw a measure of fear in the man's expression.

"Know me? Know me *how*?"

Vedas bent down to Shavrim's ear and said Jojore Um's name. Then he turned on his heel and walked away.

‡

Halfway between the square and the inn, the girl appeared at his side and took his hand. He smiled down at her, not sure if she had assisted him and not particularly caring. His mood would change, undoubtedly, to a familiar, long-worn state of worry and fear, as soon as he woke from the charitable disposition that had taken hold.

The glow of victory did not last forever: there would come a time when, for Fyra's own safety, he would have to tell her to go—to leave them to their fate, in Shavrim's hands . . .

But it would not be now.

He gripped her hand and stopped. In silence, together, they watched the slowly and swiftly spinning spheres of the Needle, the threat of the world's destruction, pass overhead. He did not see them with Evurt's eyes, but with the limited vision his mother and father had birthed to him. The components looked as they in fact were: farther away than all the steps he had walked on the face of Jeroun. The scattered entirety of the Needle could be nothing more than it always had been to a mortal, earthbound man.

Indistinct and unknowable. A blight upon the order of the heavens.

Nonetheless, at that moment, it was beautiful beyond measure. It was a decision to view it so. It was a denial of reality.

He accepted this now, understanding he would not make the same choice again.

‡

In the morning, he rose with Churls, awkwardly accepted the provisions Ual's mayor publicly insisted on gifting to him, and made his way to the docks with his three companions.

Townsfolk stopped him along the way and asked for his blessing, which he gave reluctantly. "You have it," he said again and again, grimacing more than smiling at the small, black-skinned men and women, wrinkled into early grandmothers and grandfathers by the strong, salty wind and ocean sun.

Churls failed to keep the amusement from touching her features. The people knew her by reputation, as well, and smiled warmly in response to her expression, as though she too had blessed them. Berun, also known by his association to Vedas, accepted the company of the town's few children with good grace, holding his massive arms out low so they could swing from him.

Shavrim walked several body lengths behind Vedas and company. The townspeople gave him a wide berth, likely because they had caught some news of furthering events in Danoor. Even as isolated as they were, it was clear someone had passed through recently. The mayor appeared uncomfortable next to the broad, horned man, but he listened intently to what Shavrim had to say. They had been talking since leaving the inn.

Vedas wished he could listen in on their conversation, for he did not know how Shavrim had, without violence, convinced the mayor to allow them to lower a sea-gate that had been closed for millennia. Perhaps it had simply been an exchange of bonedust, yet Vedas did not think so. He supposed he would never know, for the townspeople crowded around him, clamoring for his attention, his touch, hungry for a person he could only pretend to be.

Eventually, they reached the docks. Or, rather, the two stone jetties and Ual's sad collection of fishing vessels, not one of which looked large enough to accommodate the four of them, especially considering Berun's mass. Certainly, they would capsize the moment anything large enough to survive on the open ocean poked its snout against their hull.

Admittedly, Vedas knew little of seacraft. He had lived two miles inland of the ocean for most of his life, and learned next to nothing about it beyond the danger it presented. Golna possessed the resources of a metropolis to defend itself from seagoing creatures of Jeroun, many of which happily hurled themselves out of the water and against the city's walls. The city also sat near one of many fishable rivers stocked heavily with smaller, adolescent versions of the oceangoing monsters that gave birth to them.

Ual, however, had no such resources. It had an altogether more novel way of drawing sustenance from the sea.

Vedas shielded his eyes against the early morning glare upon the mirror-flat water (a highly unusual occurrence, numerous villagers had told him, to have such a calm day this early in the year—a good omen, many of them said, with forced expressions that belied their words) and the top of the distant inverted bowl over Osa, searching for the fifteen-foot high stone pillars of Ual's only claim to fame: its coastal wall, which extended out from the town's shore nearly ten miles and arced to either side for nearly thirty miles, creating a relatively safe haven for fishing.

Now that Vedas considered it, it struck him as odd that so few visited or even spoke of Ual, for its people were surely extraordinary. It was common to say no one set craft upon the surface of the sea, yet the people of Ual did so daily. As they had done for millennia.

Men needed to speak in definitives, Vedas knew. They needed to reduce the world to comprehensible portions. And thus, the people of Ual and their incredible, ancient construction allowing them to do the impossible, were ignored.

Men did not sail upon the sea.

The woman next to him—small, sunworn, to his eyes identical to the woman next to her—laid her left hand upon his arm and pointed with her right.

"It's not easy to see. There is a blurred line, just below the waterline." Her eyes were wide as she stared up at him. "You're really going there, to the gate? Only the wall walkers—" those townsmen and townswomen who maintained the wall's integrity, Vedas had learned "—go anywhere close to it."

"No," Vedas said, squinting to see what she claimed was visible. "We're not going to it. We're going beyond it."

She spit into the tiny waves lapping at the rocks below them. Her neighbor did likewise.

Shavrim stepped up behind Vedas, causing both women to move to the side, allowing him space to stand. The horned man lifted his shirt over his head, inflating his massive chest with salty air. He clapped Vedas on the back, beaming as though they were old friends.

"Time to go," he said.

Vedas nodded, relieved. Without looking, he reached and found Churls's hand. They moved through the crowd more easily now with Shavrim at their side.

Berun rose from the pile of children he had let play upon his sitting form, the great bell of his laugh booming loudly on the still morning air.

But for the mayor, they left the townspeople behind. As they stepped onto the second, slightly larger jetty, Churls stopped him.

"Turn around and wave. It's the least they deserve for the hospitality."

He followed her order, awkwardly.

The people of Ual waved back and cheered, though he doubted their hearts were in it. Men did not really sail upon the sea, even in Ual. Beyond the coastal wall was the haven of animals beyond the scale of man, a shallow, glass-clear expanse of certain death. And should Vedas somehow manage to defy the inevitable and reach the shore of Osa, an impenetrable wall of crystal lay between him and his mad destination.

The people of Ual waved goodbye to their prophet.

‡

He kept his eyes forward as they set off. The boat's small thaumatrugical engine chuffed and barked at his back, with Shavrim at the tiller. Berun lay between Vedas and Shavrim, evening out the weight of their cargo at the boat's head. A strong breeze kicked in as one of the few clouds in the sky obscured the sun, and then died as the sun peeked out again.

Churls squeezed his hand. She rose into a crouch, leaned over their piled supplies amidship, and made her way toward the bow. She leaned over it for a moment, and then laughed.

"Come here!" she called. "You have to see this."

"What?" he asked, not wanting to move. He had no good memories of his last time upon the water, on their way to Tan-Ten, and the boat he sat in now felt far less stable than the *Atavast* had. Of course, it was one-tenth the size.

"Just come here," she responded.

He made his way forward, far slower and more painstakingly than she had. Pausing at the port gunwale for a moment, he peered down into the depths, surprised to find the bottom of the sea so close—no more than ten or fifteen feet below him through startlingly clear water, dappled with crisscrossing lines of light. Fish and aquatic reptiles, the cousins and spawn of larger creatures, the mainstay of Ual's diet and scant industry, darted from rock to rock.

An odd sadness crept into him at the realization that he had never before stared into the sea, that this one opportunity to do so would be so fleeting. He considered what it must have been like, growing up in Ual, knowing their manmade corner of the sea so intimately that any incursion into it—be it a creature that had grown too large, too dangerous, or a breach within the coastal wall, allowing the outside ocean in—felt like a wound in one's own flesh.

To know a thing outside of oneself, so intimately . . .

His left hand went to the neckline of his suit. He slipped the tip of his index finger between the elder-cloth and the skin at the nape of his neck, encountering resistance as the material peeled back from its tight embrace of his body. It was a disturbingly invasive sensation, but he had grown used to it, like one worrying at a torn cuticle.

"Vedas?" Churls said.

He shook his head and peered back toward the shoreline, finding it had retreated further than he had imagined possible in such a short amount of time. A crowd still stood above the tide, though already it had thinned. He imagined many of them had returned home, to stare at their hands and consider an uncertain future. The mayor had looked on the verge of crying as they pulled away from the dock.

He must surely be scared, Vedas thought. *We're opening his sea-gate. We might leave it open, destroying his and his ancestors' long and meticulously held balance.*

He reached Churls on wobbly legs. She offered him a sympathetic smile but no hand in support.

The fingers of his right hand closed around what he thought to be the tip of the boat's bow. He leaned forward cautiously and looked down into the parting water. For a moment, he saw nothing, and then his perspective shifted as his eyes registered what Churls had seen. A black, cartoonishly muscular torso. Outsized genitals. Below that, water-stained legs. He turned his head and stared into one large, white-painted eye of the statue he had carried into Ual. His hand rested on its head.

It had been bolted onto the boat's prow, making of it a figurehead.

He rose into a crouch and turned, muscles taut on his frame, all trace of physical awkwardness aboard-ship forgotten.

Shavrim did not need to turn his head. His eyes were already fixed on Vedas. He stared intently, with no trace of an expression.

"What is the meaning of this?" Vedas asked.

Shavrim's eyebrows rose, but otherwise his features remained neutral. "You claim to know me," he said. "And this makes me rather curious. Did you know I would do that?" Without breaking eye contact, he reached behind him and shut the thaumaturgical engine off. "Did you know I would do that?" He stood as the boat rocked violently back and forth in the absence of forward momentum.

Berun began to rise.

Shavrim bent forward to lay a hand on the constructed man's massive shoulder.

"This is not violence, Berun. This is us coming to terms."

Vedas forced himself to stand at the head of the pitching boat. His suit stiffened around him instantly in response to his nervousness. He forced it to unclench, and found his balance. Easily.

Churls's hand pressed to his back as she rose. In support, not to steady him.

"I've been thinking since you left me in the square last night," Shavrim said.

"And?" Vedas said.

Shavrim gestured expansively. "I'm left wondering what you really think, Vedas. Do you think I want my family back badly enough to risk the entire world? Do you think I'll keep trying to summon Evurt and Ustert, to the detriment of our plans? No. Don't answer. I'll tell you. I will not. I don't know that you alone are sufficient to oppose Adrash, and I doubt my siblings are willing to share their power. Nonetheless, we won't be deterred. I'll do what is necessary to preserve this world, even to the point of opposing those for whom . . ."

He broke eye contact to stare at Churls, and then at Berun. "Do you hear me? Do you know what I'm saying?" He pointed to the bow and his voice boomed. "Do you know what that means? It is a betrayal."

He frowned, letting emotion alter the set of his features until he resembled a different man. His hands fell straight to his sides, dragging his shoulders down with them.

"Perhaps . . ." he said. "Perhaps we're all fools. We could be wrong in everything."

He sat heavily, rocking the boat. He started the engine and Vedas looked away. Churls wrapped her arms around his shoulders and pulled him close, leaning back against the hull. Berun lay immobile, staring at the sky with eyes that could not close.

The whole day open before them, windless and bright, their journey resumed.

CHAPTER SIX

THE 25TH OF THE MONTH OF SECTARIANS TO THE
1ST OF THE MONTH OF FISHERS
ASPA MOUNTAINS, THE KINGDOM OF STOL, TO
DANOOR, THE REPUBLIC OF KNOS MIN

For one hundred days, Pol slept. For four months, he dreamt of plummeting out of the sky.

He fell, exhausted nearly to death by his headlong flight from Adrash. His skin scorched, crusted over, and peeled away as he entered Jeroun's atmosphere. His arms and legs whipped about violently enough to dislocate his joints, causing him to be pummeled by his own fists and feet as they flailed, drawing blood from his sensitive new flesh and sending it in arcs around his spinning body.

The sigils he had tattooed upon himself with alchemical ink—the spells that had been brought to life, granting him the might to stand against a god—were gathered as solid black masses at his hands and feet, as a coil rope of black hair wrapped around his throat, choking him. All were inert, useless.

His eyelids had been burned away. Heat and wind had fused his one remaining amber eye motionless in his skull, and turned the empty socket of the other into an aching pit. He fell blind, his never-ending state of agony preventing him from sinking into unconsciousness.

He lived, just barely, unable to think beyond the pain.

The ground rose up beneath him, a granite fist.

When he smashed into it, blackness enveloped him.

There was a timeless instant where he felt nothing. A breath before . . .

‡

The dream began again.

And again

And again.

‡

He woke, screaming. Not a full-throated sound, but a piteous, rattling wheeze that caught in his throat the moment it emerged. He inhaled convulsively and then coughed dry, blood-flecked sputum into the cold, thin air, curling around the aching hollow of his gut before screaming again—more fully this time, a bellow of ignorant rage that lasted until he could do it no more. He breathed in and out, deeper each time, calming himself.

It took the space of several heartbeats to believe he had stopped falling, to make his right eye organize the colors before him as images.

Gravel. Fractured planes of rock underneath.

Lifting his head took a monumental effort. The muscles of his neck screamed in palsied protest. Gritting his teeth against the pain, he looked about.

Rock faces before him, rock below and to the right.

To the left and above, sky cloudless and unbroken, painfully blue.

He examined the rock floor and walls more closely. To his eye, they appeared recently fractured, white along their angles. Many bore long gashes, five-rowed and straight. Without willing it to do so, his hand reached out, spreading fingertips to fit into the gouges. He raked his nails along the channels he had created without remembering, and then laid his palm against the cold stone, exploring the concavity beneath him.

He shivered as the realization struck him.

Here is where I came to earth.

Even with the abilities the sigils had granted him, it was a miracle he had survived.

And yet . . . *where* had he come to rest?

He rolled over, slowly, and crawled to the edge of his jagged platform. Below him extended a nearly vertical wall of bare grey rock, weathered by wind and time. Below that, dizzyingly far, the angle of the rock grew less severe, becoming a surface upon which snow could cling. And further, so much further down, the world spread out in white folds, broken here and there by thrusting spires of granite.

He had seen this vista from above the world, many times. It had once seemed just another place, high and isolated, the home of goat-milkers and idiot hermits.

It had *once* seemed . . .

His head whipped around, causing black spots to swarm before his eyes. The rock face above him shielded the view, but he felt the pull of the secret he had stolen from Adrash's mind.

He tried to stand, but his legs would not support him. He fell back, lightheaded, gritting his teeth in impatience. The second attempt was no better. The third, and his legs held beneath him. He stretched his long, angular body up the wall of rock before him, peering over its lip.

The heady perspective nearly sent him tumbling backward, but his thin fingers found purchase in the stone. He blinked the sense of disorientation away, letting his gaze steady upon the mountain's summit—or rather, a broad portion of it.

He grinned, revealing small, even teeth. His legs were suddenly firmer beneath him. He knew now, for certain, where he was.

When his strength returned, he would ascend to the mountain's hollowed-out peak. He would walk into the valley of the nameless people. He would dip his hands into the clear blue lake at its center, and run his hands over the worn remains of the forgotten city of the elders, older than recorded time.

And everywhere, he would find corpses. A storehouse of power the likes of which the world had never seen. With the talents the sigils had bestowed upon him, it would be an easy thing to gather the corpses together and transport them to wherever he liked.

His grin grew wider. Dry laughter erupted from his chest as he lowered himself into a sitting position.

Lacking even the energy to access a simple spell to be sure, he nonetheless sensed a disappointing amount of time had passed since he fled from Adrash. Weeks. Months, perhaps. Regardless, his spirits were not dimmed. Without consciously making the decision to do so, he had guided himself where he most needed to be.

‡

He lay in the sun throughout the day and, after taking in one contemplative look at the broken sky as it rose above the world, slept when the sun died. The wind, carrying air cold enough to freeze water to steel, failed to even stir him in his slumber. In the morning, he felt full, though he had eaten nothing. He stood on solid legs and walked to the edge of his eyrie, staring down the wall of his prison with one corner of his mouth upraised.

Yet his hands shook. He examined them, stained black with latent magic, and backed away from the open height. A searching thought (timid enough at the beginning to embarrass him, even alone) caused the boundaries at his wrists to quiver. He looked down at his ankles and saw that there, too, the alchemical ink had become agitated, the amorphous sigils eager to rise up his legs and arms, forming shapes, covering him in the symbols of his magical will. Those spells that had gathered on his scalp, mimicking long hair, lifted from his back and shoulders as fine filaments wavering in the wind, a hundred thousand snakes woken from hibernation.

Gooseflesh rose on every inch of his naked, eggplant skin, and the open hands raised in relief on either pectoral muscle grew in definition, as though someone sought to push out from the inside. His testicles lifted as his cock stiffened painfully. His right eyelid slowly opened, allowing smoke to seep in a thin stream from the black cavity of his eye socket.

The world bloomed into dizzying color. For the space of several breaths, his hearts pounded hard enough to shudder his vision. A wave of nausea bent him at the waste. He retched, yet had nothing to summon from his stomach.

He had been afraid, yes. He had not known if the sigils would respond to his commands after such time and grievous injury.

As good as their rousing felt, he forced them to still upon his hands and feet. He would not be arrogant now, giving in to temptation before his body had fully recovered. Not when he was so close to his goal. He lay upon the cold stone, allowing the sun to soak into the roots of his body, his thoughts drifting to the knowledge he had gleaned from the dead following Ebn's assault and then stolen from Adrash's weakened mind during their battle.

He recalled the elder he had seen and encountered on the Clouded Continent, and it was an epiphany too reality-altering to do him much good—as was the revelation of Jeroun being only one planet among many: scholars had already posited this.

And the existence of an afterlife? What did this matter? The dead were insignificant, a concern only among themselves.

What he had learned about Adrash's nature, too—his existence as a man before assuming the mantle of godhood, how blind he had become to the world he once actively ruled—enticed him while remaining altogether too abstract to be of any use. Adrash was a force nearly beyond measure, answerable only to an equal force: understanding his past or madness would add little of value.

But those frustratingly blank identities, those mortals without names who had stood on a baked plain before Adrash? He worried at these like a loose tooth, trying to dredge something useful from his memory, a detail he had not seen in the moment of revelation.

The Black Suit, a Knosi, beautiful in a boring way.

The freckled woman, whose face he had disliked immediately, viscerally.

The constructed man of brass spheres, eyes glowing actinic blue.

Pol had not the slightest clue about the first two. Not even an itch of recognition. The third, however, he sensed he should know. Holding the image of the artificial creature in his mind created a disconcertingly slippery effect, as of trying to keep water from dripping through one's hands. He had heard a story about a constructed man, had he not? He had studied the creation of constructs, and there had been one particular example . . .

He tried to picture the classrooms of the Academy of Applied Magics, places he had always known. His brow furrowed in concentration. He placed himself in his own apartment, and could not remember where his bookcases had been, or whether his bed faced the east or the west.

The name of his first instructor.

The identity of the man who had deflowered him.

His mother's stern face . . .

Summoning *any* memory from before his transformation in Ebn's bedroom proved difficult. In fact, even the details of that night were blurred around the edges. She had raped him, he recalled. He winced, recalling pain and shame greater than any he had ever experienced

But what had she *done*, exactly?

Suddenly, it struck him as very important that he remember—as though, by doing so, it would unlock the other memories eluding him. As if a door would be opened inside him.

‡

Another day passed while he waited to be strong enough.

Another day, during which his memory became no clearer. Impatience pressed upon him, as though someone were staring over his shoulder, urging him to act. It built until he shook with it, impotent in the face of it.

And then, just as the sun dropped below the jagged skyline and the scattered spheres of the Needle began rising in the east, a face rose out of the mist clouding his recollection.

A broad, lavender-skinned, horned face. The face of a quarterstock. Pol had come to know it in the months before his cathartic encounter with Ebn.

Shav. His name had been Shav.

A madman, given to spells of dementia . . . of appearing to be one man and then another . . .

All at once, Pol remembered every word.

‡

The dragon and I. A halfbreed and a quarterbreed at this moment in time. The conjunction of the two is interesting, Pol. Interesting. I've seen a dragon crash into the sea, sure the animal had killed itself. Instead it surfaced, twisting its long neck and beating its wings upon the water, a great sea serpent clamped in its jaws—a sea serpent so large that it could've swallowed our tiny boat in one bite. Its skin shone like silver in

the moonlight, and its thrashing frothed the sea like a child's hand slap-
ping bathwater.

The Needle had only risen halfway, and the moon showed a quarter of
her face. I stared at the destruction coming swiftly: a wall of black water
that blotted out the stars along the horizon. I waited and told my men to
prepare themselves. Some of them prayed to Adrash, some to Orrus, and
some to the devil. Me, I just waited for the inevitable, almost wanting it.
Most likely, I would die along with my men. An odd feeling, being that
powerless.

Someday soon, I think you'll know what that feels like.

‡

The moment snapped into clarity within the dim confines his skull, creating a scene so vivid it was as though he were seated again in his apartment on an atypically hot day in the Month of Clergymen, the year previous. He stared at the quarterstock named Shav and thought it odd, what he now knew without doubt. What he should have known then:

Shav was no madman. Disturbed, but not mad.

Perhaps not even disturbed, but very clever.

Or even inspired.

In his mind's eye, Pol reappraised the broad, horned wyrm tamer, doubting every assumption he had made about the quarterstock: indeed, he now found himself wondering if the term quarterstock even applied. It had been the easiest determination to make, for Shav had never denied it. Moreover, what else existed that appeared as he did? Not a man and not an elderman, but a thing in between, a manlike creature singular in creation.

Yet the quarterstock itself was a near-legend. No one alive in Tansot—in fact, anyone in the recorded history of the city, the place where eldermen had always been most numerous—had verifiably documented the healthy offspring of an elderwoman. To assume one had suddenly appeared in Pol's life, just as he desired an asset worthy of note . . .

An asset who spoke such odd, portentous words.

At the time, Pol had dismissed Shav's rambling monologues. Surely, he had reasoned, they were merely the digressions of a precocious individual, the fictions of a talented mind severely maladjusted by the vagaries of unusual parentage. Beyond material assistance as a tamer, Shav could have no insight applicable to Pol's situation.

Now, however, he was forced to admit he had been wrong. The account of the dragon—it could only have been an allusion to events to come. Soon after the words were spoken, Pol and eighteen other outbound mages had ascended into the sky, bearing Ebn's gift to the god, a massive statue in his likeness. Before they reached the moon, Adrash appeared and with a thought shattered the statue, sending its pieces in a wave of mutilation toward the mages, killing all but the most skilled. Pol could do nothing to prevent their deaths.

Helpless.

Someday soon, I think you'll know what that feels like.

Pol lingered on these words. He had been horrified, true, but had he felt helpless?

No. No, he had not. Perhaps, at the beginning, for the briefest hesitation, he had not known what to do, but within heartbeats of seeing the statue turned into a bomb he had been filled with purpose, first to defend himself, and second to . . . to . . .

He gasped as the sigils spuns to life on his whip-thin body, rising into a whirlwind of countless long-tailed sperm on his forearms and legs, whipping around his shoulders and neck and lower belly as they recalled with near-sentience their awakening upon him. He collapsed onto the cold rock, smoke pouring from his left eye, fingers twitching one motion over and over again—the same motion he had used to release a spell upon the Needle, altering one of its massive spheres slightly, announcing his challenge to Adrash before he had even thought the wages of this action through.

Coils of concussive force leapt from his outspread fingertips.

The rock face before him fractured like a broken mirror before crumbling onto his legs. He pulled his feet free before more of the wall fell upon him, and nearly tumbled off his perch. Teetering toward death, the upper half of his back over the void. Arms outstretched, rigidly under the control of the sigils. The spell bore into the mountainside, pushing him inch by inch backward in the process.

He could find no purchase. He would fall.

"No!" he roared, tightening the spasming muscles of his stomach, attempting to sit.

As he fought to regain his balance, one of the sigils on his arm formed itself into a black circle and rose upward from his flesh as a tendril, wavering in the wind as though it were a charmed snake. Pol focused on it as its tip ballooned, stunned into immobility despite the danger.

The sigil formed a face, black on black, horned.

"Waste no more time," it said. "Learn to fly."

Pol screamed as he tipped over the edge of his perch. The wind ripped the voice from his mouth as he fell. There was no time for thought, no time even for fear. Certainly, there was no time to recall the second portent Shav had spoken to him . . .

‡

Before he leaves, my father tells me to contemplate death. He tells me to feel my mortality in the creak of my bones and the soreness of my muscles. With every heartbeat, you are closer to death, he says. He forces me to smell the stench of his underarms—the smell of the body birthing and decaying life at the same moment. He tells me to know, intimately, every sign of weakness in my body, and then reject each in turn.

He breaks my arm with one blow, kicks me as I writhe on the ground. Remember this lesson above all others, he says. The body heals. It responds to trauma, to pain—not with fear, but with purpose. So must you. You need not die, my son, but in order to continue living—

—you must suffer.

‡

Pol dropped, head first, as fast as a body must drop, yet his perceptions were reduced to a crawl, drawn out into one long howl of wind—an avalanche in his ears, a needle in his eyes. Rigid-limbed, he spun as the spell continued to pass from his fingers, warping the air before him like heat radiating above a fire, strafing the mountainside in cracks as he rotated to face its solid wall again and again.

The mountainside. It loomed closer each time he regarded it.

Spiraling, caught and stretched in a sluggish current of time, horrified and fascinated at once (at his predicament, at his foolishness for not being more attentive when events had been playing out), he found space within himself to consider Shav's words.

He placed himself, once again, in his apartment. He held a knife in his hand.

It had been near the end of the Month of Pilots, three weeks after Ebn's disastrous goodwill mission. Confident the display of power he had recently shown was only the beginning, the birthing of greater magic within him, Pol nonetheless forced himself to caution. He would not underestimate Ebn. She had swayed a god, after all, if in the brief moment before his rage returned to him. Pol would not rely upon the dimly understood nature of his sigils, but attack his superior using brute force.

A knife, cunningly crafted, intended for her skull.

Shav had offered the support he could—first the knife, second the assistance of his wyrm, Sapes—before succumbing to yet another of his spells.

You need not die, but in order to continue living, you must suffer.

Pol cursed himself for not drawing the obvious conclusion sooner.

Shav had known, or at least predicted.

A month after he and Shav's meeting in his apartment, his plan of attack frustrated, Pol had committed an act of supreme foolishness, relying upon tradition to protect him. Ebn, the more opportunistic of the two, broke into his apartment, breaching the oldest of etiquettes dictating how eldermen treated one another, and humiliated him. After ensorceling him into a state of immobile arousal, she raped him. Despite the aggression of the act, she still could not summon the rage to kill him and so resorted to greater violence.

Finally, she had torn out his left eye.

He recalled the agony, the humiliation. He recalled a pressure. Voices, calling him to transformation . . .

You need not die, but in order to continue living, you must suffer.

A sudden gust of wind pushed against him like a cold slab of glass, tipping him lengthwise in glacial motion, sending his feet into the mountainside. He braced for the pain of contact, of his skin being flayed against the rough wall.

When it came, however, it was more intense than he could have imagined, drawn out into one torturous moment. Reactions slowed, he watched in paralyzed horror as his bloodied feet rebounded from the wall and rocked his upper body toward it. The closer his hands came, the more damage his spell did to the rock, boring into it in doubled lightning lines.

When his hands finally passed into the mountainside, he screamed. The mineral, heated to its vaporization point, blackened and bubbled the skin of his fingers. His wrists. His forearms.

He fought helplessness through the red haze of his torment. Soon, his face would hit the wall and he would be dead. There would be no fractured rock beneath him when he woke. He would not wake.

Learn to fly, his sigil had said.

Learn to fly.

‡

A timeless moment before his forehead touched the mountainside, he did just that. A voice—or several voices: he would never be sure—whispered wordless directions, spoke a command Pol felt more than understood, and he remembered.

He had once possessed wings. They had carried him into the night sky from Ebn's bedroom. They had borne him to orbit.

He tipped his head to the side in slow motion, cracking vertebrae. He then tipped it to the other side. Fully inhabiting his pain now, taking succor from it, he flexed burnt hands now under his own control. He increased the power of his spell, pushing himself back from the mountainside before closing his fists and entering into a full dive.

He was an arrow, suspended in amber. *Enough*, he subvocalized.

The wind tore at him as time reasserted its normal pace. He bared teeth into the gale, grinning at the swiftly approaching ground. With a few muscular twitches, he corrected his spin.

As he spread his arms out to either side, stretching the kinking muscles of his shoulders, wings unfurled from his back. Blacker than a moonless night they grew, doubling and then tripling in width, becoming assets befitting a creature of legend, a god.

He arched, letting his wings cup the wind. His bones creaked as his body took the weight of gravity only feet from the snowy mountainside. His dive flattened into an unsteady soar over the frozen landscape.

Quickly, he righted his shuddering wings and flapped down once, twice, three times, his confidence growing as memory took hold.

He flew. It was as though he had been born with wings.

‡

Before him, an invisible wall shielded the valley. He knew of its existence from his contact with Adrash, but understood little of its nature beyond the scope of its power. It had served to hide the valley from all but the most powerful gaze for all of human and elderman history.

Until Pol, that is. He saw through it easily, first through the phantom organ of his left eye and then through his unaided right, gazing down upon the lifeless plain. Cradled at the valley's exact center, bluer than any memory of blue, was the lake. Upon seeing it, his mouth began watering. He had not drunk since before the turn of the half-millennium.

A smile rose to his lips as he recalled the taste of cold water. Water he alone would drink. Glory he would never be forced to share.

Regardless of his excitement, he forced himself to caution, angling his charcoal wings to slow his approach. The alien ache in his bones grew more severe, the closer he came to the barrier. The remainder of his self-congratulations came to a grinding halt as the fractaling sigils fled from his leading fists, en masse, flowing like ink over his sinuous torso to gather as static, as jittering ants on his legs. The sigils flowing from his scalp flattened on the ridges of his back, tapering into a point above his buttocks.

All at once, the coldness of the air registered. He shivered.

Pressure built, centering into a tight knot of resentment behind his eyes. He stopped his chattering teeth by clenching his jaw until it rang, and stretched his fists out before him.

Anger became determination. With a twitch of his wings, he dove forward.

The wall did not physically restrain him. There was no pain. Nonetheless, he cried out as he crossed the threshold, for the error—the wage of his impetuousness—was immediately clear. Ebn had been a master of dampening spells, but even she could not have accomplished so thorough an effect.

At once, the sigils were thrown into chaos on Pol's body, spreading and contracting like tides, pooling and bursting without pattern. The vision in his phantom eye faltered, flickering to him an image of the valley below and then failing utterly. His wings began to diminish. They rippled, no longer rigid along their length.

Struggling for any measure of control, using his legs as crude rudders, Pol managed to turn toward the lake.

Despite his rapid descent, by the time the water stretched beneath him he still flew too high. Soon, he would be beyond it. Possessing neither the strength nor the alchemical faculties to turn around for another pass, without considering the injuries he might sustain, he curled his wings around himself and fell.

Below, the surface of the lake was a mirror, reflecting the noon sun as a perfect circle. He kept his right eye open and focused upon it, letting its light sear into his skull, seeing his shadow become a black hole at its center just before his body hit the water.

It came to him, fully, a complete memory in the breath before impact:

He had been laid out by an attacker before. Once, years previously, a fellow mage—Pol's senior by a decade, resentful of the younger elderman's quick advancement—had nearly killed him with a simple, outsized concussion spell that blasted him thirty feet into an iron cauldron. He recalled the feeling of its impact, being slapped by a giant hand, and then the near immediate rebound of his body against an immobile surface far harder than his own body.

Then darkness.

Then, all in an instant upon waking, the awareness of the fragility of one's physical being. The sudden rush of memories . . . of bones breaking, of flesh collapsing.

He did not have the benefit of losing consciousness, this time. He remained aware as his body crumpled against the unyielding surface of the lake. His joints flexed and strained, threatening to snap. His bones, from the smallest to largest, creaked and rang. His neck bent at a sharp angle, driving his skull to the side and crushing it against his left shoulder, forcing his teeth down upon the tip of his tongue and severing it clean.

The surface yielded, as though he were a pebble dropped into molten sand. The lake drew him under. Lungs flattened, arms and legs immobilized by his wings, he could do nothing but sink through the glass-clear water, watching as the world grew dimmer. It seemed to him it took far longer to reach the sandy bottom than it should have, and when he came to rest it was as though a soft hand cupped him.

His mouth opened and closed, releasing a cloud of blood that turned his vision red. The sun, dim through the water, wavering in the turbulence of his passage, became a baleful eye.

Life flitted before his eyes, tiny and nearly translucent. His eye flicked from one creature to another as they moved back and forth through the bloodied water, and finally formed an image. Shrimp. Smaller than their cousins fishermen netted in Lake Ten.

Eldermen hated water. They wanted nothing to do with anything that came from water.

A smile formed on his lips.

He opened his mouth again, and took the lake into his lungs.

‡

Swim while you can, Adrash said, eyes flaring in darkness. *You will not get the opportunity to do so again.*

Pol stared at the stricken god, whose armor appeared slightly gray under the weight of water. Having exhausted himself, he weighed his options. There were none. The god would recover before him. And so he turned and swam, as fast as his weary body would swim, through an openness of sea that was not open at all, but which pressed upon him from all sides. Black and cold and swarming with life, he felt the weight of sinuous bodies, monstrously-jawed and behemoth, eager for any morsel of flesh.

He escaped through the most shameful of realities: only because of his own smallness, his own insignificance in comparison, did he survive. Nonetheless, smallness notwithstanding, he could not rest. There was nowhere to rest. He had to continue pushing himself, beyond the point of collapse, breathing in the sea itself, lest one of the beasts finally notice him.

All the while, at his back, Adrash fumed in the shattered remnants of his abyssal palace, injured but not yet dead.

Pol had failed in his task. Before long, the god would repay him for his presumption.

And so Pol swam. He reached land and flopped onto it, choking on air.

But even here, above ground, he had not truly escaped.

‡

How long his eye had been open, he did not know. Someone stood over him, swaying from side to side, undulating like a flag in the breeze, like kelp rooted to the sandy lake bottom. He wondered how it was a person could be where he currently lay and survive.

He yawned, jaw popping, and gasped: the air entered him as a knife.

Water bubbled in his chest and then burst forth, searing his throat: the knife left him.

He fell onto his side and curled inward, coughing and gagging upon water, mucus, and blood. He shook violently on the cold ground, breathing raggedly until he could breathe evenly. The pain remained—in truth, it inhabited him from head to toe, occasionally flaring into prominence in one area and subsiding to allow another agony to bloom—but it no longer obliterated thought.

Air.

Concentrating on the shifting ground before him, on the fingers of his clenched left hand—a hand which seemed also to shift, growing larger and then smaller—he suffered a moment of doubt. What if he had never landed on the mountainside? What if Adrash had killed him and he was now but one of the dead, waking in one of the many hells he had never quite been able to convinced himself did not exist? His mother had been fond of discussing the various hells a man might inhabit once he died.

Some among the Usterti sect believed in a place between life and death, where a person would be forced to relive an awful fate (drowning, typically: the Usterti were fond of tales of drowning)—that is, until the Goddess smiled upon that individual, lifting her free of torment.

The corners of his mouth turned down. He spit blood and mucus past the throbbing, shorn tip of his tongue. It steamed for only a moment before freezing.

I'll not start believing such nonsense now, he thought.

He rolled over and regarded the person standing over him. He blinked, and slowly the figure took on definition.

A human male. Small, naked, grey skin a hairless mapwork of fine lines. Eyes bulging out from his skull, his lips pulled back in a perpetual grimace. Shrunken-cocked, testicles nearly nonexistent. He should have been shivering with cold, moving to keep hypothermia at bay. Instead, he seemed content to simply stand and stare. The longer Pol regarded him, the less the man's body undulated from side to side, leading Pol to believe he had been drugged or concussed. Concussed, likely, oxygen deprived from his near drowning.

"You—" He cleared his throat. "Who are you?"

The man did not respond, did not appear to have heard. His eyes remained focused on Pol's, but behind his gaze Pol sensed nothing.

Pol looked from side to side, finding his wings a crumpled mess spread around him. Two wet sheets, pathetic, lacking any structural integrity. With shaking hands he gathered them, shook the water and ice from them, and draped them across his body. He shook until he was no longer frozen, and then sat up, immediately burying his head between his knees.

"What are you looking at?" he asked, expecting no response from the man.

There was none. Pol chuckled without humor and wondered if he had been wrong to dismiss the idea of hell. To spend eternity with the mindless, he surmised, would be a very effective hell indeed.

‡

Eventually, he raised his head.

He blinked.

Before him lay an elder corpse.

Beyond it, a trail of roughed earth stretched. It had been moved.

All thoughts of hell fled his mind. He peered up at the man standing over him. He could not recall if Adrash's memory of the valley had included inhabitants. Surely, it had not.

"Did you drag this here?" Predictably, the man did not answer. Pol pointed to the corpse. "You, you brought this here." He stood, looming over the man. He lowered his face until it was level with the other's. "*Is. This. For. Me?*"

The man's eyes shifted to the corpse. Pol nodded, though his companion failed to notice. The man took a step and bent, crouching toward the corpse. He extended a hand, and for the first time Pol noticed a flint, little more than a crude edge, clutched in his fingers. Grasping one of the corpse's forearms—which ended as a ragged, bloodless stump just below the wrist—the man used his primitive knife to cut a small strip of skin free. He placed it in his mouth and began chewing contentedly, then repeated the process.

He pivoted and held the flesh up to Pol.

Pol nearly slapped it from the man's hands. It was not that the thought of eating elder disgusted him. After all, he had used alchemical solutions made from the bodies of elders for much of his adult life, externally and internally. He had survived for days in the void of space on nothing but bonedust, as had all outbound mages.

No, it was the *sacrilege* of seeing an elder corpse so abused. The corpse trade had produced a variety of associated guilds, each of whom possessed their own secrets and unique paranoias, guaranteeing that few whole corpses made it out of Stol or Knos Min. The Academy of Applied Magics contained only one whole elder corpse on display in its central library—an entire city's worth of riches, a storehouse of alchemical power beyond the ability of any single man in existence to possess. Pol had spent many hours studying it, lingering on and memorizing every physical detail of the three-yard-long body as though it were that of a lover. Or a parent.

To see it treated so casually, solely as a food source . . .

He watched the man chew. His stomach gurgled and growled, and a cramp bent him double. He took the strip of skin and placed it in his mouth, surprised to find the taste immediately sweet, its texture like soft leather. Chewing on it, his mouth became wet, as if he just taken a drink of water. A coppery taste, similar to sagoli berry, replaced that of his own blood. The severed tip of his tongue tingled, became warm and then quickly numb.

He shivered in pleasure as the warmth spread quickly from his mouth, suffusing him in the space of twelve indrawn breaths. A moan escaped his lips.

The man watched Pol with no trace of understanding. He returned his attention to the corpse, now using the flat side of his rock as a rasp, sanding away at the protruding end of bone at the elder's wrist. After he had created a small pile of dust in the hollow of the corpse's belly, he wetted his middle finger and dipped it in. He offered the whitened fingertip to Pol.

Pol ignored it, and instead took his own measure of bonedust—far more than he had ever consumed at once. The familiar sensation of wellness, of focus intensified, further bolstered the steel in his legs.

He concentrated on rousing the sigils from their slumber, but found them dampened still, gathered once more on his forearms and calves, immobile. Unless he found the source of the shield's effect and put an end to it, he would not soon be taking advantage of the alchemical resources he had found. Given the singular nature of the effect, he figured it to be an artifact of elder magic. The possibility of him halting it after incalculable millennia seemed unlikely.

He turned a complete circle, examining the jagged peaks that ringed the rubble-strewn valley. On his own, it would be a challenge to climb beyond the dampening wall, but while dragging a corpse? Two corpses or three? Even with his strength returned to him, the task would be considerable.

He stretched, vertebrae popping. An itch under his skin—the feeling of walking from a cold building into the full heat of a summer's day: the awareness of a fever building in the body: the sensation of being too large for one's hide—made him shiver.

"You," he said to the man who still crouched with his finger proffered. "Do you have anything to say of value? No, clearly not. Do you have a leader, someone I can speak with?"

The man simply stared.

Pol shrugged free of his ruined wings and slapped the man, who stumbled backward but did not fall, did not cry out or grunt. His eyes widened only fractionally.

Fingers curled into fists, claw tips biting into the flesh of his palms, Pol advanced and threw his weight into a right cross that broke the man's cheekbone. Pol felt and heard it shattering, savoring the perceptions. He savored also the sound of the man's shout of surprise, his choking sob thereafter, and followed his first attack with a sharp kick to the ribs.

Four. Four snapped ribs. Pol grinned.

He took the crude knife from the man's shaking fingers and severed his wings, letting them fall uselessly to the ground. They were the stuff of intense alchemy, a product of the sigils. Once he resumed his power, he would grow a new pair more glorious, more substantial than the last.

He plunged the knife into the man's thigh.

Behind him, someone cried out. He turned to see another man—no, it was a woman, though they appeared so similar the distinction hardly seemed pressing—running toward him.

Pol's grin widened.

Pain had been a transformative factor for him. Perhaps it would inspire these fools to speak something worthwhile.

‡

In truth, he had no plan. He did not believe the inhabitants of the valley would prove able to communicate anything of value. They were clearly ancient, their meager lives extended by a steady diet of alchemicals that nourished the body extraordinarily while atrophying the mind. They had sat on the world's most valuable treasure without using it.

No. He had no plan. He merely wanted to cause pain.

As he circled the lake, he found others like the first two, and left them crippled behind him. Not one fought back, though in a similar way to the second, a few expressed concern for their neighbors without understanding what was occurring. Or, indeed, how to help. These he enjoyed hurting the most: their confused impotence amused him as much as it fueled his anger.

"Fight back," he said, repeatedly through his laughter. "Do *something*."

And so he made them scream.

Eventually, night came and he stopped. The bare ground failed to chill his naked flesh appreciably. Nonetheless, he found himself longing for a fire, a thing more alive than the creatures he had broken over the course of the day. He avoided looking into the sky for a time, and then relented to the inevitable. He had seen it before, but always at dusk.

Now, with its twenty-seven broken components stretched across the bowl of heaven . . . closer than they ever were.

Massive. Somehow, more massive than they appeared when viewed from orbit.

I did this, he mouthed.

He slept, and in the morning she appeared to him.

‡

Just like the others, though more weathered around the eyes. Wrinkles of expression, perhaps, as opposed to exposure to the elements.

He met her gray-eyed stare and recognized a depth behind it, a measure of awareness he knew did not exist in the others. Even the manner in which she crouched before him, resting her elbows upon her knees and letting her hands fall casually—it spoke of a distinct personality, something he had not yet seen among them.

She nodded, as if she had followed his train of thought, and stood. It was only a dozen steps to the lake. She walked into it up to her knees and turned.

"*Wwwwwwaa*," she said in a croak of a voice, a voice which never spoke. She lifted her left hand and stared at it, examining both sides before meeting his gaze again. Slowly, like a child doing so for the first time, she crooked her index finger for him to follow.

"Are you the leader here?" he asked.

She cocked her head to the side, doglike.

Curious, clear of the aggression that had informed the previous day, he rose.

They stood in the lake, she staring up at him, he staring down at her. Distantly, he recalled his mother. She had been a small woman, far from beautiful. Oh, how he had wished for her to be as silent as the woman he now regarded. Knowing so little of anything, she nonetheless had had an opinion on everything.

"What are we doing?" he asked.

The corners of the woman's mouth quivered, trying to arrive at an expression. She shook her head and bent at the waste, cupping her right hand to gather water. She mimed lifting it to her mouth and drinking.

"Why?"

She shook her head again, repeated the drinking gesture.

He shrugged. Obviously, the water would have some effect, either ritually for her or physically for him. Perhaps, his consumption of the water had been responsible for his confused, perceptually altered state upon waking the day before. Drinking it again might leave him vulnerable. At the same time, none of the valley's inhabitants had expressed the slightest aggression toward him.

Gazing into the woman's eyes, he found no animosity, only an intensity he could not contextualize.

He crouched and dipped his hand into the lake.

"You first," he said, gesturing with his chin.

She looked down at her reflection in the water and smiled, slowly, apparently making sure of her expression before meeting his eyes again. He winced at the sight of her toothless gums, black with untold age.

She drank, filled her hand a second time, and drank again.

He followed suit without smiling.

Remaining in a crouch, he waited, watching the still lake surface for any sign of a change in his perception. When none came and he grew impatient, he decided to stand.

Several minutes passed. He decided to stand again.

Instead, he fell backward into the water. The woman tumbled sideways, following him under. She wrapped her arms around him, pressing his arms to his sides. He did not fight her. Why he would fight her? She was beautiful, like his mother had been. He barely felt the pressure of the blood-warm lake around him. He breathed it like air.

When she kissed him, he breathed her.

‡

"Death doesn't exist here. Time is an illusion."

He stood along the shore. He turned full circle. Around the lake rose the forms of gray stone towers, tall and blank-faced, creating a skyline as severe as the peaks ringing the valley, a cityscape utterly unlike the cities of glass he had seen in Adrash's vision of the Clouded Continent—different enough, in fact, that he immediately doubted its fidelity. An elder, dependent on the sun for its sustenance, would never lock itself behind windowless walls.

This was no true city of the elders: this was the product of a stunted imagination, a recreation of a thing that had never existed.

Nonetheless, he took in with interest the groups of elders he spotted. The creatures, their naked bodies tattooed brilliantly, their large double-irised eyes liquid in the sunlight, paid him not a moment's attention as they walked from place to place. Their locomotion, stately and deliberate, struck him as awkward, wary of their surroundings.

"No," he said under his breath. "That isn't right, either."

He paused. Someone had said something to him, had they not?

With great difficulty, he tore his gaze from the oddly moving elders. Even in their wrongness, they were compelling.

He nearly took a step back at the woman's altered appearance. A lustrous, emerald-scaled gown clothed her from just below her breasts to mid-calf. Her figure, athletic and almost prototypically feminine in its proportions, bore no resemblance to that of the person he had met in the valley. They shared a similar bone structure, no more. Her eyes, also, had changed, brightening to reveal an increased awareness, a vitality she had lost.

Drinking of the lake had been transformative for her. Unlike the city extending dull and oppressive around them, she was a genuine artifact of the past.

Looking down at himself, he discovered she had changed nothing about his appearance. The sigils remained still on his arms and legs. His cock appeared pitifully small to him, as though it too had been affected by the dampening spell.

He sighed. "What did you say?"

She gestured to encompass the valley. "Death doesn't exist here. Time has stopped."

He grunted and looked away, back to the city. Her beauty unnerved him. He had never liked women, much less human women. Licking his lips, he recalled how she had brought him here.

"I'd rather not spend eternity with you and yours," he said. "And I won't. I'll be leaving soon, with something of value. Tell me, why have you brought me here?"

"You don't want to know who I am?" she asked.

"No," he said. He rethought this answer. "Unless it has value, I don't want to know."

"Fine," she said. "I had hoped the bringer of my death would be interested in me, somehow—even impressed with my vision, here, where I've kept my true self from the white god for hundreds upon hundreds of years—but maybe that's too much to ask at the end of my long, pointless life."

Out of the corner of his eye, he saw her gesture toward the city. The elders dropped where they stood. Their buildings each fractured vertically with a crack of thunder, and then crumbled to the earth. The corpses deflated, mummifying in the ever-present sun. The rubble of the city slowly wore at the edges. Soon, the valley had returned to its present form.

Turning to the woman, he found she had aged. Her gown had lost its sheen.

She snapped her fingers, and it was night.

Above them, the Needle spread in its shattered beauty.

"You want me to tell you something of value," she said. She tipped her head back to view the heavens. "You did this. I know this fact in my bones. The souls of the elders proclaimed it the moment you dropped from the sky. I've waited ever since, these hundred and six days."

He huffed in annoyance. "This is of no value. I *know* what I did, woman. Quit guessing, speaking nonsense of elders."

"Guesses?" she whispered. "Nonsense." She crossed her arms below her withered breasts and closed her eyes, letting her head fall slowly to one side. Listening. "Pol Tanz et Som: that is your name. You confronted the white god and injured him gravely before fleeing. And where did you flee? You fled here, hardly aware of doing so. Now, you desire two things: the resources you've found here, the bodies of the elders. And, second, the knowledge to apply the powers you covet."

She lowered her arms and met his stare. "Am I close?"

"You are," he conceded. "But how?"

She grimaced. "You don't listen, do you? Or perhaps you still doubt. The elders speak to me. They've grown to trust me with their secrets. We share a similar vision."

"I see only corpses."

"You see wrong."

He considered disagreeing with her—he had seen elders, hibernating yet well and truly alive—but another concern came to the fore. "Vision? What vision is this?"

She laughed and regarded the sky again.

"This conversation goes nothing like I thought it would. You wait nearly two millennia, and you have certain expectations. I thought, when you came, you would know more. I suppose it doesn't matter. I've gotten what I wanted, what I deserve for being so patient. When the world is poised so . . ." A look of rapture painted her features. " . . . so beautifully, you don't ask for more."

He slapped her. She fell to her knees, causing the vision she sustained to flicker out. For a handful of seconds, he was underwater, staring into her gray eyes, breathing her in. He fought nausea at the thought of their intimacy, the fact that he had allowed it to occur.

"Make sense," he said to her. "I don't care about your expectations. Tell me of this vision you share with corpses."

She wiped blood from the corner of her mouth. "My vision is of devastation. It is of fire erupting from the crust of the world, of dust blanketing its face for eons."

She pointed skyward.

"It is *this*, Pol Tanz et Som."

‡

They started to move, so slowly at first that he thought he imagined their motion, then perceptibly quicker as the world's anchors set in and pulled. Increasing their spin as they drifted further and further from their positions, growing visibly in size as they closed in upon the world, the spheres became objects of menacing beauty, perfectly balanced on a scale beyond human reason. As large as moons, as deliberate as death, their leading rims began glowing with the friction of entry, of pushing aside the first protective layers of the world.

Against the dictates of logic, as though possessed of their own poetic will, the larger spheres paused before initiating their plummet, allowing their smaller companions to enter the atmosphere first, dissecting the night with lines of fire.

The Needle fell, and Pol did not keep from himself a sense of satisfaction. This fate—surely, he reasoned, anyone who had lived under the Needle would welcome it. Perhaps they would not admit it to themselves, but somewhere, in untouched corners of their minds, death held more attraction than continuing to live under threat. Men desired certainty above all else.

The ground shook underneath them as the world was impaled upon the Needle. The sky roiled with red and black lightning-shot clouds.

The woman stood at his side, smiling as her vision played out.

Eventually, she pointed into the ruins.

From among them, a figure emerged: tall, over three yards from sole to crown, walking in an assured manner unlike those ill-drawn elders to which the woman had given brief life. In the flickering light of the end of the world, the elder's feature seemed to shift, the length and set of its bones fluid.

Watching it, Pol was seized by recollection. As a child, he had seen a reptile drag a fisherman into the water. The man did not scream: he did not have the time. His mates had cried out, but even at his young age Pol had known their efforts would prove useless. The man was dead—not because he was unfit, destined for death, but simply because nothing of his world could stand against a creature of the sea when it chose its proper moment.

Pol resisted the temptation to ready himself with a spell. It would not have worked, even had he not been trapped under a dampening spell. Not here. Here, now, he would be powerless. He had walked, of his own volition, into another world. He had seen that world in Adrash's mind, perpetually covered in cloud. Slumbering.

The broad-shouldered elder stopped a body length from Pol. Even halted, it never entirely stilled. Though it did not breathe, under its vein-mapped skin a colony of insects crawled.

Head tipped slightly to one side, double irises spinning, it appraised him.

An offer, it said into the interior of his skull. Its voice, like a wasp's nest fallen at one's feet, or a bass string struck violently next to one's ear.

When it did not speak again, he cleared his throat. "Who are you to offer me any—"

The elder squinted, pulling its head back on its long neck. *Do not speak to me this way. It is an insult. It is ugly.*

Pol lifted his chin. "I'll speak to you as I see fit."

The elder took two steps forward, closing the distance between them. Pol inhaled the scent of it, cumin and longras leaf, seawater and the dust of libraries—and under these aromas, a tide so closely under the creature's dark, finely-furred skin that it leaked out through its pores . . . its blood, similar enough to his own though infinitely stronger.

His sigils stirred on his forearms and calves, tickling.

Impudent child, the elder said. Instead of anger, however, Pol's mind was filled with an air of amusement. *I will not punish you for your physical limitations. Speak with your vulgar food parts. We've not slept so long that we've not grown accustomed to the sound of your speech, horrifying though it is. We need not belabor this communication.*

Pol shrugged, having accepted his role as a child. "You spoke of an offer."

Yes. An offer. It gestured to the agitated sky. *We would see the world of man end.*

Despite himself, Pol laughed. "You've likely overestimated my power."

No. We know of you, and your encounter with the white god. You yourself would be a god. Already, you are close to achieving your goal. Not one among your people, or certainly among men, could have broken the Needle as you did.

Still, you could have more. We can help you be greater than you ever dreamed.

"The god of a dead world? Thank you, but I'd pictured a fair bit more than that."

The woman at his side cackled at this. Almost quicker than his eyes registered, the elder stepped to the side and backhanded her, sending her body spinning high into the black mirror of the lake. The vision she had created did not fade or flicker. In fact, it only solidified.

The elder returned its amber gaze to Pol. *Your picture is pitiful. Imagine a world where you are not a leader of men and eldermen, but a leader of elders.*

Pol opened his mouth to speak, and found he could not utter a sound.

Enough. We do not demand an answer now. We know your mind, and it seeks dominance. You will grow tired of being a god among men. When you grow tired, you will erase this era and usher in the new.

How? Pol thought.

How is this not clear, child? The elder stepped back and held its arms aloft. *Bring down the sky. The pact among ourselves—to not reveal ourselves or wake until the world is again clean of the interloper, man—is universal, but the method of man's extinction is not generally agreed upon. Some wish to wait. Some have tried to rouse other individuals to our cause, charlatans and magicians. But I and my families are not . . . patient. And so . . .*

It gestured vaguely, in an oddly human fashion.

The muscles in Pol's jaw jumped as he ground his teeth together. "Intriguing. But this is of no value to me in my battle. Give me something I can use, or I'll not even consider your offer. Sleep forever, if it pleases you."

A horizontal line appeared below the elder's cavernous nostrils. It grew in definition and then split, revealing human teeth. Its corners turned up. As Pol fought to keep from taking a step backward (he would admit to being frightened, yes), the elder's body shed height and width. Its rawboned body thickened, taking on the proportions of an athletic man. Its skin color, already near enough to black, darkened further. It grew the pendulous genitals of a man, but these were quickly sheathed by the new skin it had grown.

No. Not skin. A suit.

Pol stared into the face of the Knosi featured so prominently in Adrash's mind.

Vedas Tezul, the elder said, its newly formed body mouthing the words.

Its body shifted again, reducing in size as its shoulders narrowed and its hips widened. In seconds, before him stood the freckled woman whose features offended him so.

Churls Casta Jons.

Now the elders body ballooned, taking on mass outward and upward. Its skin turned from flesh to spheres of brass. From under its shelf of a brow, two blue coals glowed.

Berun.

The names meant nothing to Pol.

These three stand in our way—in your way. Each possesses power untapped, though the avenues of their power are lost to us. Like the white god, they defy our abilities to read. At times, they can be seen, but never can they be heard. For days now, they have been absent entirely from our minds.

The elder returned to its original form and leaned forward, nostrils widening as it sniffed at Pol. *Like you, elderman, they are disappointingly opaque, a dangerous instability. Only their intentions are clear. They would halt the spheres in the sky or send them into the void. They would see the age of man never end.*

Pol kneaded his temples. This had gone on long enough. The sigils, restive, divided and subdivided on his forearms, forming faces that leered at the elder.

"Where?" he said. He held up a hand to halt the creature from speaking more. On his palm, a horned man grinned and winked. "Mind, I've agreed to nothing. Reason says I should enjoy my time as a god before I decide to have done with the world. However, if these individuals are as powerful as you claim, they are a threat to me. Tell me, now, where I can find them."

The elder pulled back from him. Its long finger pointed to the sigils. *Impossible. Silence these . . . abominations.*

Pol smiled at its discomfort. "I think time will prove how much power I can summon. Tell me. Now."

‡

Danoor, the elder said.

CHAPTER SEVEN

S *radir is within you, and it will come out. Soon, if I am any judge.* These words remained. They stuck. They angered Berun in their refusal to be forgotten.

Sradir—the name meant nothing to him. Surely, this fact disproved Shavrim's claim.

Surely, it did. *Surely.*

Attempting to reason the words away simply fixed them more securely within his mind. By the morning of his third day under the dome of Osa, he found himself distracted constantly by thoughts of harm. He played out the scenarios of his own assumption by an alien god—as if by imagining the worst outcomes they might suddenly strike him as ridiculous, impossible.

But it was not impossible. He knew this better than anyone.

Being taken forcibly by the will of another, pushed out of his own mind, woken to find people injured or dead at his own hand . . . it had occurred, and the nation of Nos Ulom considered him a murderer for it. Any reassurance he had taken from the death of the one responsible proved short-lived, however, for his creator would not be bound by the laws of death: on the journey to Danoor, Ortur Omali had nearly reassumed control over his creation.

169

Berun had been forged as a tool. To think he could redesign himself according to his own whims now was the purest presumption. He had not overcome Omali alone in their final battle, after all. Fyra had been there, landing the final blow for him.

What did it matter if he did not know the name Sradir Ung Kim? Had he known Omali could call him from his place among the dead?

‡

From dawn to just before nightfall, they traveled northward and upward, over a sparsely-treed landscape of folded rocks and algae-covered lakes, finally reaching the foot of their destination—the monolith Shavrim called Adrashhut. Surrounded by rubble at its base, it rose, straight-edged and severe, giving the impression of a sudden, violent upthrust through the mantle of the earth.

It looked to Berun like the tip of a sword coming out from between a man's shoulder blades.

"There," Shavrim said, pointing a third of the way up the sheer face of the mountain to a sharp overhang. "That is where he deposited the weapons." He breathed in deeply, inflating the muscular drum of his belly. His eyes widened and an unselfconscious grin lit up his features. "It smells the same here. Exactly the same. My nose, after millennia . . ."

"I'm happy for you and your nose," Churls said. "How do we reach the cliff?"

Shavrim instructed them to cover one eye and then the other before regarding the cliff face a second time. Stairs appeared, zig-zagging upward, but with each shift of the eye they disappeared again, melding back into the slate-colored stone.

Vedas looked away first, and began setting camp. He remained subdued throughout their supper, just as he had done since their arrival on the island. Churls kept his hand in hers, often leaning toward him to cast glances at the darkness over his shoulder. Despite Shavrim's assurance—"Nothing here will hurt you. Osa is a sanctuary."—she could not keep herself from caution.

Berun looked from her to Vedas, affection battling the uncomfortable awareness that he had been left out of an important discussion. He did not resent Churls for keeping Fyra a secret, yet she and Vedas and the girl had clearly interacted with Shavrim on some arcane level during their encounter in Marept. Even had no time passed after Vedas kissed Churls, their eyes would have given them away: they had come out of their trances haunted.

Apparently, they felt Berun did not need to know what had transpired.

He avoided anger in response. Anger had been a pathway for Ortur Omali to influence him in the past, and could be so for another. Nonetheless, he found his fists clenching of their own accord as he stared at Vedas and Churls.

They were his friends. They cared about him.

Surely, they did.

‡

After his companions fell asleep, Berun left them. He could not stand the thought of a whole night spent staring at their sleeping bodies, listening to their breathing.

And so he climbed.

The stairs were hardly worn by the millennia of exposure to the elements: each appeared cut to the exact same dimensions, sharp edged and straight. At every turn in the switchback, Adrash had created an alcove where one could turn and ascend the next series of steps.

In each alcove, rising from the floor, a part of the mountain, sat an altar—and upon each altar a statue. Berun paused in the alcoves before resuming his climb, again and again, examining the figures the god had carved. Predictably, the majority were warriors, men and women in assorted modes of dress, wielding swords and axes and spears. Few bore alchemical arms.

To Berun's surprise, there were elderman and constructs among them. For obvious reasons, the constructs held his attention. He had never seen such variety, had never known such sinuously elegant creatures existed. A few were nearly identical to men, identifiable as artificial only by the thin lines of their mechanical sutures.

The final five alcoves stretched nearly double the size of the others, with proportionally larger altars and statues. The first contained a tall, thin woman with claws bared at the end of each arm. The second featured a winged man, arching his back with his open mouth to the sky.

In the third and fourth, he found twins, angularly built and naked. Though their posture mirrored one another, one appeared rigid, the other relaxed.

He recognized them by Shavrim's description. He mouthed their names.

Evurt. Ustert.

The last space held the depiction of a unique creature, neither clearly man nor woman, human or elderman. Thorns grew from its shoulders, elbows, and knees. A series of knoblike growths extended down the lengths of its oddly jointed arms.

He stared at its harsh face, lingering on the wood-textured eyes, and knew its identity.

Still, he felt nothing.

He ascended a final time, the broken sky unobscured by another set of stairs above him. The spheres of the Needle spun in their orbits, and he imagined what would occur to Osa if they fell. Would the crystal covering the island shatter? Would it hold, showing the death of the outer world through its perfect lens, holding the decay within itself?

Berun reached the summit. Open to the elements and significantly worn by time, an altar sat, unmoored to the mountain. It had drifted over time, in fact, due to wind or rain or tremors: a third of its base hung over the edge of the cliff.

Upon the altar was a carving of Shavrim.

He knelt before Adrash, hands open in supplication, eyes desperate. Pleading.

Berun took it in his arms and moved it back from the precipice. He did not understand why he had been inspired to do so, but he did it, regardless, wondering if this were the moment when he ceded control to Sradir.

Shrugging the concern off, he knelt at the edge of the cliff and tried to find a measure of the calm he had once thought so easy to achieve.

He did not find it. In truth, he found only more doubt.

Yet the night passed overhead, and the sky did not fall. He resisted asking himself how many more such nights the world would be allowed.

‡

In the hour before the sun rose, he halted his meditation and watched the largest inhabitants of the island wake from their slumber.

Methodically, beginning with the westernmost individual and spreading to either side, as though they had timed it for the most dramatic effect, blunt reptilian heads rose on sinuous lengths of neck from each of the massive honeycombed nests anchored to the lower heights of the crystal dome. As many as six individuals, variously colored and sized, inhabited the largest structures.

Generations of wyrms, greeting the new day.

When the sun rose fully over the back of Jeroun and reflected in the heights of the dome downward, bathing the enclosed world of Osa in bewitched light, the creatures emerge fully. They faced the morning and stretched, their long finger bones showing through the thin membranes of their wings.

Hearing their harsh calls to one another, his features drew into a frown.

He leaned over his crossed legs and peered over the edge of the cliff. The camp his companions had set the night before remained shrouded in shadow, but his eyes were adequate to the task. He watched Vedas emerge from the tent, left hand rubbing the leanness of his belly, right hand lingering at the neckline of his suit.

The man could not accept the reality of himself, Berun knew. He refused to be at ease in his own body. Nor would he return to the time when wearing a suit felt right, for it represented a way of life he no longer lived, convictions he no longer held.

Berun shifted his brass bulk, not in pain, no (unless a component of his body became unmoored, he would never experience true pain), but certainly discomfort. He would never grow used to being confined to one form, stuck in a man-like shape, never to fully touch the sun again. In this, he felt communion with Vedas. Both had been betrayed by men they were expected to trust—Vedas's abbey master Abse, on the one hand, Ortur Omali on the other—and paid a physical toll as a result.

Vedas turned, his hands falling to his sides.

Churls emerged from the tent, shrugging her shoulders and swinging her arms. She peered into the sky before slipping her arms around Vedas's waist, laying her head against his chest.

The spheres of Berun's teeth ground together. He stepped back from the cliff's edge, surprised by the intensity of emotion he felt at the sight of her.

I never liked the bitch much, a voice said. *Evurt took all the good material, leaving none for his sister.*

Berun spun around, but he was alone on the cliff top.

Calm yourself, Berun.

Reedy and measured, the voice held a trace of amusement. It sounded utterly unlike he had imagined it would. He had assumed something colder, more estranging.

You assumed wrong, Sradir said.

"I don't like this," he said. He turned back to the thousand-foot drop. "I don't like anything that is happening."

I know. Imagine how it must be for me, though, constructed man.

"No. No, I don't have to imagine any such thing." He folded his massive arms. "This is different than what happened with Churls and Vedas. I'm awake, aware of your presence, like you're sitting across from me. How is there room within my mind? What happens now?"

A chuckle. *So many words. You believe I must do something?*

"I do. Why else would you be here, if not to act?"

Perhaps for the view. I've been waiting for the proper time, listening only, but I see I should have does this sooner. You have wonderful eyes—in many ways, better than my own. It's a pleasure to view the world from my current vantage point. Please, look down the mountain again. I wish to see my brother Shavrim as you see him.

Berun considered denying it the request, but relented.

Shavrim emerged from the tent.

His eyes focused directly on Berun.

Oh, hello, Sradir said. *That was fast. Raise your hand, Berun. Raise it. He's seen us.*

‡

They stood together on the cliff, the four of them.

"Hello, Sradir," Shavrim said. He bowed.

Embarrassed, Berun bowed back.

Tell him hello, Sradir said. *No. Just say anything. I'll correct you if it's wrong.*

Berun paused, and then said hello.

Good, Sradir said. *I like someone who can improvise.*

Shavrim stared into Berun's eyes, clearly searching. For what, Berun did not know—a sign, perhaps, that he had found a proper ally, one possessed of sufficient strength to take his or her host by force. Ustert and Evurt had been a disappointment in this regard.

It would be easier to force you, yes. But I think not.

Churls stepped forward and laid a hand on Berun's arm. He fought the urge to pull it away as Sradir recoiled within him. Quickly, he was becoming used to how Sradir would react, how it would feel when it did.

"Berun," Churls said. She too searched his eyes. "Are you . . . are you *you?*"

He forced a smile down at her, and Sradir relented a bit.

I don't hate this one, it said. *When I can see beyond the aura Ustert has placed over her, she's actually quite likable. Not beautiful, but cute in a rough way. A dull sword is an appropriate tool for her.*

"I'm fine, Churls," Berun said. "I'm me. This is not as it is for you and Vedas. Sradir is . . ."

If you call me nice, I'll kill you.

" . . . more agreeable."

Churls smiled and embrace him, her arms extending only halfway around his torso. He patted her gently on the back, meeting Vedas's gaze over her head. After a moment, the Black Suit nodded, though his expression remained sober.

Shavrim opened his mouth and closed it. He opened it again.

"Agreeable," he said. He repeated the word, as if hearing it for the first time.

‡

I've learned something, Berun, and I've made a decision. We do this, and then we leave.

His foot slipped. He formed a question in his mind.

No, don't ask why. I'm not forcing you to do anything. I'll explain, and you'll agree—for your own good. Now, concentrate upon your task.

Curious but unwilling to push the matter, he planted his foot more solidly and flexed, causing the hundreds of joined spheres in his knees and shoulders to shriek with strain. Next to him, Shavrim roared, thick slabs of muscle shaking. Gradually, the panel of stone upon which they pushed began to move, revealing the outline of a massive door into the mountain Shavrim had assured them existed. It ground shrilly in its frame, inch by inch, extending further and further into the rock face.

Berun's foot slipped a second time . . . a third time. Shavrim paused to catch his breath, repositioned himself with his back to the slab, and began pushing once more.

The door cleared its frame. Berun shot out a hand to prevent Shavrim from falling as the door tipped forward and slammed soundly home into a recess in the floor, melding again with the mountain.

Enter, Berun, Sradir said, avid. *Beat him to it. You did most of the work, anyway.*

Amused by Sradir's pettiness, Berun kept his arm out, palm pressed to Shavrim's chest, preventing the man from advancing.

"Leave it," Berun said. "I'll check."

He entered the chamber alone. Once his trailing foot cleared the doorway, six torches bloomed into life, revealing a circular room perhaps six yards across, its wall covered in relief carvings of faceless bodies locked in embraces both violent and erotic. They appeared to shift in the firelight. The longer Berun stared, the more they seemed to move, undulating in a circle around him, first in one direction and then the other. He imagined a flesh-and-blood man would become dizzy.

An impressive effect, he noted, yet it was as nothing compared to what sat under each torch. Statues, so cunningly carved that they nearly breathed in the flickering light, lifelike enough that he expected them to rise from their cross-legged posture, held weapons in outstretched hands. Somehow, Adrash (for it could only have been a god who possessed the skill to create such life in stone) had managed to convey the reluctance of the offering: the figures appeared ready to snatch back their weapons if the taker proved unworthy to wield it.

Shavrim, the first on the left, held a long, dark, silverish knife.

The winged man—*Orrus*, Sradir whispered—held a glass spear.

Ustert and Evurt held a pair of short swords, silver and bronze. *Ruin and Rust*.

The thin, clawed woman—*Bash, my dear departed Bash*, Sradir said—held a razored circle.

And Sradir, first on the right . . .

Before he had registered the desire to do so, Berun bent and took the short whip in his left hand. Though tiny in his outsized fist, he could not deny an immediate sense of appropriateness, of *utility*. His mouth drew into a sneer even as a part of him relished the feeling. He had always eschewed weapons.

Prior to his last encounter with Omali and the freezing of his form, it had never been an issue. He had been any weapon he wanted.

I'm sorry for what you've lost, Berun.

He grunted. Behind him, Shavrim cleared his throat and entered the room, with Churls and Vedas following. Shavrim picked up his knife, flipped it end over end into his left hand, and then slipped it into the sheath he wore at his hip. It was a casual gesture, but Berun had been watching carefully.

A tremor had passed through Shavrim when his hands left his weapon's hilt.

Yes, Sradir said. *Well observed. He's not immune to its touch, just as I'm not to mine. And Sroma is a great deal more powerful than Weither. It's possessed of its own mind, and he's cautious of its influence. As he should be.*

Features blank, Shavrim glanced at Berun as he picked up Orrus's spear and Bash's circle.

"You have something to say? the horned man asked.

Berun did not answer. His attention was suddenly elsewhere.

Churls and Vedas stood separated by several feet, staring down at the statues of Ustert and Evurt. Their hands stretched toward one another in the exact position of a clasp, as though they believed themselves to be holding hands.

Berun looked away and then back, trying to convince himself that their bodies were not thinning while he watched, that their skin had not taken on a metallic luster.

Your eyes aren't deceiving you, Sradir said. *They're nearly here. The bitch, especially. She's close. Can't you smell her? Like curdled milk.*

Berun took one step toward Churls.

Slowly, like an egret following its prey, she swiveled her head toward him without moving another muscle. Vedas mirrored her. Their eyes were blanks, silver and bronze.

"Sister," Churls said. "Brother," Vedas said.

Never could wrap your minds around me, could you, fools? Don't move, Berun. Don't speak a word.

Disinterested, Churls and Vedas turned back toward the statues. As one, without moving the position of the hands that still seemed to be linked, they moved forward to grip the hilts of their swords.

Shavrim paused at the doorway and turned back. His hand strayed to the knife at his hip.

Sradir sighed. *You wanted them here, brother, and now . . . what? You want to stop them at their point of entr—*

Its last word died in a fading hiss.

A light, harsh enough to briefly overload even Berun's eyes, flared in the center of the room.

It died as suddenly as it had appeared.

In its place stood Fyra, clothed in a jointed suit of blindingly white armor. In her right hand she held a sword—also blindingly white, a proper match for Ustert and Evurt's weapons, though sized for her small stature. She took four quick steps to a point equidistant between her mother and Vedas and swung her blade up, as though attempting to slice an imaginary opponent from pelvis to chest.

It was a clumsy maneuver, directed at nothing, yet it produced an immediate effect.

Churls and Vedas gasped and pulled their arms in, cradling their hands against their bellies. Shuddering, they turned toward Fyra, their movements no longer synced, their skin and eyes losing the godly hue. Vedas bared his teeth and growled, but it quickly became a wheeze. Churls did even less, merely opening her mouth to emit a constricted breath.

Without another sound, they fell sideways toward each other.

Sradir made a whistling sound that reverberated through Berun's head.

Fyra turned and leveled her sword at Shavrim. Her arm shook slightly.

You want to be separated from your soul, ugly man? I've never done it, but I'd like to try. We'll see who wins. She flipped the faceplate of her helm down, staring through the eye slits of a mask that resembled her mother exactly. *This is a place of power. You knew being here would make your sister and brother stronger.*

Shavrim nodded. "I did. And I was wrong to allow them to enter. Ustert and Evurt are too strong, too unpredictable, to allow full control. I see that now."

Fyra laughed, and sounded nothing like a child. *Good for you. You should have seen it sooner. Take the weapons out yourself, and then carry my mother and Vedas outside.*

She turned to Berun without waiting to see if her order was followed. She was tired, clearly, her sword arm dipping only to be righted with a jerk. He stared at the wavering tip of her ghostly sword, wondering how much damage she could do with it.

Good question, Sradir said, its voice near reverential. *I'd seen her in your mind, but I'd never imagined . . . how wonderful . . . How is it she's even here? The crystal should have shielded her from entering. The strain of maintaining control—*

I can't hear you, the girl said, her voice barely a whisper, *but I know you're talking.* She took two faltering steps toward Berun, lifting her sword to keep its point between his eyes. *He's my friend. I helped him when no one else could. What are you going to do with him?*

Sradir paused, a pressure building. When it spoke again, its voice held a new quality, a resonance he imagined radiating outward from the spheres of his mind.

Girl, I'm going to finish what you started.

‡

After two days of travel, Berun stood before the barrier of crystal separating him from the sea.

The sea, and his creator.

"You're sure?" he asked.

For the hundredth time, I'm sure.

He spoke the words Shavrim had taught him and waited. After Shavrim had spoken them five days earlier, the reaction had been near instantaneous, but Berun did not worry, for both Shavrim and Sradir had anticipated a delay or even a failure. The spells keeping the island closed were ancient beyond human knowledge. Only Adrash had discerned their nature, and only his children could gain entry by uttering the phrase to unwind the arcane lock.

Though inhabited by Sradir, Berun could not properly be called Adrash's child.

In truth, he did not mind the wait. He did not relish encountering Ortur Omali again.

He pressed a hand to the clear wall. The thickness of the crystal—were it a liquid, he could have reached only a quarter of the way through—distorted the view of the rocky shoreline at the foot of the dome. A long, reptilian creature had crawled out of the sea to sun itself, its back bowed unnaturally by the warping effect.

Your mind, Sradir said. *It's like this creature as you see it now. You've been distorted by the spectre of your fear. You've been warped, set up to be broken. We're about to change that, Berun. Speak the words again.*

He let his hand drop. "Do you swear? This is your true intent, to help me?"

I promise you. I won't lie to you.

"Then tell me this. Why are you the way you are now? I see Shavrim. I watch him. He clearly didn't expect you to be as you are. How can I be assured this is not an act? How can I be sure you aren't lying to me, leading me to my doom?"

That's an easy answer. You can't. You can be sure of nothing. But time passes, and we're all changed, even gods. I didn't expect to be as I am now. For the span of my life, I expected to succeed Adrash, rule with a ironwood fist. I did not expect to one day ride a constructed man through forgotten forests and help him fight his dead father.

He felt her shrug, though how such a thing could be communicated was beyond him.

But here I am. And you have to trust your instincts about me.

He nodded and said the words.

Again, Sradir said. *Together.*

"Uperut amends," he said, Sradir harmony to him. "Ii wallej frect. Xio."

A dimple appeared in the crystal and pushed toward the outside world, creating a visible tunnel through the enchanted material. It widened quickly, creating a passage large enough for a domesticated cat, a dog, a child standing upright. Berun stooped slightly and entered it.

You've never smelled the sea, Sradir said. *I just now realized. Sad.*

He paused before leaving the shelter of the passageway and gazed out at the calm water. "What should I expect?"

Sradir laughed. *A battle, Berun. Expect a battle.*

‡

Immediately, he sensed something had changed. His own awareness of himself—of his body, the relation of each component sphere to its neighbor—intensified until the world itself seemed to fade around him. He expanded as everything else in existence contracted. His chest ballooned, creating a dark space within which his two innermost spheres knocked together. A lonely, hollow sound. He had heard it before, but not since he froze himself into the shape of a man.

"Father . . ." he said.

Berun, Sradir said. *Stay with me. Focus on me.*

He fell to his knees on the cragged shoreline, his vision flickering in and out, replaced by stretches of blackness, blackness beyond which there could be no return.

If souls existed, they resided in flesh. He did not want to die, and be nothing.

You will not die, Sradir said. *But he* is *coming. Prepare yourself.*

Concentrating upon Sradir's voice, the world slowly swam back into clarity. The sea seemed to call to him, neither in the voice of Sradir nor the voice of his father, and so he stood, creaking from each of his thousand joints, and stumbled to the waterline. Seized and emboldened by an idea he would not, could not give words to, he walked.

More surely with each step, into the water. Not so much confident as resigned to his fate.

"Let him follow us," he said just before his head fell below the sea. Glass-clear shallows rose above him, twenty and then thirty feet. Sand gradually covered the stones of the shore.

He walked, and did not look back.

Sradir remained silent. It had been in his mind long enough to know he had been crushed under deeper water than that of the sea.

At first, he believed himself to be imagining the darkness brewing before him, but soon the reality of it proved impossible to deny. It became a heavy weight upon the surface of the water, appearing like the growth of distant clouds on a clear day. It spread, a droplet of ink, its fine tendrils reaching toward him.

You may have gotten this backwards, Berun, Sradir said. *He did not follow us. We've come to him.*

Berun, his father called, drawing the name out into the long creak of ship's masts bending in the storm. It reverberated as the crack of thunder.

Berun stumbled, righted himself sluggishly, and kept walking.

"Father . . ." he said. Water muffled his voiced into incomprehensibility. Nonetheless, he knew he would be heard. "How—why—are you here? Why do you plague me?"

No, Sradir said. *Don't think of him as father. He is a sorcerer, a back-alley mage. Think of him as a thing, a thing with no power over you.*

He laughed. Existence was not so simple as deciding upon ways to think.

Much of existence is exactly that simple, Berun.

Omali repeated his name, loudly enough that the world rumbled under Berun's feet.

Creatures fled from the encroaching darkness. Sleek, torsional fish snapped at each other in panic while evading the claws and teeth of equally frenzied reptiles. Their massive bodies whipped past Berun, flattening him to the sea bottom, lifting him from his feet and sending him spinning. But for a few reflexive bites, the animals ignored him.

After they had passed, he dropped to the sand unscathed and rose. Overhead, the sun showed through thirty feet of inky saltwater, appearing more foreboding than the moon through storm clouds.

When his innermost spheres tolled together in his deep chest, they created an achingly lonely sound. A familiar sound. He and Omali had once visited Corol, a northern Ulomi city caught in the thrall of plague. There they watched infected men and women walk the streets, dull chimes locked around their throats. It had been Berun's first exposure to death.

Bring out your dead, Omali called, echoing throughout Berun's body. *Bring out your dead . . .*

Berun's vision darkened. His joints loosened, sagged.

"Help me," he said to Sradir. "I'll fall apart."

I will. And no, you won't.

They concentrated together, and the spheres within his chest slowly ground to a halt. His ankles, knees, and hips solidified under him. The darkness, however, intensified around him, forming itself into a nearly solid thing against which he struggled to make headway.

Yes, he still walked. Without a glance behind, he pushed himself forward, into the darkness his creator had made. The ink swirled around him, forming and reforming half-recognizable images. It eddied around his feet and tugged his shoulders from side to side. He swayed, nearly tipping again and again, but he persisted.

Fear had not been removed from him: he felt it ever more keenly. Sradir kept itself in the forefront of his mind, but otherwise maintained silence.

It, too, he imagined, could not predict the outcome of this encounter.

‡

An orange light bloomed in the ebon distance, as of an alchemical torch being lit in the gloom of night. It did not grow brighter or larger, yet he knew it to be advancing toward him. He sensed it in the same way a ship captain sensed an oncoming storm or the wind about to die upon his sails—as a fact of living, undeniable in its potency.

When the darkness surrounded him completely, the light split in two.

He stopped. Before him stood Omali. Two brilliant amber lenses, liquid and glowing like glass fresh from the kiln, had replaced his eyes. Bubbles of light poured constantly from their surface, rising into the blackened water as two thin streams of light. His body had changed from their last encounter, as well: skeletally thin and pale, his hairless nudity revealed no trace of his sex. He possessed no mouth, no ears, and only two closed slits for nostrils. To Berun, his creator had come to resemble a creature born to inhabit caves, far from the light.

An eater of worms, Sradir said. *Say that. Now. Call him an eater of worms.*

Berun shook his head, transfixed by his creator's stare.

Your days of pretending are over, Omali said. He lifted his right hand and opened it, revealing the webbing between each finger. His open hand became a fist. *You will now submit to me.*

Sradir's voice grew louder. *Do it, Berun. Say he's an eater of worms.*

"Eater . . ." he said. "Eater of . . ."

Omali tipped his head to one side and turned it slightly, revealing an earhole Berun had not seen. The bubbles streamed more quickly from the sorcerer's eyes as he stepped back. A pair of long, thin swords grew in his hands.

(No, Berun noted. They grew *from* his hands, drawing material from his own body. His arms, already thin, became twigs as the blades lengthened.)

What is this? Omali asked. *Your mind is corrupted. Tell me, who is this interloper? It is different from the girl.*

Well apprehended, magician, Sradir said. *Attack him, Berun. Don't answer or delay. My strength is yours. Do it, now.*

Berun's eyes flared as Sradir unfolded itself and stood inside him, wearing him as though he were a suit of armor. For the space of several seconds, he basked in the sensation of wellness—a sensation he had not experienced since the days when he could bend and mold himself to any form. Each component of his body tickled against its neighbor in readiness, sliding into new configurations, moving from his interior to his surface. Dirt, gathered from months without washing in the desert, rose around him in a red cloud.

He closed his massive hands into tight fists, savoring the piercing sound of brass rubbing against brass. The simulated muscle of his frame bunched and writhed. The corners of his mouth curved upward into a grin.

He was an alchemical engine once more, primed and rumbling.

Allowing himself no time to doubt his actions, he stepped forward unencumbered by the water and wrapped his arms around Omali's shoulders, crushing the small man to his chest. His forearms and hands flowed into a fluid mass of spheres, cohering into two constricting snakes seeking to crush the life out of their prey.

But Omali would not be crushed. His frame, while frail in appearance, was harder than stone. It possessed strength to match its opponent's. Omali flexed against the bonds Berun had constructed, inexorably lifting his creation's arms. As he did so, he tapped the edges of his swords along Berun's flank. Where it touched, Berun became numb.

Candles, one by one, snuffed out.

For the first time in his existence, Berun lost contact with elements of his body.

He had heard men describe pain before, of course. This seemed far worse, however, an absence where there should have been only connection. It was worse, in fact, than the rare occasion he had been struck hard enough to remove a sphere entirely.

Worse, even, than being stuck as a man-shaped thing.

No, it's not, Sradir said. *You're being manipulated to fear, Berun. You must not—No! Hold your ground.*

Berun had dropped Omali and backed away.

You are a mistake to be rectified, Omali said, arms spread wide, the points of his swords leveled at Berun. *Clearly, I was too liberal in the freedoms I allowed you. This is immaterial now. Now, I will have you and the thing inhabiting you evicted. I have much to do, and it cannot be accomplished in this wisp of a body. It is strong, but I need something more . . . permanent.*

He strode forward.

Berun backed up a step before Sradir halted him.

I'm sorry, it said. *I'd rather see you fight this battle, but we don't have the option of losing. I need your body as badly as Omali does.*

The sorcerer's swords came down. Through no order of his own, quicker than he would have thought possible, Berun's hands came up and caught them. Immediate numbness in his palms resulted, but Sradir did not so much as flinch. The god caused Berun's wrists to rotate until, with a muted crack of bone, the blades broke.

Omali screeched as blood pumped from the wounds. Bubbles streamed from his eyes and burst incandescently. He tried to back away, but Berun's fists were locked in position. His feet were rooted to the sea floor.

Sradir opened Berun's mouth and spoke with his voice, with a clarity that the constructed man could not have achieved underwater.

"You want to know who I am, magician? I am Sradir Ung Kim, Wood Heart—heir to Adrash."

Omali shook his head. *No*, he said in a strained whisper. *There is no one by this name. There is no heir to Adrash.*

Sradir laughed through Berun's mouth and pushed Omali backward with his right hand, leaving his left clenched around Sradir's broken sword arm.

The spheres of Berun's chest erupted outward, ejecting something quickly to the surface.

His right hand—Sradir's right hand—rose from his side and closed around a handle.

Weither, Sradir had called it. Berun had not known himself to be hiding the whip.

The god brought the thin weapon low, arcing it near the constructed man's hip and flipping it fluidly into a backhanded, slanting cut across Omali's torso, severing the sorcerer from rib to shoulder.

No expression crossed Omali's face. He uttered no sound as the seam split and the top half of his body toppled backward.

Sradir stepped forward through thick clouds of blood, pushing Omali's lower half to the side. It crouched near the wounded man as the trail of radiant bubbles stopped flowing from his eyes.

"Now," it said. "Now, you die. It will be . . ." It smiled. "Permanent"

It reached forward, covered Omali's face with Berun's broad hand, and slowly crushed the sorcerer's skull.

No stranger to violence, Berun nonetheless quailed at the sight. Blood, bone, and a liquid radiance erupted from between his fingers, the last of which bent like smoke toward his face. It wavered before his eyes, a living, vital thing. His instinct was to pull away from it before contact, but Sradir kept him from doing so: it caused his mouth to open and drink the golden essence.

He fell back as the inky darkness dissolved above him. He stared at the sun through thirty feet of suddenly clear water, the vision faltering in each eye, off-time, a stuttering rhythm.

Holding himself together became impossible against the will of Sradir, and so he decohered. After each component sphere loosened its grip in the matrix he had created, his body spread out as a mat of brass upon the sea floor. Under his own control, this would not have bothered him. He had once done exactly this to gather sunlight.

Under another's control, it was agony.

You'll likely not believe me, Sradir said, *but I'm sorry.*

Apologies meant nothing. He had been betrayed.

True. But I'll apologize, nonetheless. I'll apologize also for what hasn't yet occurred, what you can't prepare for. Hold steady, Berun. You have eaten your maker. Digesting him will not be pleasant.

‡

Sradir did not lie. It was as far from pleasant as Berun could have imagined.

In life, his creator had not carried within him an ounce of compassion. No sentimentality or allegiance. No quarter given to anyone. Possessed of a vision of brutal clarity, he coerced others to his own ends without a trace of regret, trading in lives as though they were coins. Near the end of his first mortal existence, a madness had taken root in his mind, focusing the dark lens of his intellect on the deficits he identified in humanity itself.

Berun flinched from the reality, the immensity, of Omali's narcissism.

The pact he had made guaranteed the end of an entire world, the creation of a wasteland that would exist for millennia—simply to usher in an age where his hands would not be tied, where his words would be as law. He had been bound too long by the will of kings, ground under the heel of lesser men only because they possessed the resources to do so.

But the elders—the elders, hibernating away under permanent cloud cover, shielded in a state of suspension, guaranteed him a place at their table, a king among kings. A god. They seduced him with the only object of his desire, and so he planned. Alone among men, he discovered a pathway to life after death. A true life, among the resurrected heirs of Jeroun.

He had designed Berun as his vehicle.

First, to enact his will against those who would prevent the fall of the Needle.

Second, as a body in which to weather the death of the world. A place to hibernate away the long afternoon that followed.

‡

The sun set and the creatures of the sea returned to their hunting. They circled around Berun, clearly curious but unwilling to touch him. He kept his eyes to the sky as the moon rose, dragging the disjointed halo of the Needle with it. Through the rippling surface of the sea, each sphere appeared dangerously mobile, shuddering in its orbit as though eager to fall.

He imagined them falling, and wondered why he would do so.

Human curiosity? Sradir said.

He considered pointing the obvious fact out to Sradir.

It snorted dismissively. *You're more human than not. And no, before you ask: there's no part of you that desires the same ends as your maker. You're your own man. In your desires, you always have been.* It paused before continuing. Perhaps it wanted an answer he would not give, a sign he had forgiven it for its deception.

There had never been a question about the outcome. It had defeated Omali handily, and this fact angered Berun more than its assumption of his body.

You thought we were in this together, Sradir said. *Tell me, Berun—have I ruined everything?*

He grunted. "Answer it yourself. My mind is yours to read."

Not true. There are aspects hidden even from me. I'm a good guesser, and that's all.

"No," he said. "You're a good liar. And I'm bad at discerning truth."

Outcroppings of rock began appearing under his feet. On the moonlight-dappled sea floor, they appeared like the backs of burrowing creatures. He trod heavily upon them, causing his body to ring like a bell, and tried to still his thoughts.

Sradir said nothing, for which he felt gratitude, which in turn inspired annoyance.

The island of Osa proper began. He ascended the jumbled, twilit steps of stone ten, twenty, thirty feet, and rose above the surface of the sea.

Standing on the shore, a thousand rivulets of saltwater sluiced from his body. Above him stretched a wall of crystal, reflecting the night behind him perfectly.

The sky. The sea, reflecting the sky.

He said the words without Sradir. "Uperut amends. Ii wallej frect. Xio."

The passageway opened immediately. He spared the sea no backward glance.

‡

He traveled a night and a full day before Sradir spoke to him again.

Wait. Stop, Berun. Please stop.

"Stop me yourself," he responded.

His pace slowed as Sradir ground him to a halt gently. He saw no point in resisting.

I'm not doing this to show you I can. You know I can. Look up. Look around you.

He lifted his head and did so, finding himself at the foot of a low wooded hill.

"Yes? What of it?"

You haven't looked up from the ground for an entire day. Take a moment and see with these brilliant eyes of yours. This is the world we wish to preserve.

He considered refusing, but once more, what would be the point in it? Each of Sradir's displays of power served only to dispirit him.

Turning a full three hundred and sixty degrees, he took in what he had noticed only as obstacles to be overcome. Behind him lay gently sloping plains, fold upon fold of golden grass and sparse forest. Miles and miles of geography, trampled under his feet in his haste to reach his companions. In the distance before him, blue mountains rose in the center of the island, his ultimate destination.

Closer at hand, a creek wound down the slope of the wooded hill. It met another creek at the hill's foot, and together they formed a narrow, swiftly-moving river that disappeared into the forest to the south. He imagined how a man would have viewed it—as unthreatening, idyllic, a place to rest a body after a long walk—and decided on a proper response.

He shrugged. "It's beautiful."

Sradir kept him from lifting his foot and moving on.

It is, yes, but that's hardly all. You're being willfully dense, ignoring the fullness of what's before you. Curiosity is not something you've ever had to force yourself to feel, so don't start pretending disinterest now. How do I know you're pretending? I haven't been in here, wasting time. I've observed you. Fact is, I'm the closest you'll come to a lover, a true friend, or a parent.

"You could equally well be an enemy. A very good enemy, I'd add."

Sradir sighed. *What occurred between us, I regret. If there had been another way, then I would have chosen it, but there wasn't another way. To assume I mean you harm is ridiculous. I don't ask for your thanks, but I expect you to realize the threat Omali posed to you. Ask yourself, would I have done what I did if I meant you harm? I'm here to help us toward a shared goal. That's the entirety of it, Berun. That's all I want you to see.*

"You said you needed my body."

I did. I do. I need your physical form to enter this world. Otherwise, I'm little more than a shade of my former self, content to wither away as time counts down to a close. When the threat to the world became clear even through the haze of that half-life, I focused upon the one soul attuned to my own.

You, Berun.

I fought the inertia of death and immortality both, because there's something about you. I wanted to return, yes—the world still holds its sway—but if not for you I wouldn't have found the strength to do so.

He shook his head and tried to raise his foot again. This time, Sradir relented. He climbed the hill, descended its other side, and continued. His gaze remained fixed on the mountaintops rising over each successive summit. Overhead, wyrms corkscrewed through the sky, calling to one another with nearly human voices.

As the waning sun sent tall shadows before him, he finally relented to his desire.

He stopped and tipped his head back.

"It's beautiful," he said.

Yes, Sradir answered. *It is.*

‡

As promised, the land led him to it. A mile due south of the weapon repository, Adrash had carved a roadway into an ancient lava flow. It descended ten miles into a verdant thorn bush and cactus-studded plain, ultimately depositing him at the entrance to his destination.

He passed a hand over the finely pitted surface of one massive basalt pillar that helped form the entryway. It and its neighbor rose fifty feet over his head, the crossbar at its height extending nearly twice that length. An army could have passed through, thirty men across. A family of wyrms could have roosted upon it. He wondered what Adrash's intentions had been, creating such a massive monument. Had he been so bored with existence?

Yes, Sradir said. *That's it, exactly.*

He climbed a broad stairway of black stone, gazed down into the partially cloud-covered valley, and found his sense of scale confounded a second time.

Though he had known a valley to be his destination, a ridge of stone had shielded it from view during his descent along the lava road. Nothing from Sradir or Shavrim had led him to expect anything other than a natural feature of the land.

Surprise, Sradir said. *Welcome to Shavrieem, useless monument to my brother.*

Berun rocked back with a shrill creak.

An entire nation could have attended games in the coliseum Adrash had carved into the immense, almost perfectly circular depression. Danoor's Aresaa Coliseum, itself the most massive stadium on the continent, could have fit inside the terraced space alongside a hundred of its reproductions. Row upon row of stands, divided by staircases that plummeted the better part of a mile, circled the walls of the valley.

Even the lowest seats possessed a spectacular view, rising nearly three hundred feet above the earthen floor. Gated entryways, each large enough to sail a galleon through, were spaced at regular intervals in the walls below them, leading Berun to believe that more construction existed beneath the valley itself—immense tunnels, holding cells, and training areas.

He sensed amusement, but also a measure of annoyance, from Sradir. *Adrash never was one for half measures. Boredom drives even a god to extraordinary measures. This pleased him for a time before it too became something of a sore subject. We once shared this place as a sanctuary together, a place removed from humanity, but after the creation of Shavrieem . . .*

It waved Berun's arm in a vague gesture, almost as though it had for briefly forgotten itself.

Silent, he wondered at the odd intimacy of the moment.

One of the low-hanging clouds shifted to show a greater stretch of the coliseum floor. He immediately focused upon the temple revealed at its center. Roughly hewn from red stone and open to the elements on all sides, it stood out from the clean, complete lines Adrash had crafted.

Shavrim's answer, Sradir said. *Not that Adrash ever noted its existence.*

"They were not happy with each other?"

Frequently.

He started down the nearest staircase, the spheres of his feet automatically conforming to the steps. More and more sure of his balance, he moved ever faster while keeping his eyes focused on the temple. Shavrim had been no more specific than to say they were to meet in the valley, but Berun felt confidant that he meant the temple.

As if in answer to his assumption, Shavrim walked out of the temple's shadow. Shirtless, newly scarred over the length and breadth of his torso. Carrying the black knife Sroma in his left hand.

From miles away, their stares locked. Berun kept his features carefully composed.

Hello, brother, Sradir projected. *We return in triumph.*

Shavrim closed his eyes, as though weighing these words. He nodded slowly, stone-faced, then turned away and re-entered the temple.

Sradir made a clucking sound. When it spoke, Berun knew it was only for the two of them.

Oh, Shavrim. You always knew how to ruin a good thing.

‡

The dynamic between the three had changed: Berun recognized this the moment Churls and Vedas stepped from the temple's interior to greet him. Though both had thinned further in his brief time away, they appeared well rested, far from frail. Indeed, they appeared harder, knifelike, every muscular twitch more defined on their frames.

Shavrim followed several paces behind, breathing heavily, three long wounds raked across his chest. There were lines on his face that had not been present only days ago. His red-rimmed eyes scanned the heights of the valley as if he expected an attack.

Churls ran to Berun, light-footed in a way he had never seen her, ready to leave the ground. She wore calfskin leggings and a thin, tight vest, revealing the hairline cuts on her arms and shoulders, most of which had already scarred over. Her skin tone struck him as subtly wrong, too even, without the warm redness she had always possessed after days under the sun. The freckles had faded to nothing on her shoulders, upper arms, and bare scalp. They remained on her face only as a spattering over the bridge of her nose.

He had always admired her freckles. So few humans possessed them.

"Berun," she said, wrapping her arms as far around him as she could. "You're free now." She released him and laid her palms flat upon his chest, her eyes bright and clear. "And you're warmer than when you left, like a fire's inside you.."

Yes, you silly bitch, Sradir said coldly. *He's got me now. I'm the fire inside him.* The god stretched partway into his limbs, and—for all the good it would do—Berun braced himself against another assumption of his body. Sradir relaxed, however.

She's closer to the surface, Berun. Ustert. You can feel her just behind your friend's smile, can't you?

He could, and it pained him to recognize it. He forced himself to rest his hand upon her head, fighting the revulsion Sradir made no attempt to hide.

"It's the sun here, under the glass," he said. "It seems to have an un-usual effect over time."

Vedas did not quicken his pace like Churls had, but he smiled warmly. Barring the severe angularity of his face and body, he appeared much the same as he always had to Berun.

That is, until the man stood within touching distance.

Close up, Berun could see the fine lines raised in relief upon Vedas's suit. Repeating vortices, geometrical patterns upon patterns. They shifted subtly as Berun watched, growing and reducing, birthing and dying. Vedas could not have created such intricate work on his own. No man could have done so.

Berun made sure to keep his stare from becoming obvious. He composed his features into a pleasant expression and gestured to encompass the valley.

"This is our training grounds? Is it not rather overlarge, Shavrim?"

The horned man's smile did not reach his eyes. "Likely. But I know of no better way to attract Adrash's attention than to return to this place."

Berun looked from Shavrim to Churls, Churls to Vedas. "This is the extent of your plan?"

Shavrim nodded. "You expected more, constructed man? Some elaborate plan to lift us from the earth and hurl us into the void? No." He stamped his foot, causing the heavy muscles of his thighs to jump. "He comes to us. We force him to fight us on the earth we've claimed for ourselves."

He flipped his heavy black knife twice, and then threw it at Berun.

Berun lifted his right hand to slap the weapon from the air. Upon contact, a great blast washed out the vision in his eyes and threw his body backward thirty feet. Senses scrambled, he tumbled end over end, throwing up great clods of grass and dirt. He came to rest, and though the thought of getting to his feet occurred, he could not make himself do it. All at once, he had forgotten where he was, how he had come to be on the ground.

Footsteps. Berun levered himself up and stood, swaying as he sought to reorganize his thoughts.

A threat. There was a threat. Footsteps.

He fell over, tried to rise, and eventually managed to sit.

Someone slapped his head, righting it. It had turned completely around on his shoulders.

Shavrim swam before him.

"Yes, Berun," he said. "Light and sound and violence. We'll need more of that. After thousands of years, I no longer remember how *not* to shield myself from Adrash. Thus, it's up to us to shout our challenge as loudly as we can." He crouched, a not unkind expression on his face. "And you—you'll need to learn to defend yourself a bit better. Death will come wielding more than knives."

‡

When his companions' breathing changed, signalling the depth of their slumber, he rose and walked a mile west from camp. He sat, cross-legged in the grass, and slowly let his spheres uncouple and spread out. The glowing blue coals of his eyes focused on the temple as his body undulated and then began forming itself into a replica of the building. It proved taxing work, for it had been some time since his form had been fluid enough to do so.

Sradir remained silent, undoubtedly aware of his intent.

It took numerous attempts, but finally, on the seventh, he toppled one of the pillars and allowed it to detach completely from its neighbors, achieving the separation of his being into two distinct parts.

Sradir gasped as the wave of pleasure crashed over them.

Berun fought to hold himself apart, as two entities, sustaining the sensations. The thousand spheres of his body rang a wild harmonic tone, repeating and intensifying in waves to match his wildly stuttering senses. His eyes flared on and off in the darkness, pulsing from brief star to cold stone over and over again. He became aware of Sradir, sharing the moment, lending him the strength to draw it out longer.

Time stretched from the two poles of his reality.

When both of his and Sradir's efforts could maintain the division no longer, the sculpture he had created of himself dissolved into a pool of brass once more. The components he had separated were reabsorbed into the greater whole, and the sensations wound down.

He rested in companionable silence, vision rotated to the sky. Much like the wyrms he had seen on his way to the valley, the beauty of the Needle could not be denied.

Yet it took him several minutes to notice the change in it.

One of the largest of the spheres, which had for months been positioned over the constellation Indusc, had been moved further back and closer to the moon. He stared at it, dumbfounded by this change—by the change, but also by his own willful ignorance. A god moved the heavens according to his own whim, and until that point he had not bothered to consider how odd a thing this was.

He had always observed men, noting the ways in which Adrash's existence altered the course of their lives.

But the very fact of Adrash? This, he had not considered.

He formed a mouth. "Has it always been this way, Sradir? Is it this way elsewhere?"

Elsewhere, Sradir said. *Where, elsewhere?*

He focused his eyes on prominent individual stars, on the wispy backbone of the sky (each miniscule speck of which, Omali had claimed, was itself a star), and finally on the bright smudges and whorls scholars claimed to be the immeasurably distant homes of other stars.

Entire collections of stars, millions upon millions, each with its own collection of worlds.

Sradir chuckled. *What do you think death is? There's a world of the dead, as you well know, lying under and above this world. There's a way to other places, as well, but no one returns once they've left, and thus no one can say what lies beyond.*

It's a place of theory, Berun. Perhaps Adrash knows, but he's never told.

"You didn't answer my first question. Has it always been this way?"

Sradir let him feel a portion of its discomfort. Or, possibly, it no could no longer easily hide itself from him.

I wasn't born. I was created. I held the jar that housed my body before its decanting. It was a small clay container, no higher than a man's knee, no heavier than a water barrel. After my creation, my education—he could hear the sneer in the word—*began in earnest. Adrash, no more a father than Omali was to you, dictated the terms. I learned what he'd have me learn. Even after millennia, I still doubted . . .*

My point, Berun, is that I am . . . I am . . .

"You don't need to finish, Sradir. I understand what you—"

I do, and you don't. You persist in believing we're quite different, but there's a reason your mind resounded with mine. We are much the same. Despite having spent so much time with my creator, having witnessed his moods over the span of many human lives, having inherited so much from him, I look at the sky now and I wonder what passes through his mind. I pretend to know, but in reality?

I know nothing. I'm here with you, wondering. Has the world always been this way? Does each world possess a god it must overcome to achieve adulthood? There are no answers to these questions. We fight, you and I, against what we can see.

‡

"Drivel," a flinty voice spoke. "Answers are for the taking, Sradir. You merely need to know which screws to put to which thumbs."

Berun's eyes swiveled to the source. In the moonlight stood a tall, pale-skinned man, naked from crown to sole. Creatures crawled upon his sinuously muscled torso, and an odd darkness flowed from his back, obscuring the land behind him.

No. Berun reappraised what he saw.

This was no man. At least, not fully. Before him stood an elderman, though unlike any elderman he had previously seen. What had first appeared to be creatures crawling over him were in fact black shapes, one-dimensional images of wyrms and wolves and tentacled creatures. They shifted from form to form, chasing one another around the angular length of his body, avoiding only a hands-print deformity on his pectoral muscles and a massive scar raked across his abdomen.

The darkness at his back revealed itself to be broad wings, deep and without mark or feature.

One double-pupiled, amber eye appraised Berun. The other was a smoking pit.

Unnoticed at first glance, a gray-skinned, naked woman lay crumpled at his feet. Her chest rose and fell in fits. Blood leaked from her left ear.

The elderman stretched his arms lazily, like a man recently woken.

"Get up," he said.

Hello, Orrus, Sradir responded.

‡

Berun did not question if Orrus was an enemy. He did not need to.

Without a word exchanged, they began circling one another. Berun expected Sradir to take control, but it seemed content to let him lead. He remained aware of the god within him, of course. He felt the strength of it at his fingertips, a potential violence he knew had only been hinted at with Omali. The spheres of his left forearm shifted, sprouting outward from his palm, pushing Weither into his hand.

Orrus's right eye widened at the sight of the whip. Smoke poured in gouts from his left. With a muscular twitch of his shoulders, his wings snapped wide, lifting his feet briefly from the ground. The black images spun faster upon him, ripping themselves to shreds only to re-form in other shapes. He bared small, sharp teeth.

Berun refused to be put on the defensive. He coiled his legs and jumped forward, closing the distance between them by half. Lengthening his right arm into a hook, he swiped at Orrus's chest, making minimal contact but still managing to spin the elderman to the side.

He ducked as the elderman's wing hissed toward his head and continued moving toward his opponent. Just as Orrus turned fully to face him, Berun's right shoulder plowed into Orrus's lower belly.

His arms wrapped around Orrus's hips, trapping the elderman's left hand in the process. Causing the spheres of his feet to flatten and broaden, he prevented himself from tumbling to the ground and arched backward, lifting the flailing elderman into the air before slamming him into the earth.

A second time. A third. Orrus snarled and struggled to break free.

Watch his hand! Sradir shouted. *If he gets it loo—*

Orrus pulled his hand free as he rebounded against the ground a fourth time. More rapidly than Berun could properly register, the elderman gestured with both hands.

A violet light erupted and Berun was struck, thrown forty feet into the air. He spun end over end, spraying uncoupled spheres from the gaping hole in his left shoulder, roaring in the only sensation analogous to pain he had ever known.

Hold on, Sradir said just before he hit ground. He felt the god enter his limbs, forcing him to deform slightly to absorb the impact. Nonetheless, more components shot from his wound.

He growled into the soil and levered himself up, spheres flowing from his chest and back to mend the hole in his shoulder.

Orrus stood before him, ink-covered arms crossed.

"Should have had your puppet use the whip," he said. "He's quicker than I thought. He could have had me with that first blow."

Berun sensed Sradir's question before it was spoken, and relaxed his jaw.

"He's no puppet," it said. "Can't say the same about yours. Who are you, brother?"

Orrus—or the elderman Berun thought of as Orrus—grinned. "*Who are you, brother?* What a wonderful thing it is to be asked such a question. Two days ago, I was a rather charmingly awful young mage named Pol Tanz et Som. Now, after a tangle with a rather temperamental dragon, not to mention the burning of a city, I'm still him." He shrugged. "Him, and not him. I've taken the best of what I found in his mind and incorporated it."

Berun's mouth drew into a sneer. "You've become a talker in your old age. Oh, and a fool. We were not enemies. We need not be enemies."

"Much has occurred since the death of my original body. This is an understatement. Had you returned to existence before now, like Evurt or Ustert, perhaps you'd have become something more interesting than the sorry, sentimental thing I see cowering in this . . ." Orrus chuckled. "Pile of rubble. Adrash favored you above us all. To see you now, like this—well, it's satisfying, is what it is. Almost as satisfying as replaying Bash's death. She, like you, had no true resolve."

Berun's brows drew together. "What of Bash?"

Orrus waved his hand dismissively. "As I said. Dead, at Pol's hand. Her puppet had her way with him. Instead of taking the opportunity in two hands, Bash simply watched. She always was too seduced by pleasure. You need an appreciation of pain to truly make something of yourself."

Sradir pointed to the woman, who still lay crumpled on the ground. "And her?"

"A key to this place, no more." He shook his head, an expression Berun could not name altering his features. "I've never had the benefit of being one of Adrash's pets, privy to all the secret words."

Sradir stared at the woman, intensely curious but unwilling to say more.

Instead of speaking again, she chose surprise. She caused Berun to lunge forward, arm raised to slash downward with Weither.

Just before the weapon made contact, Berun's body collided with a spell neither he nor Sradir had seen, a piece of the night distilled and propelled so slowly that all Orrus had required was a target unobservant enough to walk into it. He had found that target, and once struck by the spell Berun's body ceased to move. He struggled against it, but it was as though he had been encased in concrete. Only his eyes remained under his control.

Fuck, Sradir said.

At his back, a shout. He recognized the voice as Churls's immediately. He concentrated and heard the pounding of three sets of feet.

Orrus took a step to the right to look past Berun. "Too late, fools," he said, and reached up. Taking Weither in his right hand, he snapped his wings open to their full width. The muscles in his legs jumped as he crouched to leap.

Oh, no, Sradir said. *He doesn't have the strength. He's not about to try—*

Orrus left the ground, dragging Berun into the air with him.

‡

I feel I've underestimated him.

It was expressed with a trace of sad amusement, but Berun could not bring himself to see any humor in his situation. Orrus had lifted him far above the earth—so far, he could not conceive of a way in which he might survive the fall. He watched the moonlit ground below, looking for a last sign of Churls, Vedas, or Shavrim, but they had risen to too great a height. He imagined they would near surface of the dome itself soon.

I'm sorry, Sradir said. *Again. It seems I've let you down.*

He could not bring himself to be angry with the god. It had allowed him to attack on his own.

It had been he who failed, ultimately.

No. I won't hear anything about failure. Sometimes, you're simply not strong enough. There's no shame in fighting and losing. Everyone must experience it at some point.

Sradir spoke quickly, aware of the time. How little time.

I remember the moment of my death. I struck Adrash only once, merely scratching his armor. He laughed at me and then, as easily as a man swats a fly, killed me. I was no failure in death. The moments where I failed had all been in life. I didn't even recognize them as failures. That took many thousands of years to see.

He took little comfort in this. No second life awaited him beyond the veil.

Sradir, now fully inhabiting him, made yet another attempt to break free of Orrus's spell, flexing her own phantom limbs in time with

Berun's efforts. Nothing gave, and they both collapsed inward upon the other, their consciousnesses co-mingling. Together, he felt an immense weight lift from him.

Will you let me say something to you, Berun?

He would, but before anything could be said Orrus cursed.

A white light bloomed above them, and the elderman swerved suddenly, rocking Berun from side to side beneath him. For a moment, he imagined he would be dropped, but Orrus held firm. As Berun swung, he lifted his eyes to the light.

Sword in hand, she hovered above Orrus in full armor, flapping wings to match her opponent's, blindingly white to his depthless black. He could not see her face, but he assumed it held the same expression of grim determination he had often seen grace her mother's.

Behind her, he saw her reflection in the dome. They had nearly reached it.

Before Orrus could move, Fyra dove downward, her blade arcing into his left wing where it joined his back.

He shrieked and dropped Berun.

Sradir, sensing the failing of his spell, lengthened Berun's left arm, reaching.

She wrapped his fingers around Orrus's ankle and dragged him down.

‡

Wrapped in Orrus's wings, they fell. Stunned by Fyra's attack, Orrus quickly lost any advantage he might have gained.

Berun bound his hands. He flowed into the form of an iron manacle and enveloped the winged god's body, crushing it until he and Sradir felt the give of his spine.

It snapped.

Orrus screamed and they formed an arm with Weither gripped at its end, drawing the weapon savagely across his throat, severing skin and cartilage, setting his blood free to the wind.

Next, they ripped his wings from his body and let them flutter away.

Orrus's mouth gaped open. His one eye rotated backward into his skull. Still, they would see him not mortally wounded—they would see him dead, never to return.

Small spheres flowed from Berun's body, swarming over Orrus's face. They entered the elderman's empty eye socket and made jelly of the interior of his skull. Neither Berun nor Sradir relished the task (he keenly sensed Sradir's regret: it and Orrus were not true family, no, but they had not hated one another in life), yet they would not be dissuaded.

Blackness emerged from Orrus's nostrils and reached toward Berun's face. Understanding Sradir's intention—the nature of its grisly talent— he did not object when his mouth opened to drink the essence of Orrus and his puppet, Pol Tanz et Som.

Neither would live on, but their memory would exist in whatever remained of Sradir after Berun's death.

Berun envied them all their legacy.

Finished, he and Sradir pushed Orrus's corpse away and aimed toward the earth. Berun's body became a teardrop shape, his two eyes at its leading point, watching the darkness approach.

How long could they fall?

Soon, now, Sradir said. *Goodbye, Berun.*

"Goodbye," he said. He could not hear his own voice, yet it hardly mattered. Sradir had always heard him, regardless of whether or not he spoke.

‡

A breath before impact, she appeared below him.

Unarmored, smiling, arms reaching out to him for an embrace.

Not goodbye, she said.

He hit the floor of the world and shattered into a thousand pieces. Housed in each component sphere of his body, his consciousness was thrown upward and outward.

Thoughts skittering into dissolution—

—he felt himself coming down as a shower of stones—

—and then felt nothing more.

CHAPTER EIGHT

THE 7TH TO 9TH OF THE MONTH OF FISHERS
JEROUN ORBIT, THE ISLAND OF OSA

Adrash drifted in a slowly decaying orbit above the surface of
the moon.

Every muscle stood out in tension upon his tall, broad-
shouldered frame. Twisted by grief and anger, the features of his face
were made ugly even under the flawlessly smooth exterior of the divine
armor. The light spilled from his eyes as his passion crested and broke,
again and again. Now and then, he reached up to press his right palm
flat against his chest.

To count his heartbeats, as though seeking to confirm his own existence. As though fearful of losing the one link tying him to reality.

Orrus died.

Sradir died.

He forced himself to relive the moment of their deaths, saddened by
the loss but more stunned by his ignorance. Only in their final seconds
had their identities been revealed to him, had the full implication been
apparent. The fact of his children's existence—how could such a thing
have been hidden from him for so long? How could he have heard
their voices, killed their hungry avatars on so many occasions and still
failed to recognize them? Pol Tanz et Som had come to him, fresh
from the murder of his mentor—an elderwoman who must surely have
housed the soul of Bash.

Adrash had stared the ascendant god in the eyes, yet had not truly seen.

Clearly, his mind had blunted over the course of his long life. Perhaps he had never possessed an intellect equal to his godly pretensions.

His right hand returned to his chest. He pressed fingertips against the heavy muscle of his left pectoral, testing its firmness. He prodded the ridges of his belly as a coldness settled in his gut. His fingers slipped over his genitals. He squeezed, grimacing at the thought of his impotence and only releasing his grip when the pain became too much.

Turning away from the moon, he let his gaze fall frustrated upon Jeroun.

Just before Vedas Tezul's party left Danoor, a void had opened. Once as easily read as words printed on a page, Vedas's mind and those of his companions had become all but impenetrable. Adrash could still observe their actions while under the open sky—just as he could for all men, no matter how talented at masking themselves.

He could do this, but no more. Not any longer.

The near perfect recollection of their minds remained, however, and it pained him to realize how obvious their inhabitation should have been to him. Mere mortals did not think such thoughts, or come to know one another so thoroughly despite their insecurities and moral divisions. Regardless of the arcane magic he had assumed existed at their disposal, they could not have developed advanced martial skills so easily.

Most tellingly, they could not have found themselves under the dome of Osa, holding the marvelous weapons he himself had crafted for his children.

As he watched Vedas and Churls mourn for their fallen comrade on the floor of Shavrieem, he was shocked to discover they had come to resemble Evurt and Ustert. Both were considerably thinner, hardened to familiar blades. The woman had even begun shaving her scalp.

Had he really been so blind as to ignore bodies . . . faces?

It spoke of more than a faltering mind. It spoke of a willful disregard.

And yet, surely, he had needed a period to recover after Pol's attack. He had expended much of his strength keeping the spheres of the Needle from spinning out of control. Was it not conceivable that exhaustion had kept him from the revelations that now struck him as plain?

No, he thought. *No excuses.*

Another concern nipped at him. For the first time, he found his interest aroused by the third remaining member of Vedas's party—the wyrm tamer whose name had never been spoken, who confounded analysis by appearing as a blank in Adrash's mind, defying curiosity with his frank lack of distinguishing features. Individuals such as this had been known to exist. They cropped up now and then, though rarely in positions of influence.

But this one? He had ruled over a portion of Danoor. He had sought out Vedas and Churls, and thereafter held his ground during their encounters on the way to Osa. At times, he appeared to lead. What had seemed to Adrash the simple effect of an opportunistic individual, one seeking to take advantage of Vedas's fame after the tournament in Danoor, suddenly seemed noteworthy.

He focused on the broad, ugly tamer, and discovered he could see no further than the first layer of the man's swarthy, sun-reddened skin. The harder he concentrated, the more the man's mind slipped from his grasp.

Even the man's appearance was an assumption: it too could not be focused upon. The second his attention was elsewhere, he fought to remember the man.

Adrash's brows knit together as he poured his strength into the effort of seeing.

‡

The tamer helped Vedas and Churls gather what spheres they could from Berun's dismembered body, but did not otherwise interact with them. When they stood around the pile they had created, he said nothing in remembrance. After several minutes, he left them to their sorrow, returning to the temple Shavrim had built in adolescent protest so many thousands of years previously.

Passing near the entryway, he retrieved a dark, indistinct object he had set against one of the temple's columns. A moment later, he returned from the building's interior and sat on its front steps, running his right hand along the length of the object positioned across his knees.

No. He was not running his *hand* along the object's length. He held two objects, one applied to the other. Ignoring the man, Adrash concentrated upon the longer object.

When it suddenly swam into sharp relief, he nearly gasped.

The man held a blade as black as night, whetting its constantly renewing edge as gently as one stroked a lover's thigh.

Sroma.

Less a fabricated thing than a creature in its own right, an elder-artifact outdating humankind's habitation of Jeroun, it was the one weapon Adrash had not created for his children. In the earliest days, when he alone had stood upon the surface of Jeroun, recovering from the long navigation between a home he had never known and a place he had been created to rule, it had called to him.

It had called, and so had another—a four-fingered glove, whiter than snow.

He had weighed both in his hands and chosen the divine armor, thus eschewing the knife. Each would not inhabit the same space as the other. No, not even to be held. Eventually, Adrash had bequeathed the knife to Shavrim, creating a name and lying about its provenance. His first child had never known the value of the thing he held, had never known he alone had been created to wield it.

Adrash returned his attention to the man, imagining his gaze as the searing tip of a poker, fresh from the fire. He slammed his focus into the shield protecting the man, willing it to fail.

‡

The man paused in his task and looked up, expression unreadable, head cocked as if listening. He then stood and shrugged the illusion away.

Adrash's heart stuttered. It quaked, painful in its intensity.

The man could be no other than Shavrim.

The seconds lengthened as Adrash realized the depth of his first child's deception. How it had been accomplished did not matter. All that mattered were the millennia that had passed.

Alone. They had both been alone.

Neither had needed to be alone. Together, time could have been a cure.

Instead, it had only rotted the framework of Adrash's mind.

The white god ground his teeth together and turned back to the moon. A furnace was stoked between the walls of his skull, was released from his eyes as twin columns of fire. Below him, a half-mile circle of regolith turned into a boiling lake. Vapor shot upward and immediately cooled in the airless void, rebounding against him as an iron rain.

When his rage finally exhausted itself, he closed his eyes.

The lake settled, fused into a shallow bowl. He descended and lay upon its swiftly-cooling surface.

‡

With the full acknowledgement of his foolishness, came resolution.

All three would die. He would not particularly enjoy it, just as he had not enjoyed ending their lives nearly thirty thousand years prior, but this was immaterial. He would see their bones bleaching in the sun, and realize his work done.

He dug his fingertips into the iron floor beneath him and arched upward, attempting to ease the pressure lodged in every muscle. His nostrils twitched as the divine armor filtered the merest particles from the void, tailoring it to his mood, his unspoken needs.

Death was not his sole concern. Duties yet remained.

The smell of blood filled his head, and he opened his eyes again to take in the nearest sphere of the Needle. The seventh largest, it spun only a few hundred miles from him, looming massively in the star-shot darkness. Had it been placed before him, it would have obscured his view of Jeroun entirely.

If he neglected it any longer, it would soon begin a rapid descent into the moon.

He gestured toward it with his open left hand, drawing further from the well of power within himself, but also from the armor sheathing him in its cold embrace. The muscles of his arm flexed and shuddered with the strain.

The sphere quaked in its spin, and slowly backed away.

One, five, twenty, a hundred miles. It appeared to him as if it were waiting, impatient.

He sympathized, but it would have to wait a bit longer. He would briefly rest, and then he would kill what remained of his children. Only with that assuredly behind him would he allow himself to return to the question that had plagued him for so long:

Had the world proved itself worthy, or had the spheres of the Needle waited long enough for their promised day of destruction?

‡

He allowed himself to move at a leisurely pace—the very pace at which an outbound mage such as Pol Tanz et Som had once traveled to and from Jeroun. Hurrying would afford Adrash no advantages, and moreover, by not taxing himself he took full advantage of the divine armor's unique capabilities. It warmed itself in the sun as did a freezing man before a fire, replenishing itself and stoking the flames that existed deep in the crafted core of Adrash's heart.

For perhaps the hundred-thousandth time of his existence, it struck him as odd that his body worked in such perfect concert with the armor, that together they had crafted a god. He could conceive of no way for his creators to have anticipated such a fusion.

Of course, he had never known his creators. By the time he woke, alone and soulbound to the iron egg *Jeroun* as it sailed the void, carrying the descendents of humanity, his creators were little more than shades of living men, a collection of ghosts wandering the long rust-pitted halls, muttering to themselves, standing forlorn watch over the rows upon rows of unborn men.

Nonetheless, their intent in his creation was clear. It could not be denied, for purpose drove him in those unimaginably early years. Slaved directly to his mind, the caravan of vessels stretched one hundred miles and occupied every bit of his attention. Its navigation, while largely intuitive, ensured his constant preoccupation: he learned to care for it as intensely as a father cared for his children.

This obsession nearly proved disastrous, however. Once deposited upon the surface of Jeroun (no, he knew nothing of the world his people had left, and so christened the new world with the first name to mind), he procrastinated on his next mission. He knew it must be done—indeed, a part of him ached for it to be done—but nonetheless he kept those he had transported closed within their caskets and bottles.

For a decade, he walked the face of the world he had named, longing to return to the cold spaces between worlds where he alone had been master.

Despite the distance separating them across the face of Jeroun, the eggs would open as one. Once opened, they would not be closed.

His creators had not been stingy in his makeup: though in appearance and spirit a man, his body could withstand considerable damage. It would live for eons, storing its memories within the split courses of his marrow. He possessed an inborn desire to lead, an instinctive awareness of how to coerce. With violence, if necessary.

And it would be necessary, he knew. During his journeys over the continent of Knoori (the second vessel that had followed *Jeroun*), he had seen the modified men outfitted for war in the various holds, arrayed like blades fresh from the forge. He had seen their beasts of war, their machines of destruction. There existed factions he had never anticipated, and they would challenge him as readily as they fought amongst themselves.

He delayed the inevitable.

Yes, because he was a coward.

Only when he found the armor had he roused himself to do what must be done.

‡

Now, as he moved between the moon and the world he had guided and then abandoned, thinking upon events he had not let his mind fall upon for millennia, he came to several inescapable conclusions—conclusions, he could not avoid admitting, he should have reached long ago.

For all his strength, he was a coward still. The armor had been his crutch.

It should have hurt. He did not like this word, coward.

Yet it did not hurt. It hardly mattered, for death awaited him.

He saw this, without avoidance. Whatever decision he reached after the murder of his children, he could not allow a coward to continue living in his body.

The world would die, or it would continue living. Free. With no god to dictate its course.

‡

He entered the atmosphere directly above Osa, slamming himself against air compressed into steel by his swift passage. His body neither flexed nor snapped in two. Flames hotter than those of the sun cocooned him but did not obscure his sight, which remained focused on his destination.

Once within breathable sky, trailing smoke, he outraced sound to the accompaniment of a massive clap that shook the earth below, flattening trees and causing rockslides.

Osa lay fixed before him, a circle of jade in an aquamarine setting. It expanded in his view rapidly, taking on detail. He smiled grimly, recalling its beauty from within the dome, regretting his next action while fully committing to it.

He would not walk into the island as he once had—not now, after so many eons away. He would arrive as an agent of destruction. Pitiless, without remorse.

A fraction of a second before impact, he finished projecting the words.

Uperut amends. Ii wallej frect. Xio.

It was a finely calculated move, potentially dangerous even to one such as he. The dome, he had discovered over the course of several centuries after arriving upon Jeroun, was neither a solid nor a liquid but a state between, granting it permeability and immense structural integrity—tensile strength enough to withstand even a direct blow from Adrash.

Whenever a passageway into it opened, however, the surrounding area became brittle.

Arms crossed before his face, he flew into the dimple marking where the tunnel had begun to form, slamming through the elder-forged material as though it were a thin pane of glass. A halo of crystal scattered around him as he slowed fractionally and turned in the air to view what occurred in his wake.

Cracks branched out from the hole he had created. They were thin and regular at first, each extending no more than a few hundred feet before stopping.

For the briefest of moments, he thought the dome would be able to repair itself.

But no. The cracks thickened, spreading, spider-webbing to the sound of thunder.

In the space of one second, the dome went from glass clear to opaque with innumerable fractures.

Halfway through the following second, the entire structure liquified and fell.

He turned back to earth and outraced the crystal rain, coming to a stop and righting himself a mere foot above Shavrieem's killing floor. Relaxed, arms crossed over his chest, feet slightly pointed toward the ground, eyes dimmed to a low radiance. He remained in this position a moment, utterly still, staring at the temple Shavrim had built.

He gestured, toppling it over.

At his back, a familiar soul spoke his name, and it began to rain.

‡

"Shavrim," he said, speaking aloud. His own voice was much as he remembered it. He did not turn away from the ruined temple.

"Do me the favor of showing your face before we begin," Shavrim said

Adrash smiled within the divine armor, turned, and obliged his first child. The enchanted material opened as a pin-sized hole at his scalp and grew, flowing over his features like oil over ice. He turned his black-skinned face toward the sky and let the rain—already diminishing to a light misting—enter his mouth. He tasted Osa, his smile growing wider.

He breathed. The air smelled, felt on his his skin, much as he remembered it.

"Have I changed?" he asked, lowering his gaze to lock eyes with Shavrim. "It has been a good while, after all."

"No," Shavrim said quietly, stare fixed on his creator. "Some things never change."

Adrash bowed his head and set his feet upon the earth. "As with you, though it looks as if you've recently taken some beatings. It's a consolation, is it not? There are few constants in life."

Shavrim shrugged his heavy shoulders, expression blank.

To either side of him stood Vedas and Churls. Adrash looked from one to the other, left eyebrow raised. At once, he determined that Evurt and Ustert had not assumed control, merely influence. Though both humans bore the signs of their inhabitation, from this distance neither could be confused for truly ascendant gods. They stood stiffly, shoulders thrown back, chins up, Ruin and Rust clenched tightly in firm fists, yet to Adrash their fear was obvious. He could see it, smell it.

Regardless, they did not flinch from his gaze.

In another era, discovering two individuals able to defy the will of his creations would have overjoyed him. Simply to relieve the tedium of observing the cycle of human existence, he would have studied them, turned them to his advantage or set them up against his own interests.

Now, it was an insult. He had come to ground to greet his children before their deaths. To look at them through clouded glass, through . . .

"You're beautiful," he told Churls. It was no lie. Few, if any, would call her pretty, but there was a coarse allure to her. He nodded to Vedas, amused to note something of his own appearance in the man. "You, as well. Welcome, both of you."

"Your welcome's a bit late," Churls said. "We've been here a while."

Adrash's smile did not diminish. "I welcome guests, even when they trespass."

Vedas lifted his horned hood over his scalp. The elder-cloth flowed to cover his face. His suit was a lovely thing, Adrash noted, filigreed with slowly-altering designs the man could not have produced on his own: surely, an external sign of Evurt exerting what control he was able.

"I think you've confused which of us is trespassing," the man said.

Adrash laughed.

Shavrim made a cutting motion with his open left hand. "Enough. I wanted to see your face one last time, and I have. Cover it and let us begin."

"No," Adrash answered. "I want to feel my naked fingers around your throat, Shavrim."

Holes opened in the divine armor, at all twenty fingertips and toe-tips, retreating up his forearms and calves, thighs and biceps. It slipped to uncover his genitals, his sinuous torso. Before long, the only white that remained was an egg shape upon his chest.

He was more beautiful than any man had ever been. His features were generous, almost prototypically masculine. No hair marred his sculpted perfection—no scar, no blemish. He appeared as though he had risen whole from a lake of cooling obsidian.

He stretched languidly, feeling their eyes upon him, and then planted his feet.

"Now. First one, then the other. Or all together. It makes no difference."

‡

They surrounded him. He faced Shavrim, but his awareness extended well beyond himself—far enough, in truth, to render sight unnecessary. Even without his armor actively covering his body, the three presented little actual threat. During the earliest years of mankind's history on Jeroun, even with his own enhanced makeup, he had been appallingly vulnerable when unarmored, but experience had only made his bond with the artifact stronger, more efficacious.

A small part of him lamented this fact.

Vedas broke line first, coming in low with Rust in his right hand. Assisted by Evurt, he covered the twenty feet separating them quickly. His thrust, while graceful enough to catch most opponents unawares, was nonetheless pitifully inadequate against an opponent such as Adrash. He watched it coming in, no more rapid to his perceptions than dripping sap.

He let Vedas in close, then spun and slapped the blade away. He softened his blow to the man's temple, but it still sent him twenty feet in the air to land it a heap near his lover's feet.

She helped him up.

Adrash returned his attention to Shavrim. "This is what you've been training them to do, boy? Hurling themselves against a wall might have serviced your cause equally well."

Tight-lipped, Shavrim raised Sroma and advanced. Adrash strode forward to meet him, arching backward to avoid Shavrim's first downward strike at the last possible moment, savoring the cool wind of it on his chest and belly. Gooseflesh rose on his forearms and inner thighs, a nearly erotic sensation.

Shavrim shuffled his right foot forward to pivot before Adrash and levered his blade upward, aiming its edge between the god's legs. Adrash bent at the waist, head-butting Shavrim while thrusting his arms forward to catch the blade between his palms.

The enchanted metal rang in his hands. As expected, loathing radiated from the weapon at his touch, suffusing his body with its cold fury.

Yet it was not quite what he had anticipated. The force of Sroma's hatred, so much greater than he recalled, nearly brought a gasp to his lips. It seemed it had found more reason, during its long entombment, to rage. Perhaps the armor had changed, as well, so gradually that he had failed to notice. The thought trouble him mildly.

His grip faltered and Shavrim pulled Sroma free. Adrash turned in time to slap the blade to the side as Shavrim tried to disembowel him, and stepped into his opponent's guard, laying his left palm flat upon the Shavrim's chest.

He straightened his arm, snapping Shavrim's sternum, sending him flying backward.

Adrash ducked. Churls's sword, aimed to take his head from his shoulders, passed less than an inch from his scalp. Before her swing had completed its flat arc, his hand shot up and gripped the blade. It sliced into his palm to the bone, yet he hardly noticed the pain (indeed, before he registered it, his body had begun to heal, pushing the blade out from his flesh) and wrenched the sword forward.

The woman held on, allowing herself to be hurled over his shoulder. He threw her sword to the side.

She rolled cleanly and popped to her feet, fists up. He was there before she stood, however, standing at her back. He wrapped his right arm around her neck and lifted her from her feet. Burying his nose in the space behind her ear, he breathed in the aroma of her stale, ordinary human sweat. His cock moved against her bare leg, but it was only a stirring.

Vedas ran at him. Adrash backhanded him to the ground with his remaining hand, almost as an afterthought. The man's right arm lay across his chest at an odd angle. He did not rise.

He frowned, spoke directly into Churls's ear. "You'll be the first to die. Goodbye, Churls. Goodbye, Ustert, for what you've been worth."

He tightened his grip. Her fingertips dug into his forearm. Her heels slammed into his thighs. He leaned his head forward as though he would kiss her cheek, peering at her eyes as her life fled, hoping to see something more—a sign that either she or Ustert had more fight in them.

She pursed her lips and tried to spit, but could not summon the breath to do so. Drool ran down her chin, onto his arm.

"This is all too fast," he whispered. "I'd hoped . . ."

Her body stiffened, and he grunted in surprise.

Her nails had bitten into the flesh of his forearm, drawing blood. He watched in shock as the cartilage of her windpipe pushed against his flesh and forced his wrist out. She sucked air into her lungs, arching against him. White light poured from her eyes and her grip intensified convulsively, the tips of her fingers slipping like sharp teeth between the corded muscles of his forearm, nails scraping over bone.

Pain. Shocking in its novelty. Fury in its wake.

He roared and flung her from him. She flew, carrying a pound of his bloody flesh in her hands.

Cradling his arm, he witnessed with wide eyes as her body failed to impact the earth: it came to rest like a feather stopped in midair, horizontally, four feet above the ground. She sat up and swung her legs to the side, as if she were getting out of bed. When she stood, her feet did not quite touch the ground. Her eyes lost some of their radiance yet still glowed, as if a light had been struck in her skull.

He assumed, momentarily, that Ustert had finally achieved greater influence over the woman, but the assumption quickly proved false. No child of his had ever possessed such a bearing. Or such a light. He fought the ridiculous temptation to shield his eyes from it.

He glanced at his mangled forearm, horrified to find it had not yet begun to heal. A substance, blacker than the night, blacker than the void itself, mixed with his own blood deep in the wound.

As he watched, it disappeared. Into his body.

A memory tugged at him upon seeing it.

Pol. During their battle, the elderman had hit him with a spell composed of a similar substance.

With a thought, the armor flowed from Adrash's chest to cover the injury.

"Who are you?" he asked. He gestured to her with his unarmored hand as though he were choking her. To his puzzlement, no strength came to his aid. Though he had so recently moved the spheres within the void, he could not lift her from where she stood.

"Answer me," he said through gritted teeth.

The woman only spread her arms.

Lights bloomed to either side of her, and rapidly coalesced into forms. Into figures, shades of white upon white. An old Knosi woman, unbowed by her age, a defiant cast to her jaw. A second Knosi woman, perhaps in her mid-twenties, alluring, as hard as a knot of oak. After a shamefully long pause, Adrash recognized her. She had died, just before Vedas and his companions arrival in Marept.

Both women stood weaponless, with arms crossed, no trace of nervousness about them.

The younger one spat. The fluid fluoresced into nothingness before hitting the ground.

"I told you to answer me," Adrash said. "Who are you?"

"Me, plus a couple trespassers," Churls said with the faint trace of a smile. "You'll never know their names. But these two? Say hello to Jojore Um and Laures Kasoert." She looked at one, then the other. "Go. Get them up."

Quicker than their steps would suggest, the ghostly women moved to Shavrim and Vedas's sides. They reached down to both, *into* both, their arms cut off at the wrists in each man's chest, and then lay down, disappearing completely into the men's bodies.

Shavrim and Vedas shuddered. Screams tore from their throats as they bridged up from the grass. Their eyes opened as spotlights. Adrash watched, fascinated despite the clear threat, as they regained their feet. Shavrim winced as his sternum snapped audibly back into shape. Vedas gasped as his arm straightened with a resounding pop.

Churls cracked her knuckles and grinned.

‡

One came after the other, closing him in, reigning blows upon him at speed, as quickly as he could deflect them. He returned the violence, landing hits through their lesser defenses while admitting the tide had taken an inconceivable yet undeniable turn.

How such a thing could be done—he did not bother asking. He did not allow himself the room to wonder who could have such power. There would be time to determine what had occurred once the threat had been neutralized.

With a thought, the divine armor covered him completely. He batted his opponents' hands and feet away, and with three open-palmed strikes pushed them back. Turning in a circle as they stumbled, he allowed the blast furnace within him to crack its seals and overflow. From his eyes and mouth it came: a fountain of flame, engulfing his opponents.

No. Not engulfing. Flowing around. The shields they had formed flickered against his fiery onslaught, limning their bodies in shifting, actinic blue as their spells counteracted his attack. Regardless, their defense was not entirely effective. The heat demonstrably wore at Vedas and Shavrim, causing them to fall back under the blaze.

Churls, however, kept her smile in place and lunged forward, landing a viciously quick punch to Adrash's gut. He grunted, and the fire from within faltered. She blocked his clumsily upthrust knee with her left forearm and jabbed stiffened fingers into his throat.

The fire died as he choked for breath.

She followed with a flurry of punches to his jaw and cheeks. Shavrim and Vedas returned, battering him from side to side. He slipped on the wet grass, falling beneath their fists and heels. The white light of their eyes bathed him.

Pain, so odd that it quickly became an abstraction, a wave, a feeling to lose oneself within, became his reality.

His children pummeled him into the ground. Into a grave.

‡

He did not make the decision—that is, he did not consciously resolve to move.

Yet move he did. He shifted from one place to another, a near-instantaneous maneuver he had never used anywhere but within the void, where no atmosphere impeded his progress. (Moving so quickly, even against something as insubstantial as air, had never seemed an advisable course of action.)

He stood for only a moment, in the position his unspoken desire had deposited him, before his legs collapsed and he crumpled upon the ground.

Further agony.

It felt as though a massive hand had slapped him from the sky, pulping every bone in the right side of his body. He groaned into the night, and then screamed when he rolled onto his back. Broken bone-ends ground together, clicking in his hip, his shoulder. Breathing in and out produced pain so sharp that his vision blurred.

A figure obscured a portion of stars above him, staring down with radiant eyes. Churls. A second figure came up beside her, placed his hand in hers.

They were a good pair, he noted, equally broken, beautiful in the same frail, human way, neither bending to what fate appeared to have in store.

They had retrieved their weapons. Churls put the edge of Rust to his throat.

Vedas caused the elder-cloth to unmask his features. He flipped back the hood of his suit.

"It all seems to be happening so quickly now, doesn't it?" the man said.

Adrash did not answer. It did indeed seem that way. A life could be so long, yet it still failed to teach one about death. That moment, he had always known, would not be meditative. Time would not wait, but hasten the end. It would come too fast, rendering all the periods of one's life into a fleeting memory, no more substantial than any other life.

He had lied to himself. He would have let a coward continue to live in his body, as long as it could. He would not have chosen death.

For the world, yes, but not for himself.

Vedas crouched at his side. "Not the wisest move. You've crippled yourself, and for what? A hundred yards? You've gotten nowhere, for no reason. Should have let us kill you. Now, you're going to die here, in this undignified position, throat slit like a hog." He frowned. "For all that you've done to shape the world, no one is here to remember you, to mourn for you."

Adrash ignored these words. They were meant to offend, and he could be offended no more. He willed the divine armor to retreat from his head, and spoke through a broken jaw.

"How?"

"How, what?" Vedas asked. "How are you beaten?" Grim-faced, he tapped the flat of his sword against Adrash's ribs, sending twinges through the god's torso. "Through superior forces. With the help of others who wouldn't see the world made a grave."

"That's not . . ." He paused, embarrassed by the slurring of his words, the trail of drool that ran from his mouth. "That's not what I meant. These others . . . You're not Evurt. You've pushed my child out completely."

"Evicted, without remorse," Churls said. She shrugged. "We couldn't have done it on our own. As Vedas said, we had help. It almost seems like there's a lesson in that."

Vedas gazed up at her with an unreadable expression.

"Let him see the victors in this battle," he said.

She nodded, and the light fled from her eyes as two radiant, phantom figures stepped from within her. One did not have to stoop as she emerged, stepping to the side. The other very much did, unfolding his broad form from within her and stretching to his full height.

The girl bore an unmistakable resemblance to her mother.

The constructed man—the constructed man resembled no one but himself.

‡

He admitted to himself: he was afraid to die. If there was a life beyond death . . .

"What are you?" he asked.

The girl smirked. "I'm a dead girl." She pointed to Berun. "He's a dead person."

Adrash tried to shake his head, and gasped. The relief he had been counting on, the immediate easing of pain his unique physiology had always provided, appeared never to come. The body he had known as his own, a constant over the long course of millennia, was now infected. His awareness of the divine armor dimmed, too, until the artifact no longer felt a part of him. It was as if he had been swaddled in wet sheets, encased in plaster.

"That's no answer," he said.

"I'm fairly sure it is," the girl countered.

Shavrim appeared above him and crouched opposite Vedas. He gripped Sroma in his right hand, tapping its flat against his left palm. His expression held a measure of regret.

Adrash's first child had never been as callous as his siblings. He had tried. He had rebelled. But he never was the leader he desired to be. He had been an odd choice to lead a revolt against his maker. Love, the desire to be a family in more than just words, clouded his vision.

"Some mysteries go unsolved," Shavrim said. "Even you, observing from on high, privy to so many secrets, don't get everything you want."

Adrash moved his uninjured arm carefully, arousing as little new hurt as possible. He gestured to the sky, the scattered components of the Needle.

"What will you do with this? Left alone—"

"They'll fall," the girl said. "We know. We're not fools."

Adrash allowed himself a chuckle. It turned into a cough, which speckled the white of his armor with red. The cough turned into a scream as something shifted within his chest cavity, pressing down upon his heart. The organ pumped against the intrusion. With each rhythmic shudder, agony erupted, coursed throughout his body.

The girl looked to her mother. Churls nodded.

The torment stopped when the girl reached into his chest. Warmth suffused him, blissfully.

Leaning in close to his face, the girl whispered. "I know what you think is so funny. How will we, weak little things, get up there? Even if we did, what would we do?" She smiled. "You have no idea what I'm now capable of. I've stolen skills from your children, and from one hateful elderman. They knew things—things you never suspected they knew—some things *they* didn't know they knew."

Her smile widened even further. The light pulsed from within her.

"I've learned better than you what it means to be a god."

She stood, removing her hands from his chest. He gritted his teeth against the pain that abruptly resumed, breathing shallowly against the scraping of bone in his right lung. The world dimmed perceptibly, vibrating to the rhythm of his spasming muscles.

"Do it," Berun said, nodding to Shavrim.

Shavrim rose, Sroma in hand. He regarded the knife for several seconds, turned it over to grip its blade, and passed it to Vedas.

"I can't," Shavrim said. "Or I won't. It makes no difference."

Vedas stared at the weapon. "You lived for thousands upon thousands—"

"No," Shavrim said. He shuddered. His eyes closed, and when he spoke it was with an altogether different inflection—an accent Adrash recalled intimately.

Speaking modern words, Shavrim nonetheless spoke in the manner of the ancients.

"It will be you," he said. "It will be now." He stretched his arm toward the Black Suit.

Though doing so caused new hurts to bloom, Adrash held his breath. No human had ever touched Sroma. He doubted anyone gathered suspected what it meant to wield it. Adrash himself did not know what end the elders had sought in crafting the knife.

Vedas did not move. He paused.

In that pause, another stole his fate.

‡

She dropped her own sword and stood, taking the knife from Shavrim. She weighed it in her hands.

"Balance," she murmured. "It has a nice balance."

Her knees bent. The blade flipped vertical in her calloused grip.

Falling upon Adrash, Churls plunged the blade into his chest.

EPILOGUE

They labored on a vast concave plain, under the pale rose moon and her five smaller children. Side by side, the four of them: she, her mate, and the two men who had become like brothers to her. They pulled sweetroot, depositing their vegetables in the long furrows that ran poleward to poleward for nearly forty leagues. It was repetitive, backbreaking work, but they were content.

Particularly content, for they were tipsy. The sweetroot in the far uppoleward rows had fermented over the course of the immensely long night, and they sampled it liberally. As per usual, they did not talk in their work, yet still they managed to communicate, stepping jokingly upon one another's toes, jostling one another with their hips as they moved down the line.

Seasoned by three days and nights on the plain, the two men did not look up from their work. The black-skinned man no longer stared fixedly at the moons. The lighter-skinned man did not steal glances at the black-skinned man.

They were focused on their task—yes, even drunk, or even when a gulling croaked and lifted from the ground only a few feet away from them, re-depositing its long, land-awkward reptilian body a bit further away. The first night, both had been fascinated by the creatures. She

223

understood, of course: in their southern climes, people did not train animals to fertilize the sweetroot fields during the night. They woke to shit on their own soil.

She smiled, thinking of the joke she had told about southerners. It amused her to see how a world modified its inhabitants, to make light of the variations between people. Some would foment hate over such things, but having known a thousand types of person, not all of them human, guaranteed she could not summon an ounce of indignation over their divisions.

This did not mean she loved mortals easily, however. Time had made love for anyone but her mate and the two whose arrival she always anticipated difficult. She no longer sympathized with their limited awareness. She could be brutal, unfeeling, and so left the easy tenderness to her mate, who had retained through his lifetimes a sense of commitment to charitable work.

She alone bore the burden of remembering. Though her mate would quickly locate her in whatever place they found themselves, he needed to be reminded of who he had been. It came as a great relief to him when she told him. The story fit. He had been a hero, after all.

But the two men?

They came to her and her mate in peace, but also in need, knowing only two things—two things they had struggled to put to words their entire lives. They had lived before. She had been there when they died.

Beyond this, they held their suspicions.

They had not been good men, had they? For all their trying, they were missing something – had always missed something.

Could she help them find it?

‡

They became hungry at the same moment, and sat in the dirt and grass. From their packs came roasted corn, honey-cured boar, and cakes formed of the ever-present sweetroot. Somehow, the food became more delicious with each passing meal. Now that their gathering was complete.

(Of course, drunkenness might have had something to do with it, as well.)

They ate quickly, each of them grinning through their packed mouths, each eager to have the story at its end. Picking up where she had left off at the end of the previous meal, she nodded to the lighter skinned of the two men and finished the tale in two sentences, without fanfare.

"And so I killed you, because you asked me. You wanted to come with us."

He nodded, rough features settling into contentment. He had spoken only a handful of words since arriving, and never asked a question. Of the two, he never required further clarification.

His companion, on the other hand . . .

"Is it still there?" he had asked the previous night, head tipped back to stare at the moons. "Is the Needle yet in place?"

"What of the elders?" he had asked. "Surely, they tried again."

"Why would you save me?" he had asked. "I deserved no compassion."

Now, he said, "But your mother—you loved her enough to do what none of the dead had done before you. What became of her? What of Vedas, and all the others?"

She answered these questions the same way she had answered the others.

"Not everything has an answer."

He shook his head, smiling through his frustration. "You're not curious? What if there's a way to know, an arcane science or magic to determine . . ." He gestured broadly, to encompass the world. "There are only so many places for a soul to go. You might see her again!"

She cut a sliver of fermented sweetroot free and placed it in her mouth, relishing the tart fizz of its juice. A second, third, and fourth slices went to her companions. She sensed each person's mood as her own. Her mate, satisfied after a long period of work. The lighter-skinned man, appeased to know what he now knew.

The black-skinned man, frustrated but unable to rouse the rage that defined every life he lived.

Her hand, sticky with fermented sweetroot, pressed against his warm cheek. She called him by his old name, and he shuddered slightly at the sound of it.

"I'm going to tell you what your friend—" she nodded to the second man "—told you, just before your first death. He said, *Some mysteries go unsolved*. This doesn't mean there's no truth to be found. Courageous acts aren't erased simply because you don't know what their ultimate effect was. Most importantly, perhaps, the existence of a mystery negates no love anyone has ever felt."

"But don't you want to know?" he asked. "Don't you want to see her again?"

"I suppose," she responded. "Eventually. But for now, I think I chose my fellow travelers wisely. We can be a family, even if just for this moment. A hundred, a thousand years hence, I bet we'll be sharing the same moment, or one just like it. This is enough."

"Is it?" the lighter-skinned man said. "Is it enough?" His hand moved toward the black-skinned man's knee, as of its own accord, but stopped short of contact. He drew it back to his own lap.

She willed him to move it again, crossing the border between the two.

She willed them to be a family, if only for now.

A GLOSSARY OF TERMS

Academy of Applied Magics—The Kingdom of Stol's most well-respected academy for the study of magic, and also the only known center for the study of outbound magics.

Adrash—The god of Jeroun, wearer of the divine armor. Thirty thousand years ago, beyond the memory of man, he cracked mankind from iron eggs and helped them populate Jcroun. He is rumored by some to have once been a man. The divine armor—an artifact of unknown origin, superficially similar in some ways to elder skin/elder-cloth artifacts—affords him powers beyond any man or elderman, to the point that he can survive in the void and create the planetoid-sized spheres of the Needle from the raw substance of the moon. He is rumored by some to have once been a man able to father children, demigods whose roles have long since been forgotten or altered into sectarian myths.

Adrashi—One who believes in Adrash's benevolence and his intention to redeem the people of Jeroun. In general, Adrashi are more organized than Anadrashi. In Nos Ulom and the Kingdom of Stol, Adrashism is the state religion.

Alchemical (Solution)—A broad term for all solutions composed of materials harvested from elder corpses. Alchemical solutions are the base for every spell. Alchemical ink is a particularly regulated—and highly expensive—form, as it is quite dangerous to the uninitiated mage.

Anadrashi—One who believes in Adrash's malevolence and his intention to destroy Jeroun. Anadrashi also believe in mankind's fitness to rule Jeroun on its own. In general, Anadrashi are less organized than Adrashi. In Toma, Anadrashism is the state religion.

Baleshuuk—The highly secretive corpse miners of Nos Ulom. A dwarfish race of men, Baleshuuk have for thousands of years used their magics to extract elder corpses from the ground. Primarily stationed in Knos Min and Stol, where the largest mines exist, their existence even in these places is largely unknown to the general populace.

Bash Ateff—The second demigod created by Adrash, and the wielder of the razored circle Jhy. She is worshipped by a very small minority in Dareth Hlum, Casta, Stol, and Knos Min. Bashest sects worship her as the mother of Adrash, and believe that she will ultimately convince Adrash not to destroy Jeroun.

Black Suits—A martial order of Anadrashi found in all nations of Knoori except Nos Ulom. Marked by their black elder-cloth suits and the distinctive horns they cause to form on the hoods of these suits, their primary goal as an institution is to fight White Suits and win converts to the Anadrashi faith. By doing so, Black Suits believe they strike a blow against Adrash, keeping him from attacking Jeroun. Black Suits orders are relatively uncommon and secretive outside Dareth Hlum and Knos Min.

Bonedust / "Dust"—Pulverized elder bone used for various purposes, including currency. Rubbed on almost any surface, it acts as a protective, shielding the material from damage as well as extremes of temperature. It is also a base material for many alchemical solutions. When ingested, it hydrates the body. In many areas, bonedust is contaminated—sometimes purposefully cut—with other substances. Like every other elder artifact, bonedust is subject to periodic inflation due to supply issues.

Casta—Newest of Knoori's nations, a democracy having no official state religion. The capitol of Onsa, located on the northern coast, is its second largest city after Denn. Unless locally enacted, in Casta there are no laws prohibiting gambling, prostitution, or drug usage, but there are strict laws prohibiting sectarian violence. Castans of the north are generally light skinned, often freckled, while those of the interior and south are generally darker, shading into slate colors in the badlands. Geographically, Casta is split between the fertile rolling hills of the north and the semi-desert and desert badlands of the south.

The Cataclysm—The decade-long winter caused by Adrash sending the two smallest spheres of the Needle into the ocean to the east and west of Knoori approximately one thousand years ago.

Construct—A magically created intelligence, housed in a variety of different body types. The body and mind are typically composed of bonedust, metal, and a collection of more esoteric materials, the exact "formula" of which is the construct-maker's closely guarded secret. Casta and Toma are the sole nations that do not regulate the creation of constructs. They are most common in Knos Min.

Dalan Fele—Dareth Hlum's five-hundred-mile-long defensive wall, which forms the nation's western border with Casta. Seventeen gates allow access to and from the interior of Dareth Hlum.

Danoor—The oldest inhabited city on Jeroun, and the third largest by population in Knos Min. It is situated on the plains just east of the Usveet Mesa, and has for hundreds of generations hosted the Tournament of Danoor.

Dareth Hlum—One of Knoori's nations, a democracy having no official state religion. The capitol of Golna, located on the eastern coast, is its largest city. Generally, Dareth Hlum allows public, organized fights between Adrashi and Anadrashi sects as long as no onlookers are harmed. Citizens vary widely in appearance, but skin hues are generally darker than the people of northern Casta, Nos Ulom, or Stol. The most geographically diverse region of Knoori, the various mountain chains that cross the nation contribute to many different types of climate and terrain.

Elders—The extinct race that preceded man's birth on Jeroun, whose artifacts and landworks are of a scale beyond the means of mankind's magic to reproduce. Little is known of their culture, but many uses have been found for their buried corpses. Primarily, they are used to create alchemical substances. Their eggs and sperm—next to skin the most prized of all elder substances—can be used to inseminate any living animal and produce a hybrid creature. Extrapolating from the nature of hybrids and manufactured elder artifacts, scholars note that elders must have been extremely long-lived and hardy, as well as photosynthetic. Due to their continual harvesting for thousands of years and the increasing depth which miners are forced to go to acquire them, elder corpses are ever more expensive. Some fear the supply will soon run out.

Elder-cloth—Any material containing thread made from the skin of an elder. Far stronger than normal fabrics, over time elder-cloth binds itself to the wearer, assisting in limited biological functions. If close-fitting and of a high grade, elder-cloth makes the wearer stronger, faster, and less subject to physical harm. Like all elder artifacts, cloth of this kind must be exposed to sunlight often in order to continue functioning. Elder-cloth can be dyed any color.

Elder Skin—Skin harvested from elder corpses. The second most prized and thus expensive of all elder materials, elder skin is used almost exclusively for the production of clothing, being used as thread to make elder-cloth and as a leather item itself. When worn as leather, it grants its wearer increased strength, speed, and protection from injury. Though not as malleable in nature as elder-cloth, leather of this kind forms a bond with its wearer to such a degree that it can be commanded to move remotely. Because of the damage it causes to the brain, ingestion of elder skin is illegal throughout Knoori.

Elderman / Elderwoman—A hybrid of man and elder. Exhibiting great intelligence, physical stamina, and speed, without age-nullifying spells their average lifespan is somewhat less than forty years. On average, their magical talent far outstrips that of humans.

Evurt Youl—The fifth demigod created by Adrash, twin to Ustert Youl and the wielder of the short sword Rust. He is no longer worshipped on Jeroun, but among the Usterti he exists as a small figure in her mythology—a forgotten or deceased twin.

Hasde Fall—The wooded hills west of Ynon in Knos Min. Rumors say that the Knosi government possesses magical facilities and training grounds underneath the earth in these hills.

High Pontiff of Dolin—A man or woman elected by his or her peers to head the Orthodox Church of Nos Ulom. In many ways the most powerful of Knoori's religious heads, his or her position is neither hereditary nor guaranteed for any length of time; he or she may be elected out of office at any moment. Due to the nature of conservative Adrashism and its role as the official state religion, the Pontiff exerts a great deal of secular control in Nos Ulom.

Hybrid—The product of an insemination of elder sperm or egg and another animal's sperm or egg through artificial means. The resulting creature generally exhibits greater intelligence and physical stamina than its non-elder parent, but also diminished lifespan and deformities. A large percentage are stillborn.

Iswee—Home of the hibernating elders, located on the other side of Jeroun. Hypothesized about by the outbound mages of Stol who have seen the constant cloud cover, its existence is unknown to others.

Jeroun—The home of man and elder, a highly habitable planet with one moon.

Knoori—The largest continent of Jeroun and the sole home of man, composed of the nations of Dareth Hlum, Casta, Nos Ulom, the Kingdom of Stol, the Kingdom of Toma, and the Republic of Knos Ulom. Though several large islands lay off of its coast, none are currently inhabited.

Knos Min—Knoori's oldest nation, a republic having no official state religion. The capitol of Grass Min, located on the northern coast, is the third largest city next to Levas. A haven for intellectuals and expatriate professionals, Knos Min is the most magically advanced nation of Knoori, possessing roughly half the continent's elder corpse reserves. Long rumored to have a corps of outbound mages and other martial mages, the strength of the nation's military is rivaled only by the Kingdom of Stol's. Knosi are only marginally less uniform in appearance than the Ulomi, displaying dark brown skin tones and wiry black hair. Generally flat and arid, the nation nonetheless possesses several great mesa ranges, atop which the ground is quite fertile. Old-growth forests grow in the southeastern lake region.

Lake Ten—Knoori's largest lake, from whose fresh waters Knos Min, Toma, Stol, and Nos Ulom take a great deal of their sustenance. Officially, its waters are not the property of any one nation. Its shorelines are, however. Its sources are the Thril Rivers, which begin in the Aspa Mountains in Nos Ulom. Its sole outlet is the Unnamed River of Toma.

Locborder Wall—A defensive wall that extends three hundred and fifty miles along the western shore of Lake Ten, from the foothills of the Aspa Mountains in Nos Ulom to the screwcrab warrens of Toma. Its length defines the greatest border along Lake Ten that Knos Min ever achieved. The vast majority of its length still belongs to Knos Min.

Lore—The combined skills, practices, and traditions of a particular mage or mage group.

Mage—A human or elderman whose education grants them a great deal of knowledge about spell creation and casting. Mages are both self-taught and formally trained, though certain nations and regions discourage the independent practice of magic. The most specialized of all mages—the outbound mages—can perform feats of almost incalculable power, lifting themselves from the surface of Jeroun and surviving in the void of space.

Magics—The creation and casting of spells. The word is nearly synonymous with Lore.

Medicines—The branch of magics that deals with the physical form of the body. Often considered the least demanding of all magics due to the great efficacy of elder alchemicals on the body, medicines is one of the most common and necessary of all magical disciplines.

The Needle—Twenty-seven iron spheres Adrash created from the material of the moon, held in orbit as a visible threat to the people on Jeroun. Though they have maintained a stable arrangement for a thousand years, for the first five hundred years of their existence the spheres were arranged in a number of ways.

Nos Ulom—One of Knoori's nations, an oligarchy having Adrashism as its official state religion. The capitol of Dolin, located in the central valleys just north of the Aspa Mountain chain, is a relatively small city of less than fifty thousand souls. Of all the nations of Knoori, Nos Ulom is the most repressive, its government the most autocratic. Ulomi are the continent's most uniform people in appearance, displaying unblemished, cream-colored skin and generally curly, straw-colored hair. Geographically, the nation is mountainous in the south and composed of high, fertile tableland and pine forest in the north.

The Ocean—Variously known as the Sea, Jeru, or Deathshallow, the ocean is shallow and laps upon the shores of many islands. It harbors a startling variety of marine life, much of which is quite dangerous to man. Due to this danger, it has not been navigated by man for many thousands of years.

Orrus Dabulakm—The third demigod created by Adrash, and the wielder of the glass spear Deserest. He is worshipped within a few rural, isolated communities In Dareth Hlum and Casta. Their myths tell that he is the son of Adrash. Orrust people believe that it is not Adrash moving the spheres of the Needle, but Orrus—and that by destroying Jeroun, he will give birth to a new paradise.

Osseterat—Hybrid apes of near-human intelligence that are rumored to live in Hasde Fall.

Outbound Mage—A mage trained specifically to achieve orbit and travel in the void. Stol alone openly uses this type of mage, though rumors suggest that Knos Min also possesses outbound mages. Though a few outbound mages have been human, the overwhelming majority of them are eldermen, who exhibit a greater potential for magic and greater stamina. Each mage wears a vacuum suit—composed of leather made from elder skin—on which he or she paints sigils. The mage also wears a dustglass (bonedust-reinforced glass) helmet. The suit and helmet protect the mage from vacuum for a brief period of time should his or her spells fail. The purpose of the outbound mages is to monitor Adrash, though much knowledge of Jeroun has been gained by the activities of the corps as well.

Osa—A large, circular island in Uris Bay. It is covered by an artifact of high elder magic, an immense glass-like dome upon which a variety of life clings. Wyrms and other large creatures, most not seen on the mainland, live near the dome walls. With intense magnification, abandoned cities can be seen on the slopes of Mount Pouen, the island's largest peak. No openings appear to exist in the dome.

Pusta—An exclave of Stol. The capitol is Ravos, located on the northern coast. Differing from Stol in many respects, the culture of Pusta inherits much from its multiethnic fisheries, which are the most technologically advanced in Knoori and extend along the entire coastline.

Quarterstock—The extremely rare offspring of a hybrid. The majority of hybrids are sterile, and the vast majority of their offspring never come to term. Even if they do, a very small percentage live. Of those that live, an even smaller percentage are unaffected by mental or physical retardation. No comprehensive study of a healthy individual—human or animal in origin—has yet been conducted.

Shavrim Thrall Coranid—The first demigod created by Adrash, ostensibly the leader of his siblings, and the wielder of the sentient silverblack knife Sroma. Though a pivotal part of the early history of

Jeroun, nearly all vestiges of Shavrim's identity have disappeared from the minds of mankind. Among the Tomen people, however, a legend is told of an immense, immortal man with remarkable skills—particularly, the ability to tame animals or keep them at bay, allowing him to take to the air on the back of a wyrm and even navigate the sea.

Sigil—A particular type of spell that is painted on a surface using alchemical ink. It is usually "activated" by the recitation—verbally or, if the mage is sufficiently powerful, mentally—of a specific set of words.

Sorcerer—A mage.

Spell—An alchemical solution that—when activated by thought, incantation, or physical action—produces a magical effect. Hundreds of thousands of such spells, each varying according to the particular mixture of elder components, are produced and cast every day for a variety of tasks. The easiest spells to produce and cast affect inorganic materials: moving the elements, creating a current, etc. The most difficult spells to produce and cast affect living substances: changing one's structure, extending one's life, creating constructs, etc. The efficacy of a spell decreases the farther away the mage is, a fact which makes influencing an object over long distances—as in the sending of a message—difficult.

Sradir Ung Kim—The fourth demigod created by Adrash, and the wielder of the oilwood and leather sambok Weither. All vestiges of Sradir's identity have disappeared from the minds of mankind.

Sroma—A large, silverblack knife found by Adrash before the birth of mankind on Jeroun. A sentient elder artifact similar to the divine armor, its existence appears to stand as a counterpoint to the armor, acting as opposing forces. Shavrim is the only being to ever hold it other than Adrash.

The Steps of Stol—An earthwork monument created by high elder magic. It begins in the fertile southern plains of Stol, extending some eighty miles to the coast and more than four hundred along it. Ascending to a height of twelve thousand feet in seventeen evenly spaced, gently sloping rises, the Steps stop abruptly at the ocean. Most of Stol's elder corpse reserves are buried within it.

Stol—One of Knoori's nations, a kingdom having Adrashism as its official state religion. The capitol of Tansot, located on the eastern shore of Lake Ten, is its largest city. Moderate Adrashism is the general rule and all Anadrashi sects are allowed to live peaceably within the kingdom's borders, though they suffer persecution in the central valleys. After Knos Min, Stol is the most magically advanced nation of Knoori, possessing roughly forty percent of the continent's elder corpse reserves. The only state with a known outbound mage program, the strength of the military relies much upon magical developments from the Academy of Applied Magics. Stoli people vary widely in appearance, but are generally light skinned. Geographically, Stol is generally hilly in the north, descending into fertile valleys in the central region, and rising to great heights on the Steps of Stol in the south.

Tamer—A mage who specializes in taming and controlling large, exotic, and hybrid animals. Their lore is far more esoteric and difficult to master than the many readily available spells used to help control draft animals, entertainment animals, and pets. In rare cases, the tamer achieves a type of telepathic bond with his or her animal. In Casta and Stol, the most daring and specialized type of tamer exists: the hybrid wyrm tamer.

Tan-Ten—The island at the center of Lake Ten. Oasena is its only city. The people of Tan-Ten have never shown interest in power or political maneuvering, but have on many occasions successfully defended their island from invaders.

Thaumaturgical Engine—A construct used to create kinetic force. Unlike constructs that mimic biological creatures, an engine is rarely imbued with more than the most basic intelligence needed to follow simple directions. Due to the expense of creating and maintaining engines, those produced are most often used in barges or other large transport vehicles.

Toma—One of Knoori's nations, a kingdom having Anadrashism as its official state religion. The capitol of Demn, located on the southern coast, is its largest city. Possibly the most religiously militant of all the people of Knoori, Tomen nonetheless value the personal, non-dogmatic expression of Anadrashism more than any other. The people vary considerably in build, but are generally dusky skinned and rust-haired. Toma is the most arid nation of Knoori and, but for the Wie Desert in the southwest, the hilliest.

The Tournament of Danoor—The decennial tournament between Knoori's White Suit and Black Suit orders, which occurs on the last day of every decade. A fighter is chosen from every town numbering more than 2000 souls. He or she then travels to Danoor and is allowed to fight in the tournament. In the end, one Black and one White re-main. Accordingly, along the way fighters will inevitably have to fight brothers and sisters of their own faith. The New Year celebration starts after the tournament champion's speech, wherein he or she typically extols listeners to convert to the winning faith. Usually, secular fight-ing tournaments begin the next day.

Ual—A small town in eastern Knos Min, positioned on Uris Bay. An otherwise unnoteworthy locale, it is remarkable only for the singular-ity of its coastal wall, which creates an enclosed pool of seawater thirty miles long and ten miles wide. Though it is common to say no men set craft upon the ocean for fear of what resides in it, the men and women of Ual have kept their sea-gates shut for millennia in order to hunt juvenile fish and reptiles before they grow to dangerous proportions.

Ustert Youl—The sixth and final demigod created by Adrash, twin to Evurt Youl and the wielder of the short sword Ruin. She is worshipped by a relatively large minority in Casta and Knos Min. A loosely orga-nized sororal community of mages and apothecaries (often referred to as witches, though this term is widely used even in Adrashi and

Anadrashi contexts), Usterti profess a variety of beliefs, bound only by the understanding that the goddess governs all existence. Due to this ambiguity, a great deal of mystery surrounds the community.

The Void—Near-Jeroun orbit and outer space.

White Suits—A martial order of Adrashi prevalent in all nations of Knoori except Toma. Marked by their white elder-cloth suits, their primary goal as an institution is to fight Black Suits and win converts to the Adrashi faith. By doing so, White Suits believe they encourage Adrash to redeem Jeroun sooner. Orders are relatively uncommon and secretive outside southern Nos Ulom, Dareth Hlum, and Knos Min.

Wyrm—A dragon of immense size. Highly intelligent and extremely temperamental, they do not come into contact with men often. This is due mostly to the fact that most food is taken from the open ocean. Only a small minority of dragons hunt large prey on the continent. Hybrid wyrms are not common, but do exist in Stol and Casta.

ACKNOWLEDGEMENTS

Thank you to my wife, Sophia, and my son, Dominic, my mom and dad, my sisters and brothers, and my mother-in-law Rosemary Papa.

Thank you to all the people—too many to list, really—who encouraged me to keep going on this second book without any prompting or cajoling (okay, maybe a little prompting and cajoling).

Lastly, thank you to my agent, Michael Harriot, my editors, Jeremy Lassen and Cory Allyn, the behind-the-scenes Night Shade Books crew, and all the other cool folks who made this book a physical and digital reality.